Anything for you, ma'am

An IITian's Love Story

Anything for you, ma'am

An IITian's Love Story

Tushar Raheja

Srishti
PUBLISHERS & DISTRIBUTORS

SRISHTI PUBLISHERS & DISTRIBUTORS
N-16 C. R. Park
New Delhi 110 019
srishtipublishers@yahoo.com

First published by Srishti Publishers & Distributors in 2006
Anniversary Edtion (First Impression) 2007
Copyright © Tushar Raheja, 2006

Ninth Reprint 2008
ISBN 81-88575-86-0

Typeset in Kuenst480 9.5pt. by Suresh Kumar Sharma at Srishti

Cover design: Kajal Kumar, Career Launcher

Printed and bound in India

Reviews for 'Anything for you, ma'am' from National dailies:

'Tushar has this instinctive ability to hold your attention with narrative deviations that illuminate disparate subjects ....the charm of campus life, pig-headed Professors, the advantage of sisters, the adventure of train travel in India, the joy of an early winter in Delhi ....What Raheja does is to very cleverly localize the Wooster persona. So English aristocracy, the idle rich, the lad sent down from Oxford, the young man with great expectations and little ability, the chappie whose only survival tool is a smart gentleman's gentleman called Jeeves — all this is turned into rich material for humour of a local kind ....Some of the humour is side splitting ....'

— *The Hindu*

'Remember Bertie Wooster? ....the humour – most often arising out of situations poor Bertie gets himself into ....Anything for you, ma'am works on same lines .... Well, it would be too presumptuous to compare a fourth year IIT student Tushar Raheja's attempt at witty writing to a classic Wodehouse, but he does manage to get some laughs ....a laugh-a-minute book ....'

— *The Times of India*

'Raheja writes a touching book about a young lover's story ....that engrosses the reader, with its high speed rather hilarious turn of events ....Amidst all the chaos are the sweet love moments ....be it their date or their telephonic conversation ....It is the story of a boy-next-door, which any youngster can relate to. Raheja moves back and forth in time, reminding of ace writers like Virginia Woolf and Amitav Ghosh ....'

— *The Pioneer*

'The difference lies in the treatment of the subject ....the narrative is devoid of lofty idealism ....the lingo and its texture is very close to what students use in colleges ....a good attempt by someone writing only his first novel ....'

— *Hindustan Times*

'Anything for you, ma'am is a delicacy of feelings with dollops of mischief and fun ....Infused with the sepia tinted fragrance of life at IIT Delhi campus and turbulent love terrain of tweeny days, the book is for those who are romantics-at-hearts and nostalgic about the good ol' college days ....'

— *Society Magazine*

'With all the masala of a Hindi movie, the story has interesting plots, interspersed with humour, enough to keep you glued to the pages ....'
— *New Indian Express*

'The author smears Tejas' life philosophy with a veneer of middle-class respectability and manages to bolster the book with the help of an extremely indulgent plot ....one must hand it to the young author for an enterprising race to the finish ....' — *Deccan Herald*

'The story takes many intriguing turns. It has been penned in a language that is perfectly suitable for a story placed against a campus background, perfectly setting the mood and verisimilitude ....an enjoyable read ....'
— *Seventeen*

'As one goes through the book, there is just one feeling that a reader gets. The feeling that a movie is being screened before him, scene by scene ....'

— *Vijay Times*

Dedicated
to
Dadima
who told me so many wonderful stories

Before I Begin....

I must thank my parents for bearing with an eccentric son like me. I must thank Chhavi, my dearest sister, too in that regard. For years I have worried them with my strange and sudden whims but they have gladly faced it all. While my peers were busy finding jobs, I was busy writing and it wouldn't have been easy had I not got their support and encouragement. They deserve an applause.

Notable, also, for believing in an unlikely writer like me are Yogesh, my brilliant brother; my worrying sister trio – Chhavi, Priyanka and Nalini didi; Jaideep, another supportive brother; and my bindaas friends who believed me, though after raising an eyebrow each, when I told them that I was writing a novel – Anshul, Mukund, Rohan, Rumit, Shitij, Siddharth, Sumeet, Vaibhav (in alphabetical order) and many more. Praiseworthy, also, is their patience. I didn't allow any of them to read a word before the book was printed. Long live their 'blind' faith.

I am grateful to my editor, Mrs. Purabi Panwar, for allowing in the book my 'incorrect' English, yet refining my grammar. I am happy for the encouragement I got from my publisher's team who, by taking this manuscript seriously, gave this youngster a chance to see his wayward writings in the form of a book.

Apart from my family, I must thank Mr. C K Jain, Mukund Sanghi, Harpreet Singh, Rohan Gupta, Mr. Arjun Wadhwa, Ms. Kajal Kumar, Mrs. Satjit Wadva, Ms. Trupti Gupte, Mr. Nilanjan Das, Dr. R.N. Malik, Rahul Sharma for the help that I got from them in various forms. The list doesn't end here but I can't possibly name all.

I wouldn't be here without the blessings of my *dadima, babaji* (the literary genes come from here), *nanima, nanaji, mummy, papa, tayaji(s), tayiji(s), mama(s)* and *mami(s)*. I couldn't list all my brothers and sisters here, but I'd like to thank all of them – seven brothers and five sisters in all after adding contributions from both my parents' sides – for the smashing fun we had together as kids. Those were the days.

And the biggest thanks to the genius of R.K. Narayan, P.G. Wodehouse and Arthur Conan Doyle who got me interested in stories and inspired me to write my own.

And finally, thanks to the ma'am in my heart, wherever she is. For you, wherever you are:

> I wake up in the morning
> To the sound of raindrops,
> And I wonder where you'd be,
> And I wonder if it's raining there.
> Wherever you are, I hope you think of me,
> When it's raining there.

October, this year.

Now, when driven by emotion, I get down to prepare an account of my extraordinary voyage, I cannot help but wonder what Professor Sidhu, Rajit and Dr. Prabhakar, those fateful men who were meant to be a part of it, were doing at that hour. That hour, my choice for opening this account, was when I truly sprung into action. I recall distinctly: it was a typical October noon; there was a cool breeze all over the place, and the sun was mellow. It does not get any better in Delhi, the city of extremes.

I lay on my back, my mind not without trouble, when the October air, the type that lulls you into sleep, without you actually making any effort, did the trick. My eyes closed, my thoughts scattered, when, suddenly, my cell phone buzzed. It was Khosla, our Class Representative, one who does all the running for a particular department; in my case, the Industrial and Production Department, Indian Institute of Technology, Delhi.

"Hullo!!" I said yawning.

"Were you sleeping, Tejas? Get up, *yaar*, I couldn't get your ticket; there was this long queue and little time. Do what you want to quickly. I guess only about fifty tickets left." That woke me up.

"Only fifty?"

"Yes."

"Anyway, thanks, *yaar*, I'll book mine. What are your seat numbers?"

"Bogey S-9; the first twenty-seven are ours."

I got up quickly. I had to rush to the nearest travel agent at once. Bookings opened ten days back and the moron could find time only now to book the tickets. What if I didn't get mine? I grabbed the essentials: money and my itinerary that I had so meticulously prepared on Microsoft Word. I kick-started my Scooty; it coughed, jerked and finally started. I headed for the Sector-15 Market of Faridabad, a peaceful place juxtaposed with Delhi where I live with my papa, mummy, *dadima* (grandma), *babaji* (grandpa) and Sneha – my dearest sister.

It was a spacious office. A huge multi-coloured banner announced 'JFK Travels – Always on the move'. A baffling name, indeed. I recalled coming across a certain JFK Tailors once and wondered what the properties of the ingenious brain behind this JFK chain could be when the man inside the office called me. He looked like a typical businessman.

"How may I help you, sir?"

"Train reservations?" I asked in return. He didn't bother to say yes. He simply pointed towards the board that said 'Rail Reservations' at number three. Rest were air travel related. I was not that rich. I took my seat. Without wasting any more time I asked, "Can you book me tickets from anyplace to anyplace?"

"Certainly, sir!"

"I mean, for example, sitting here in Faridabad, can you book me tickets from Timbuktu to Honolulu?"

"If there is such a train, then, yes sir!"

"Fine!" I took out my itinerary and showed him the train numbers and names and times. "I want a ticket from Delhi to Pune for 10th December. The train reaches Pune on the 11th. Then, I want a ticket for the train from Pune to Chennai, 11th midnight or 12th whatever you wish to call it, which reaches Chennai on 12th night, 8'o clock."

He eyed me suspiciously, I thought, and said: "Only one, sir? For you?"

I replied in positive, coolly and asked, "Are they available?"

A torrent of computer keys later, he said, "Plenty!"

"I was informed that only about fifty remained!" I said.

"No, sir, about a hundred and fifty!" he said, smiling and I cursed Khosla. I hate being woken up, especially woken up like that, with a shocker.

"Sir, name?" he asked.

I had thought about that. I wouldn't give my real name.

"Leave not a speck

That may cause a wreck,"

has always been my slogan. My name wouldn't have mattered but my surname might have. What if he turned out to be my father's patient? My father is a doctor, by the way, and so is my mother. And one can never afford complacency when one's parents are doctors. All sorts of people flock to them and while showing a sore eye or a loony pimple, they can always blurt out things that they should not. My father, over the years, has formed a tremendous network of his patients, without any spying intentions, of course. And its wretched members seem to be everywhere. Or at least their sons and daughters are; who, being my schoolmates, contrive to expose, without fail, that latest zero I scored in my Moral Science or some such paper. Thank God, I am in a college now, far away from the network which mercifully has its limitations. So, playing safe, I said what I had thought:

"Rohit Verma." Not a bad name, I reflected; common, and easy to remember. But just as I began to feel good about my enterprising skills, foresight and all that, he bowled the next googly.

"Address?"

I hadn't thought of that. I took a pause.

"Do I have to give it?" I shouldn't have said that.

"Yes."

I tried to correct my expression.

"Actually, I... I... I don't live here. I came to visit a friend for Dussehra holidays. I stay in Delhi. Can I give that address?"

"Yes, sir"

"Fine! D-24, Karakoram House, IIT, Delhi."

"Contact number?" I coolly gave my mobile number. Thank God, I have one.

"Well, I want the aisle seats. And, from Delhi to Pune, I prefer a seat in Bogey S-9, if and only if, the seat number is beyond 50. Otherwise, book me in bogey S-8 or S-10. I hope you get it?"

"Sir, I have been in this business for ten years," he said with pride and would have vomited matter sufficient for his biographer had I not tactfully shouted, "Wonderful," and pressed his hand. Yet I repeated all my instructions. I wanted to make sure that they were followed. I wanted *those very* seat numbers. I'll explain all that and other plan details, but, for now, we'll be patient. Here, it would suffice to say that I didn't want to be very close to my college group as one of its constituents was a professor, whom one must avoid. Yet I wanted to be near enough to two of my friends who knew it all. My department was going on an Industrial Tour to Pune.

The agent informed me that I'd get the tickets the day after. As I got up, satisfied, I remembered in time to ask him:

"What does JFK stand for?"

"Oh, they are the initials of my grandfather's name!"

"What!" I uttered incredulously. The world was strange. How the great man's grandson could be employed in a travel agency across the seven seas was beyond me. But as I began to feel good about finally establishing an acquaintance of importance, he elaborated with pride: "Yes sir, Jahangir Fateh Khan, he was a great man. Always on the move. Hence this travel agency, dedicated to him, and our slogan too: Always on the move!" Funny was the world, I reflected.

"Do you know another great man shared his initials with your grandfather?" I asked.

"No, sir, I have no knowledge! Who, sir, may he be?"

"Oh, doesn't matter, he was a small man compared to your grandfather," I said, smiling. He smiled too and I moved out.

The cool wind greeted me, stirring in me splendid emotions. I had the gait of a soldier who is finally on his way to meet his lover after a ten-year war. And it is a different matter that mine was a somewhat similar case. I had a song on my lips which is usually the case. There is a song for every occasion, glad or sad. I cannot recall the song but one may bet on it being a merry one. The first stage of the plan had been executed and well. I could hardly contain my excitement. I had to tell her and tell her then. The moment should not pass. I dialled her number.

"Congratulations Shreya! I am on my way..."

September, this year.

It would be convenient, here, to rewind our tape a little. To a month back approximately. Mid-September that is. Shreya's number hadn't been reachable for over three hours now. We hadn't spoken since morning. Our life had been punctuated with jinxes lately and these were not good signs. My heart beat faster each time the call didn't connect. Finally the bell rang. I thanked God!

"Hullo!" I said.

"Hullo!" said she.

"Where have you been the whole day? I have been trying your number since morning. How many times have I told you to inform me that you are busy and can't talk?" I said in a tense voice mixed with anger.

"The network was down. And I couldn't call from home."

"Why?" I fired.

"Mom and dad were around."

"The whole day? You couldn't even find a minute to call me?" I should have tried to understand her position but my temper took over, "How foolish is that! You know very well that I'll be worried. Every time you don't call, I think, not again, not another shocker! But no, you won't call. You are never bothered!"

"Right. I am never bothered," she said irritably.

"Shut up!"

"No, you are right, I am never bothered and why should I be!"

"Now, don't begin. Tell me, all well?"

"How does it matter if it is or not. I am not bothered. And you shouldn't be, either."

"Shreya, please tell me. All well?" I asked a little worried.

"I can't, right now, I'll call you at night. Around eleven-thirty," she said in a melancholic tone. Something was wrong.

"Just tell me if everything is fine!"

"I won't be able to, now. Please."

"I can't hang up like that, Shreya. You make me nervous. At least give a hint," I summoned all my guts to say, "I hope you are coming to Delhi in December."

"No," she said after a pause, her voice on the verge of breaking.

I couldn't talk any more. I needed some time to absorb that shock. I knew that it was on the cards, still I needed time.

My mind sprang into the past...

It was July end and she was back in Chennai – that is where she lives, a good two thousand kilometres away from me. Back, I mean, from Delhi. We had met quite often while she was here and those surely had been magical days. And after she left I had missed her sorely. So I decided, or say erred, like many other victims of love have since time immemorial and will continue to in spite of my well-meant warnings, to write a letter to her, pouring out my feelings. My first love letter! I wrote under her friend's name and she got it alright.

But not many days later she called to tell me that the letter had been discovered. By her parents, of course. Like a fish out of water, my game up, I asked, like everyone does in such situations, an inconsequential question:

"Didn't you lock the drawer?" I had asked.

"I had!"

"Then? You said there were two keys, both in your possession!"

It so happened, she told me, that a third key existed. Her mother kept it. She wasn't aware of it too until she came into her room after college and found the drawer open and the letter removed. And they say – ignorance is bliss!

Well, rest of it is the usual. Her mom played a passing-the-parcel, and gave the letter to her dad and any dad, on discovering a letter written by a lover to his daughter addressing her dangerous things like darling and sweetheart, leaps in the air and so did Mr. Bhargava, her father, and in that process hit the ceiling impairing his brain forever. I don't blame him. It is perhaps natural, for I have seen documentaries that study a dad's reaction on the discovery of his daughter's darling and they all show the same thing. The *dad* goes *mad*. For him it is not merely a letter, but a time bomb, ticking away, threatening to blow his daughter away one day. And when a dad goes mad, he decides that his daughter must be kept in strictest of custodies, with barbed wires and all.

Tough times ensued and I reluctantly admit to have become something of a philosopher. Such was my condition that I managed to write a song on life, playing which on my guitar, brought me comfort. Though scarcely better than a crow's serenade, it was of help, and so I reproduce it for you:

> *You haven't paid your rent,*
> *Landlord isn't much of a friend,*
> *He wants his 50 dollars 3 cents,*
> *Or you'll be booked for offence.*
> *You'll be kicked out, but*

Find new house, new town.
For life goes on.

Her name is Alice,
Yesterday you got your first kiss,
Today she tells it is all over,
She saw you with another miss.
Before you tell her it was only your sis,
It's a bye-bye-Alice.
Alices will go but Sallies will come,
Don't worry; life goes on.

You've finally found a new job,
Good pay, not much work on the shop,
Your pocket's picked on the morning train,
"Oh my God," you're late again.
The boss doesn't listen, says you are outta job
You are a rolling stone again.
Don't worry they say "It can't get worse."
And life rolls on.

Got no girl to call your own,
No job, no money, no home,
You've been searching for a bench to sleep on.
Everything's so bleak 'n forlorn.
Life's a rollercoaster, with its ups and downs,
Life goes on.

There's one thing you've got to learn,
Life's full of twists 'n turns,
You've got to break the rocks in the hot sun,
For the tide to turn.

If there is night, there has to be dawn.
Life goes on.

Yesterday may have been shit,
Today you may be a complete misfit,
But tomorrow's a new day,
So don't give up that weeny ray.
You've got to pray, dream, hope and move on,
O-O-O Life goes on.

The band's gone; the applause over, let us return to the story. Around two months had passed and like all matters, however hot initially, this one too cooled down, and life had indeed gone on. We (which strictly includes only Shreya and me) had hopes that her dad would allow her to come to Delhi in December as had been the plan. We managed to talk once a day and were satisfied. There had been no shock for a long time, until this day when her father had, no doubt, for some reason, ordered that his daughter must not be allowed to go to Delhi. And so, it was required that his daughter's love must go to Chennai, of course. So, that's the story of my first love letter and, well, the last.

Back to October, this year.

Well, now if you are not as dim as the hundred watt bulb that struggles to light up my room for want of sufficient voltage, you must have gathered the reason behind my voyage.

My decision was spontaneous. I *had* to go *there* as she was not coming *here*, because we *had* to meet. It was that simple. Those who have never been smitten by the love bug may find it a little difficult to comprehend the obviousness, but if they only lie coolly on a sofa and think about all the movies they have seen, and all the crazy things in them that lovers often do, the fog would begin to clear up.

After all, I am not building a palace in my lover's name, and cutting the hands of the artists thereafter or, for that matter, not even writing letters in blood, my own of course. I am merely undertaking an expedition, harmless but risky all the same. When you have not met for about six months the one who, as the sayings go, makes your heart beat faster and steals your sleep and peace, it becomes impossible to go on and you think you'd rather die than suffer this agony. It is wise, therefore, to try and do anything that makes the union possible. Hence this journey.

The intellectuals will be quick to spot that though it is all very merry to say "I'll go", the real thing lies in the doing. Although far from being

11

an intellectual, I am glad to tell you that this fact struck me too, and like a hammer. When circumstances are as they were with me, you do say a lot of things to yourself in an enhanced state of mind and become aware of this boring world of reality only a bit later. Suddenly, you battle with such concepts as feasibility and practicality and —zoom— you come crashing to the ground!

And so I was hit, indeed.

But then I must tell you that, although bereft of intellect, give my mind a task which cannot be done the straight way, and it starts to do better.

After talking to her, I finally got my act together and decided firmly that I had to go to Chennai. I thought about all possible ways to go to Chennai in my winter vacations and short-listed some. I decided to call her. Poor thing, she must have been crying. I wanted to tell her that I would come and we'd meet.

"Hullo!"

"Hi!" I said, trying to gather as much happiness I could.

"What happened?" she said with her innate sweetness.

"Nothing, just wanted to apologize for hanging up like that. I am sorry. But I couldn't talk then."

"It is okay. I understand."

"Now, at least tell me what happened, why are you not coming?"

"I told you I'll call you around eleven-thirty, Tejas."

"Tell me something at least. Your dad said something about us?

"Yes!"

"What?"

"Do I have to tell now?"

"A little."

"Okay, Raju *bhaiya* is getting married..."

"Raju *bhaiya*..." I tried to place him among her numerous cousins, "The one who used to carry you piggyback all day long?" I asked and she chuckled.

"Yes, the same..."

"Where is he these days?"

"Pune."

"Where is the marriage? Pune?"

"No, here in Chennai. The dates and all are being decided. When mummy came to know about it, she asked papa if we could visit Delhi in November as we'll be stuck here in December." She paused.

"Then? Go on and please don't cry!"

"Papa told her that she could go if she wanted to but that he won't allow me. He said he was sure I'd lie again and meet you!" She managed to say that.

"Don't worry, I'll come."

"You? How can you come?" she asked, stunned.

"I'll explain all that when we talk at night. Bye, love you and don't you cry."

⌒

She called at eleven-forty. Late as usual. But I don't mind that. In fact, I sort of like these typical cute habits that accompany a typical cute girl. Coming late, taking hours to dress up, irritating you and getting irritated at small-small things. Yes, sometimes when your mood is not receptive, these things do get on to you, but mostly you smile inwardly and marvel at the uniqueness and beauty of a girl. Charms unlimited!

It is so lovely to talk into the night with her. We lose all sense of time and surroundings, and become completely lost in each other when, suddenly, one of us glances at the watch – it's been rather long; it's been two hours! A trifle if you take into account the other long twenty two hours of the day, but absurdly long when you realize it is an STD call. It is so difficult to hang up. We have so much to talk about and it seems we have just begun, when the damned watch proves us wrong. How lovely things pass so quickly and boring things seem eternal, will always remain a puzzle.

So she told me as promised, in detail, about why she was not coming. There was her cousin's marriage and that, too, in Chennai. These coincidences kill you. You wonder if it is a game going on. How, of all the zillion places, can her brother choose a girl in Chennai? And just as we were discussing our eventful life, getting sentimental, I told her again, that it is fine, if that's the game, then we have to play it. I'd come to Chennai. She replied lovingly and crying, "But how will you come?"

"Don't worry, I have many options. I told you about my Industrial Tour in December. I can fake it at home and come to Chennai. Then we also have our Inter-IIT meet scheduled at IIT Madras this year. I can try my luck there. Or I can apply for training in some company in Chennai. Or maybe, I can come with my friends. You see, ma'am, for your genius lover there are options unlimited. No worries."

"Please don't lie at your home. If you are caught, there'll be more problems. Right now, only my parents know. What if your parents come to know as well?"

"See, that's a risk that we'll have to take. And, God willing, it'll all be fine."

"But, better if you don't have to lie. I don't see how you can come!" she said, worried.

The mere thought of going to Chennai and meeting her had dispelled every bit of droopiness in me. I was already looking forward to my adventure. My tone was now brimming with exuberance and *filmi* spirit. I told her as Mr. Shah Rukh Khan, himself, would tell his heroine:

"Shreya, you want to meet me or not?"

"Of course, I do. But how will you come? It is so risky. What if something happens?"

I repeated, "You want to meet me or not? Say yes or no and nothing else."

"Yes."

"Then, stop crying and stop worrying. I will come, darling. And besides, what is life if it is normal and boring? It must have some adventure, otherwise all thrill and enjoyment will be lost," I said philosophically, "And you know how much I love movies and things that happen in them, so it'll be fun. And, if we pull this through, won't we have nice things to tell our grandchildren?"

"Yes..." she said in a low voice.

"So, when God is giving us such a good chance to live a movie, why should we despair?"

"But, how much more *filmi* can it get?"

"Don't know that, I hope it is normal sometimes too, but yes, right now it is a perfect script for a *masala* movie."

"You'll come this far, Tejas, just for me?"

"Anything for you, ma'am, anything!"

And we went on talking into the night. About cute things, silly things; telling each other the love that we had for each other and how much we missed each other, over a million times. And never once did it sound stale; each time we felt the same joy hearing it, our souls so lost in each other's. Tough times, however unwelcome they might be, how much we may curse them, do one good for sure; they bring us closer. They remind us all how much we need each other and that we are incomplete without each other. They test our love and it is so beautiful to sail together, hand in hand, enduring storms, and in this effort if we may perish too, our love will live on forever.

S aid Rishabh: "It is best that you apply for a month long training in some Chennai firm. They excuse you for the Industrial Tour, then. No suspicions."

The green lawns of IIT stretched out in delight. The trees smiled, the birds sang, the tall MS building shone and, our lectures over, we chirruped at the Holistic Food Centre, a cosy mess in IIT.

The month of October is ideal for plotting and planning. The weather invigorates you thoroughly. The mind is fresh and a smile adorns your face all day. In the heart joys abound, and in the mind ideas. You don't have to worry about wiping the sweat off your brow, nor about crossing your arms to counter the winter chill. You don't have to bother about anything, just lie dormant in the mellow sun, while the mind ponders and does the necessary planning. The cool breeze brings with itself fresh ideas and the feeble sun is warm enough to ripen them. The breeze this year was sure an intelligent one.

All I had done for the past two days was stretch out in the sun and let the mind wander and ponder. And now, I discussed the possibilities with two of my friends. "No way, yaar," I said in response to Rishabh, "My dad knows what a sloth I am. I wouldn't train for a day, he knows. One month and that too in Chennai! It will tell him all. 'Who's the gal, son?' he'll straightaway ask me.

16

Pritish, a sports freak like me, who was listening to it all quietly, suddenly erupted, "What about the Inter-IIT sports meet at Chennai in December? Perfect, man, perfect. No more discussion," he said rubbing his hands excitedly, as is his habit.

"You mean I should tell at home that I have been selected?" I asked disapprovingly.

"Why not?"

"I can't."

It pricked my conscience. I bet some of you will laugh at this sudden discovery. "Are you not betraying your parent's trust already?" you'd, no doubt, jibe and rub it in. But let me tell you that even the biggest knaves have some scruples. They all draw a line somewhere. Robin Hood never swindled the poor. Billy the Kid never murdered innocent women and children. And Tejas Narula would never hurt his father's pride in him and his achievements. If I'd tell him that I was playing for the college, he'd hug me and say, "Well done, son," and those very words would kill me.

He has always been so supportive and encouraging. A perfect dad. And to lie to him, who has blind faith in me, pains me no end. But you do understand, I hope, that meeting my love is not possible without keeping him in the dark. So I have no choice. But I better lie in a proper manner. Lie morally, you can say. It is not that bad to lie about what you did on a one-paisa tour; but to lie about winning gold in a marathon is too much. No, sir!

Rishabh reiterated, "I still maintain, get a training there."

"I told you, I can't" I said peevishly.

"Fine, your wish," he gave in, irritated.

"See, you don't need to get into all that hassle. You don't want to lie about Inter-IIT, you can't train, then just fake the Industrial Tour," summed up Pritish.

"Yes, I'll bunk the Industrial Tour and instead go to Chennai. That's the best chance I have. Only the risks involved are high. If, by any chance, my parents come to know, I'll be dead," I said.

"But how, man? How? They won't doubt you. And if they don't see anything fishy, they'll be normal," Pritish spoke, excited.

He had a point. And I knew it well, too. Over a life of lying and frauds one comes to know the importance of staying confident and calm. You can sell a ton of brass as gold if you have the right look on your face.

"The main problem is that if my phone is not reachable and they call any one of you, I can be in trouble."

"That we'll manage, *yaar*. We'll tell him that you are not with us but busy in some factory where your cell is not reachable, and that we'll ask you to call them..."

I felt I was closer to my Shreya already. As Pritish and Rishabh fought over my plans, as if it was they who were going, I sat back, withdrawing from the conference and was transported two thousand kilometres across the country – blue sky, blue sea, cool breeze. And there I could see Shreya, with her hair blowing in the breeze, twenty paces from me in a white dress, angel like, adorned with the slightest of smiles, waiting for me to wrap her in my arms.

"Shhh," said Pritish suddenly, breaking my dream "There comes Pappi..."

"So?" I asked.

"He is the tour in-charge."

"Who is in charge, brothers?" came a booming voice from behind. It was Tanker – 'The Lord of IIT'. Take note, you all; two critical characters have just made your acquaintance.

For now though, let us keep aside these men of importance. The air is magical, the mood romantic; and all that comes to the mind is Shreya.

January, this year.

For a long time now, I had wanted to ask her the question. Again. I had already asked once before. I had been preparing myself for days now. "I *have* to ask her again," a part of me said to myself, "I cannot let her play with my heart any longer." But then another voice shouted from inside me, "You moron, it's been only three months since you last asked the question. Don't be hasty again."

These conflicts are the worst. These voices, they fight like unruly street boxers and in the end leave you at sea, for no one wins. But then however much ambivalent you might be, you *have* to decide on something. You've got to play the referee and, after twelve good rounds, raise one voice's hand, forgive me for being abstract, and slip a garland around its neck.

I decided that I would ask her again. I was nervous as hell. She messaged me at about one in the noon that she'd call me after she got back home from college, that is, at around three. I was at home, it being a Saturday again. Between one and three, I visited the loo an absurd number of times. That, my readers, elucidates best the kind of effect a girl produces on a boy. And, in our case, a boy endowed with courage of no small measure. You must have gathered as much from the facts of the previous chapters. You must have silently appreciated my guts and said to yourself, "Boy! He is fearless," and now you must be let down by my attitude. Well, all I can say is: have faith in my audacity. Even the bravest of souls totter sometimes. I bet that Hitler, himself, would have gone weak in his knees, faced with such a daunting task.

Bertram Wooster would have gulped in one of the famous Jeeves potions at a time as stressful as this. But I had no Jeeves by my side and am not much of an ethanol consumer. But the occasion demanded some. So I went to my refrigerator and took out a two-litre bottle of Coke. I poured it into one of my father's beer mugs which I sometimes use for cold coffee. I added some lime and drank my preparation just as Wooster drank Jeeves's to soothe his nerves before any enormous task. Coke, I am told, has caffeine; so it is bound to calm you down. It was the closest thing to vodka or rum that was available.

I glanced at the clock after each second. I walked up and down my room nervously, time and again felt a strange sensation in my stomach again and kept visiting the loo. This went on till three. I finished the entire bottle of Coke between these visits. But it did no good.

All this while, memory of the last time kept coming back to me. What if I get a "No!" again? I comforted myself by arguing that this time around things were better and surer. But hadn't I thought the same the last time too? Boy! That had been a painful night. I still remembered vividly the kind of effect it had on me.

It is worth recounting the story to you all. And I will begin from the beginning this time. It is high time I told you about myself more, about how my romance started.

January, the year before.

January. What a lovely month! The month that brings with itself a fresh year. The month in which are born new hopes, new joys, new ideas, new expectations, new resolutions, new everything. The month which is as fresh as the early morning dew.

January. The month that brought her.

⤿

Now that we've arrived to this point in the narrative where I must unfold before you a most unique episode, I must tell you all, my readers, that I was once a sceptic, a ridiculer of this thing called Fate. You may prefer to call it destiny or kismet or coincidence but since the mentioned episode I have known this entity as Mr. Fate. Though guiding my life since birth and, no doubt, yours, his movements were all but obscure to my eyes, until he chose to show up and how!

Now, lie back, all you lovers and let your mind slip back to that fortunate accident, that ingenious stroke of fortune which enabled you to meet your love. I do not talk about the moment you fell in love; no, I talk about the *accident*, that singular coincidence, when he or she, not yet your love, bumped into your life. Now, forgive me, I ask you all to delete that incident from your life, though from it hinges your entire life; it is a scenario you shudder to contemplate, but do it; what remains is an *aloo parantha* without *aloo*.

So it was that Mr. Fate had planned a similar accident for me and had it been absent, no doubt, you would not be reading this book and I would still be a sceptic. But now a believer, as I continue the story, I urge you to become a believer too in the strange workings of Mr Fate – destiny, kismet, coincidence et al – in whose hands we are mere puppets.

It was the eve of my birthday, I distinctly recall. Vineet, my dearest brother, was here on a vacation from US, along with our *bhabhi* (not Vineet's wife) and it was going to be a grand birthday, what with their presence gracing the event after a long time. Although a character of significance in this story and my life, my brother has only a guest appearance here and I will talk about him in detail later.

We were planning the morrow after my classes at *bhabhi*'s place when she suggested going to a movie.

And, now, I shudder to contemplate the scenario if she hadn't done so. Would someone else have? If not, then how would I have met Shreya? There are other ifs and buts – the cinema halls could have been different, the show timings...what not... That it was meant to be is all that comes to my lips.

And so it was that *bhabhi* uttered:

"Let's watch a movie tomorrow. Is that SRK starrer out?"

"Yes, it is good, I have heard," I said.

"Great, we'll watch the eleven o'clock show and then head towards your home to celebrate your birthday with *Chachi's* yummy cakes." My mom is famous for them.

"Tejas, call Palak and ask her if she can come tomorrow; it'll be fun if all kids get together. But Sneha will have school, I guess," said *bhabhi*.

"Yes, Sneha won't be able to come, but I'll ask Palak right away." Time to start the introductions, I guess. Sneha and Palak are my younger sisters, and if you are curious about the whole real sister and cousin sister thing which interests me the least, you'll say that Palak is my cousin and that Sneha is the real one. For me both are sisters, dear and loving. We are of the same age group being born within two years of each other. As with all sisters, they are hugely possessive and do not approve of my uncivilized habits and frivolous nature. Their ultimate aim remains to tame me into a presentable young man. A pursuit which has borne no fruit and that despairs them most along with my mom and my *didi*, Ria *didi*, who is another cousin sister, the only one older and seven years that. There'll be more on her later. A lot more.

So I called up Palak without wasting any time. She had been at odds with me and Vineet lately because we were spending most of our time roaming here and there, and not with her at home. And well, God save a brother when his sis has drawn the sword.

"Hi sis! College over?"

"Yes, I just entered home. And you must be *enjoying* yourself," she said with sarcasm.

"Of course, you know I enjoy myself everywhere."

"Blah-blah... People like you and your brother, who have no other work in life but to hop from one place to another..."

"Like a cat on a hot tin roof..."

"What?"

"Nothing, an English saying you may not be aware of. What was it that you were saying, dearest sis? That Vineet and me, who have no other work in life..."

"...always enjoy. At least you think you do. Mad nomads," she said, mocking.

"You mind that? And don't you be jealous."

"Please, jealous and me? I am enjoying a break from you two. Stay there as long as possible and relieve me from the stress."

"But sis, so unfortunate, that we have to meet tomorrow again, for my birthday."

"I know, even I was getting depressed thinking about that. Anyway, I treat it as a part of life. Sorrow follows joy. But joy will follow soon. But yes, I am excited about tomorrow..."

"Precisely! You should be. After all, it is your dearest brother's birthday and it calls for all the zeal you can muster. So, good! But let me increase your excitement a million fold by informing you that tomorrow we all are going for your favourite Khan's *'Kuch Nahi Hota Hai'*. We'll pick you up from home..."

"Excuse me. First of all, how did you get in that thick head of yours that you are my dearest brother? Sorry to dispel all your illusions for the millionth time; you are not," she thundered. I could sense that her mood was such that she could break my neck and not feel sorry about it. I thanked God I wasn't in her vicinity, "And sorry, again, to tell you that I am already going for that movie. And not with *you all*. That is what I was alluding to when I said I am excited about tomorrow."

"What? Now with whom are you going for the movie? Got a boyfriend?" I bantered.

"None of your business that, but tomorrow I am going with my friends."

"Wow! What preposterous planning is that," I said in anger, "You can go with your stupid friends anytime, sis. It's my birthday. Tomorrow all of us are going. So, you have to come and I won't take no for an answer," I ordered.

"Well, that is what you'll get from me. A flat *no*. And don't you call my friends stupid."

"But you can go with your *highly intellectual* friends later. Who can be more special to you than your brother?" I asked emotionally.

"Well as a matter of fact anyone would be. But yes, my best friend is here after a long time and so I got to meet her; and we all just planned a movie."

"May I ask which one of your best friends is this now? You change them as frequently as one changes socks. Is she someone I know of or have you got a new one again? Girls, the funniest creatures." Now I was getting hot too and I decided to take her on.

"Shut up! I am talking about Shreya. My school friend."

"Oh, the same girl that went off to Chennai? Leaving her best friend here, alone," I said agitated. Inwardly I cursed her friend. How idiotic of her to come to Delhi and meet my sister on the same day that she should be with me. All of us were going together for a movie after such a long time. And this girl had to ruin the celebration.

"Shut up and bye," she raged.

"Fine, bye. But just an advice: You better go to the movie with me than hop around with pseudo friends."

"But I am going to do exactly that."

"Fine," I said angry but saddened.

"Bye..."

"*Arre*, wait a second. You sure, you're not coming? We'll not book your ticket."

"Yes, I have my ticket in my hand."

"So which theatre and show?"

"At the Grand. Eleven AM show."

I jumped out of the sofa on hearing that. We were going for the same show.

Which completes the accident. But Mr. Fate's job over, it is a man's duty to do his work and so I did. I tried to recall what Shreya looked like. She was pretty, if I had placed her right in my head.

"Wow, we are going for the same show. How fortunate!"

"Most unfortunate. Don't you dare speak to me there. It'll be ignominious for me if my friends see that I have a cauliflower like you as my brother."

"On the contrary, it'll be most honourable. I can see your friends talking to you – "Your brother! How charming!! Can I have his number?"

"Yes, why not! Don't dream; get a mirror if you haven't got one."

"By the way, how many of you are going? Someone pretty?"

"Four of us. And what will you do if someone is pretty?"

"Change parties. I'll entertain you and your dearest friends."

"Thanks. But we are better off alone."

"Your wish. By the way, is Shreya the one whose picture you showed me last time?"

"Yes. So?"

"She seems interesting," I said full of hope and joy.

"Tejas, don't you get ideas. If you come up and speak to me there, I'll kill you."

"I will not talk to you, of course. Shreya will be enough. So don't be bothered."

"Don't you dare!"

"You know me, sis, I will."

"Good, make a fool of yourself in front of them. Your wish. Besides she has a boyfriend. So no hopes, Romeo."

"Well, not a worry for me, they come and go, boyfriends...

Yesterday he,

Tomorrow me,

Day after I don't care

If she has any.

Sounds like a poem! Wow, I can speak in verse, sister. Wonder what Shakespeare would have said about that."

"Shut up! I'll warn my friends about you – what a flirt you are."

"Do that. Bye for now, see you tomorrow."

"Bye, but behave yourself tomorrow."

"Let us see."

"Tejas, hurry up!" shouted *bhabhi*.

"Coming," I shouted from inside the loo.

"Even girls don't take that long to get ready. What's taking you so long?"

"Just a minute!"

I looked one last time in the mirror. And set my hair one last time with my hand. Boys like me don't fancy combs. I should have had a hair cut last week, I thought, when mother was after my life and had threatened to chop my mop while I was asleep. I had wisely slept with my door bolted for the entire week. How I wished I had listened to her; for once she was right.

She is always too finicky about my hair and hair length and if she has her way, she will soak my hair in a gallon of oil and then comb them back, firmly adhered to my scalp, and then proudly announce me as her *'babu beta'* or in simple terms her innocent, smart and ideal son. A typical Indian mother. And I, who have grown up admiring the dishevelled mane of Paul McCartney and co., naturally suffer irreconcilable differences with her on all hair related subjects, which have threatened to disturb the peace of our home, time after time.

But, today there was no doubt about it. She was right. Blessed are the souls who say 'listen to your mother', I thought. The more I looked, the more I felt like Conan, the famous barbarian. Anyway, I gave up shaping the superfluous mass into something remotely civilized. As dad says, one has to do the best with what one has. I gave one last fleeting glance at the other parts of my face which I had forgotten in the wake of the hair crisis. I had three pimples on my nose. Bloody hell! Hardly the sort of thing that cheers an already blighted soul. What a birthday gift that was! I was wondering at the injustice of God, when, again, shouts came from everywhere. I shot out of the bathroom that very instant.

A step out in the sun was just what the doctor would have ordered for me. As I inhaled the fresh breeze I could feel my woes fading away and a balmy feeling abounding me. I looked up. The sky was blue, absolutely blue and there was not a spot to be seen. The whole canvas was lit up by a splendid sun. Just the sort that brightens up your soul on a winter day. Sunny winter mornings, wow! It was the kind of morning when a bloke after stepping out in his pyjamas, stretches his arms, yawns and mumbles to himself, "Ahaaaa". And I did as much.

The vivacious ambience struck the right chord and sent a signal to the brain which sent a song to my lips. It was no more than a reflex. '*Summer of '69*'. Though hardly what you'll call a summer, the song suited the spirit. The air resonated and sang along with me. I wished that I could play my guitar. So I moved to the car with a hip and a hop. My mind was lit up with the prospects of the morning.

The movie theatre was a half-an-hour drive from home and we reached well before time. The attendance in the morning show is thin and the moment we landed, I could see Palak with two friends. The others spotted her too and our group moved towards hers. I finally saw her friends clearly. Shreya was missing. Palak wished me 'Happy Birthday' again, this time in person. Preliminary introductions revealed that the two girls were Saumya and Kamna. Palak eyed me with the dare-you-flirt look. But I wasn't interested. Period.

"Almost half an hour to go, why don't we all grab a bite?" someone asked. I was too lost to notice.

"Palak, why don't you join us?" asked *bhabhi* I believe.

"No, not yet, *bhabhi*. One of my friends is yet to come. So we'll wait outside. We'll join you when she's there," Palak replied.

"Shreya is always late," complained Saumya or Kamna.

I glanced at my watch. There was about half an hour to go; more if you take into account the advertisements and all. Plenty of time to play around! While entering the food court, I could almost have shouted, "Brilliant!" as my mind gave finishing touches to my plan.

I excused myself out of the group. "I am not hungry, *bhabhi*. I'll look at the magazines and enjoy the sun for a while." No one complained. "*Bhabhi*, give me your mobile; Vineet, give me a missed call when you are through," I said. Back then I didn't have a mobile. *Bhabhi*'s mobile was of strategic importance as she had acquired a new sim-card and I was sure no one had her number.

I avoided the path where Palak stood, still waiting. I was relieved. I chose a vantage point and dialled the number. My heart was full of mirth. It was a lovely morning and I was doing what I like to do the most. Playing Mr. Holmes. Disguising, impersonating, plotting, conning...

"Hullo!" said a sweet voice.

"Hullo!" I changed my voice to a gruff one and drew immense satisfaction with what I sounded. "Is that Palak?"

"Yes."

"*Beta*, I am Shreya's dad. I had some work, so she got late. Sorry for that. She just left with the driver and will reach in ten-fifteen minutes."

"Oh, *namaste* uncle! No problem."

"*Namaste beta*. That main road leading to the hall has a jam. So she'll come via another. She told me to inform you to wait at the back entrance."

"Okay, uncle."

"And yes, she doesn't have her cell phone. That's why I called to inform."

"Fine, uncle."

"*Beta*, please wait at the back. She doesn't know much about the area. And doesn't even have a phone. So wait there only."

"Fine, uncle."

"Hope you are fine, enjoy the movie."

"Thanks, uncle, we will."

"Bye."

"Bye."

I saw them moving. Going, going, gone. I let out a breath. Job well done. I prayed that Shreya would come soon and not call Palak on her own. And given the thin crowd, I'll figure out her figure easily.

⌒

Standing there, after successful execution of the first phase of the plan, I started feeling nervous. These girls always give you jitters. It is no easy task dealing with girls under normal circumstances, and, today, the circumstances being trying, it was depressing. It is one thing when you are standing in the sun, abounding in your life's calm, when suddenly you sense a slap on your back and, turning, find yourself eye to eye with your childhood crush. But the scale of enormities, when you have told a hundred lies to intercept an unfamiliar beauty, is a unique one. You can still utter, in the first case, life-saving hi's and ya's while the mind is holidaying. But the second case is hopeless.

All my inhibitions assumed the form of a giant demon and punched me in my face. Bang! How messy I looked! Bad hair, pimples... I began to feel like an idiot. What a foolish plan I had devised! The bright sun and the cool breeze gave no respite. I was hardly aware of them. I was about to give my plan a serious second thought when lightning struck.

Her majesty appeared.

Well... you must have read countless books, seen innumerable movies celebrating with fanfare the arrival of the heroine. Strong winds start to blow, thunderstorms strike and as if this noise was not deafening enough, loud music erupts and the *tapori* in the front row acknowledges it all with a sincere whistle.

Poets write lyrics heralding the descent of the divine beauty from heaven. One reads incomprehensible stuff about rosy cheeks, coral lips and starry eyes, entwined with the indecipherable thee(s) and thou(s) and thy(s). I have neither the ability of the poet nor the flourish of the dramatist. But I must admit that I was floored.

I pick up again from the passage where I mentioned that lightning had struck. I cannot explain it better. She looked amazing. She was like a painting, a song. Everything about her was so graceful and fluid. Like breeze, she flowed towards me, her hair flying and ear rings dancing. She was the breeze. With a whiff of perfume. And I was stunned.

One can never say if it was love-at-first-sight or not but, admittedly, the dent she left in my heart was a big one. These beauties hit you like a storm and you never recover. Never ever. That was my case, entirely. I was completely lost, enraptured, mesmerized... The moment will remain with me forever, framed and gilded. When I close my eyes, it all comes back to me, and my heart dances with delight; the perfect picture... her glowing face, her shiny, flying hair, her smooth walk, her dangling ear rings, her mirror-work bag by her side, her red pullover, her blue jeans and her searching eyes.

She looked around for her friends and looked confused. I had to move before she took her cell phone out, if she had one. I regained consciousness and composure. There was no use worrying. She'd not eat me; nor was she the last girl on earth. I had to act, now, that I had planned so much. Be a man, Tejas. I looked at my clothes again. Nice jacket, nice sweatshirt, nice jeans. Cool, I thought. "Be a Man!" I said to myself again and walked towards the heavenly creature.

The close-up only enhanced her beauty. Her searching eyes were innocent and beautiful. She had a fresh, milky complexion, and her red pullover made her look all the more radiant. Winters, oh lord! Girls, they have never looked better. They look so fair and bright, and the skin seems flawless. Their lovely, glowing faces peer out of the bright woollens so cutely. Girls indeed blossom in winters.

And blossoming she was. The red dress made her look so pink and lovely. I could almost have kissed her cheeks. Despite the heavy woollens, I could see she had a lissom figure. She had shiny, black hair and was wearing silver ear rings. She was simple. And beautiful. Perfect.

I gave her a slight pat on her shoulder from the side. She turned towards me drowning me in her sweet aroma. And I was lost again in her brown eyes and light perfume. Magic! She had a hint of *kajal* in her eyes.

"Yes?" she asked, breaking the spell. 'Talk, idiot!'I said to myself.

"Shreya?" I asked.

"Yes," she said surprised, obviously.

"Hi! I am Palak's brother," I said and forwarded my hand.

She shook it. Her hands were soft. It felt really good. She smiled and returned the greeting. She had beautifully chiselled pink lips with a hint of gloss. Extremely kissable. I ventured into solving the puzzle for her straightaway. "I can see you are surprised. Don't be. Palak will be here soon. Actually one of your friends, Saumya, I suppose, had lost her way. So Palak has gone to fetch her with the driver. I had come to drop her but your friend thought I should stay and keep you engaged till she comes back. So here I am." God, I spoke too much.

"Well, thanks!" she smiled again. She had a lovely smile. She didn't say anything else. Why don't these girls speak?

"I am Tejas, by the way. Hi again. I hope this was a better introduction." I once again shook her hand and she laughed.

"So, how much time will she take?" she inquired.

"Not much, I guess." What to talk about, I thought. Yes. "So, how is Chennai?"

"Well, not bad. But yes, nothing like Delhi."

"Absolutely! Nothing like Delhi. This winter will be a pleasant change, I suppose, from boiling Chennai."

"Yes, a lot better. It is really hot there."

"And it is really cold here. I think I'll have something hot."

"Okay."

"What about you? Tea? Now don't be formal and all," I said like an aunty, "I don't like that. Tea?"

"No, I prefer coffee."

"Oh, wow! Me, too. There is time; let us have coffee then." I hated coffee. How much lying goes into impressing a girl! An extremely tedious task.

I took her to a corner so that we were not visible. I bought two coffees. And furthered the conversation. "I believe you are pursuing management. Palak speaks a lot about you." I hoped she would ask what I was doing, and then I could tell her about my prestigious college. And she asked.

"Yes, I am. What about you?"

"Well, I am studying Industrial Engineering."

"From?"

"IIT Delhi," I announced grandly. I hoped to see an open mouth or a twinkle in her eye but there was nothing. Again, just her lovely smile. She hardly seemed impressed. I was running out of topics and time now. She was not helping either with just her monosyllables and her smiles. I hadn't expected her to be gregarious the very first time but I hadn't expected such reticence. She took her time, I supposed. Unlike

33

the aggressive girls that one sees so often these days. I liked that, but she should at least say something.

"So it must be really difficult... leaving all friends here and settling in a new city," I said, trying to strike a tender chord.

"Yes, it was difficult initially; but now it is better."

"Yes, one has to adjust. I saw some of the snaps you sent to Palak the other day. You looked nice," I said, trying to compliment her in a subtle way. I couldn't say, "You look hot," straightaway.

"Thanks!" she smiled again.

And it all went off again. There was a silence, an awful one. It kills you. You feel so awkward. You feel so conscious. It is so damned hard with strangers and harder still with stranger girls. And you want to pull out your hair in agony when the girl is so indifferent. You strain every part of your brain to search for a topic, yet you find none. It is like the world is void of everything and nothing exists. There is nothing in this damn world that can be talked about. Zilch. As the strain was becoming a tad too much, she spoke. Thank God!

"Hope they come soon. Just about fifteen minutes left. Let us have a look at some books in the meanwhile. You like reading?" she asked and proceeded towards the corner book stall.

"Yes, I love it. Nothing like books. So who's your favourite author?" I asked, happy that we had found a common liking.

"Well, no favourite as such. I haven't read that many books. But yes, I like Grisham and Eric Segal."

"Love Story..." I said, knowing that every girl loved it. I had loved it too. Since, I had read many more Segal books. I hadn't read any Grisham.

"Yes, it was amazing. In fact, that's the only one I have read of Segal."

"And that's his best. It is so touching. I almost cried in the end."

"Oh you did! Boys don't usually. I cried so much."

"Well, I am a little different. Being a little emotional is not bad, I

34

guess. But yes, boys usually loathe such books." She was impressed. I could see it in her expression.

"So, who's your favourite?" she asked, picking up a Grisham novel. The Firm.

"Well, I love R.K. Narayan. Have read all of his books. He writes so close to life; about the simple joys of life."

"I guess I have read one of his too, Coolie."

"No, that one is by Mulk Raj Anand," I said politely, trying not to be condescending, yet being impressive. Her knowledge about books was poor. Had read only one of Segal and yet he was her favourite. How funny! I wondered if she had read only one of Grisham's as well.

"Oops. You are right. But yes, I saw Malgudi Days on TV. I loved that."

"Same here. That remains my favourite serial. So real and subtle! And nowadays, you have these stupid, mindless and boring *saas-bahu* sagas. Those were the days..." I sounded like an octogenarian, I thought.

"I swear. They are so yuk! I wonder how my mom watches them. And all of them are exactly the same."

"Yes... it's better to read books... so do you like any?"

"Yes, I think I should buy this one. I'd like to read more of Grisham."

"Right. After all he is your favourite author," I said teasingly, "Like Segal. I bet you have read only one of his too."

"No, actually two," she burst out laughing. And so did I.

Well we had struck a chord now. The topics were coming naturally and we seemed to have some similarities. She was not indifferent now but a keen talker. And I loved that. I was becoming too lost in her. And there were ten minutes to go. Alas!

She bought the book and I bought one too, of Sir Wodehouse. I told her about his great humour and that she must read his books. It was nice haggling for the books together. Seemed like a work of collaboration. And what better than to team up with a girl!

The topic shifted to likings and all. She told me she loved dance. I told her that I was hopeless at dance and all I could manage was *bhangra*, which, therefore, I had to employ for western numbers as well. She laughed. I told her that I loved music.

"Well, nothing like music. It is my life. For your information, by the way, I happen to play the guitar." Thank God, she was at least impressed by this. I was always told that nothing flatters a girl more than a guitar-playing guy, but till date I hadn't been lucky. I had given up all hopes.

"Wow," she said. "I'd like to hear it sometime."

"Hmm, I think I should grant you the privilege. Not everyone is so lucky, Shreya." I must have said that about myself.

"Well, thanks. I am deeply honoured."

"So, when do you leave? I'll try and find you an appointment out of my busy schedule."

"I am sorry, Tejas, I leave tomorrow. Next time, perhaps. Don't forget then..."

"No, I promise I won't. But you should return the favour."

"Hmm, so what should I do?"

"Teach me to dance. I am pathetic."

"Only if you teach me to play the guitar..."

"Deal."

"Deal."

We shook hands again. Her soft hands. It had turned out to be wonderful. My God! I thought... Learning dance from this angel. I was lost in my dreams. Lost in her. Lost in her perfume. Lost in the moment. I lost all sense of time. I wished our meeting would never end. I wanted to talk on and on with her. I could have never imagined that we'd gel so well and be so comfortable talking. That such a pretty girl could be so affectionate with an imbecile like me. My reverie was broken when I heard her say excitedly, "Hi Palak!"

All I could manage to say through a few broken sentences was this:

"Hi... Palak... So you... Are back... Good... This is Shreya, by the way... A good friend... I guess you two know each other... Shreya... This is my dearest sister... Palak." I was dead.

"Hi Shreya!" Palak said, smiling at her. Then she turned towards me. "By the way, she is *my* friend."

"Oh! What a coincidence. I could never have thought that we'd have a common friend. Extremely gratifying to learn that." Saumya and Kamna intervened saying a 'Hi' each and asking Shreya what she was doing *here* at the entrance when she was supposed to be *there* at the back.

"What!" Shreya uttered, surprised.

"Yes, your dad called and said that you'll arrive at the back entrance. But we had waited for long, so we came back here to check again," explained Palak.

"My dad? Palak, he left yesterday. Mom and I will return tomorrow. How could he have called?" asked Shreya, surprised again.

Well, the director of the scene would have wanted to me to quit the stage, now, and I itched to do the same. "Sounds like a confusion to me. The movie is going to start soon. I better go. You also hurry up or you'll miss the beginning," I said and looked at Shreya.

"Yes, we should move. Nice meeting you, Tejas."

"The pleasure is all mine, Shreya. And don't you forget the deal," I said smiling and she smiled back.

"Well, you are the one who is busy. I hope I get an appointment," she said, teasing. That killed me.

"Well, you will. I am always free for pretty girls. Bye."

I smiled at her and she blushed a little and said bye. I shook her soft hand again for the fourth time. I wondered when I'd hold her hand again. I hadn't the slightest clue that it would be so long. I looked at Palak. She gave me a dreadful look. I smiled at her too. One of those I-won-you-lost smiles. Saumya and Kamna looked disgusted. But, I was on cloud nine.

They turned and moved away. I faintly heard Shreya asking them, 'So, Saumya, where were you stuck?" They proceeded and I watched her go. Her silky hair and silver earrings and her petite figure. I longed for her.

As they went farther, I noticed some unrest. I could not make out their conversation but assumed it to centre round me and my antics. Their battalion suddenly stopped and they turned around. It was not unlike the synchronous about-turn of the *jawan*s on Republic Day. And 'about-turn' did I, and started walking in the opposite direction, when Palak called out, "Tejas, just a minute."

"Yes," I said, turning around. They were right in front of me. Four of them. All furious. Right then I heard *bhabhi* calling out my name. Her battalion marched towards us. I had been cornered and how!

I felt like Chhota Rajan or Chhota Shakeel or *Chhota ya Bada* whatever, *yaar*. It must be a trying experience for them, the moment of trap. All those ingenious plots they must have devised, the dangerous plans they must have executed... the joy they must have derived from their successes... all must have dissolved and disappeared in a flash, in this moment of truth. I could sympathise with them. I drew comfort from the learning that popularity in my case wouldn't be of such impressive magnitude. The clan that would learn about my exploits was thankfully much smaller. As I saw the battalion approach, I felt as Bin Laden might have felt watching the FBI march towards him. One felt like a wanted gangster. One needed to act, urgently; things could be controlled even now. All was not lost. One required tact.

"Palak, let them go and watch the movie. I'll explain every thing to you," I said coolly to Palak.

"Oh! Don't be afraid, Tejas. Let *everyone* know about your glorious deed." She was boiling.

"I'll take a minute to explain. Let them go. If you want to tell them something, do that later. Don't create a scene here."

"Fine," she said angrily.

I told *bhabhi* that I'd come in a minute. She teased me: "Flirting around, Mr. Tejas?" I smiled and said, "I am glad you understand, *bhabhi*." I gave her the mobile phone and took my ticket. Vineet whispered to me, "You rascal, mend your ways. I'll kick your butt when you come back."

I returned to the furious four.

"What did you tell Shreya?" Palak got ready for the court martial.

"I saw you leaving this place. So I assumed Shreya might not be coming for the movie. But when I saw her here, I thought, might as well talk to her a little and then tell her to join you. So... I just told her what she told you that I told her. It was harmless, sis."

"Come to the point, Mr. Tejas. What about the phone call?"

"Which phone call? How do I know?"

"Of course, you know. It can't be a coincidence that we are asked to go at the back while you flirt in the front."

"Excuse me. I didn't flirt. Ask Shreya. I merely talked to her nicely."

Shreya was puzzled. She didn't know what to say. She didn't look at me nicely at all. Palak moved away and did something with her mobile phone. She dialled 'Shreya's dad's' number, I guess. A series of awkward expressions followed. I couldn't hear her but knew all. She came back red as a tomato and shouted"

"That was *bhabhi's* mobile."

"Which mobile?" I asked innocently.

"From which Shreya's dad called."

"But how did Shreya's dad get *bhabhi's* mobile? Do they know each other? Small place, this world, extremely!"

"Stop your nonsense, I mean someone called from her cell acting like Shreya's dad!"

"Oh my God, I can't see why *bhabhi* will do this. Something's fishy.

And I fail to see how you could mistake her sweet voice as a man's."

"Tejas, stop joking. I can't believe you would do that," she said, looking hurt. "I am sorry, Shreya. I didn't know he could do such a shameful thing." My heart winced at hearing 'shameful'. Some words are like pocket bombs. My sister was hurt. I should have known. Palak does get emotional at such things.

"It is okay, Palak. Don't feel bad. You didn't do anything," said my darling, comforting. She was not even looking at me. I moved towards my dear sister. "I am sorry, sis. I didn't realize you'd feel so bad. Honestly, I did this just to get even with you. And please ask your friend, I talked properly." Her friend still wasn't looking at me.

"Tejas, you have crossed all limits this time..."

"Palak, I did this just because you talked like that on the phone yesterday. I didn't feel good that you were going out with your friends on my birthday. I am sorry. I went too far..." I lied. Of course, I wanted to flirt with Shreya. But I had to lie. She was seriously hurt. I may have been instigated into doing this because of Palak's tone but the real reason was different. I took Palak's hands in mine and said sorry again. I meant that, though. "Now, please don't spoil my birthday, sis. Cheer up. The movie is about to start. You haven't missed anything. First fifteen minutes are ads."

She was still cross, I could see. Saumya and Kamna looked away in disgust. Shreya looked at me, without any anger, I guess. Then she said to Palak. "It is okay *na*, dear. Honestly, I don't feel bad. So please don't fight with him and cheer up. And yes, his behaviour was fine." She was sweet.

"I am sorry, Shreya. Can I talk to you for a moment? In private," I dared to ask her.

"Yes," she said. Thank God!

We moved away a little. Rest of them proceeded towards the hall.

"I am sorry," I said looking into her pretty eyes.

"It is okay. You are quite a prankster though," she commented mockingly.

"Yes. But today it turned out to be horrible. Generally, I like to make people happy."

"Oh?" She had a sarcastic expression.

"Well, I know you won't agree. I am really sorry if I hurt you. But it was really nice meeting you. And I mean that."

"Fine. But honestly I don't like boys who are after girls like this." An acid comment.

"Please! I am not after you," I said, trying to be polite. But I was after her. Now, yes, I was. "I am sorry if I gave you any such impression. I just tried to be a little friendly; turns out I already have spoiled so many people's day," I said, trying to gain sympathy. She did soften.

"It is okay, Tejas. Just be a little careful..." We started walking towards the hall.

"And yes, please pep up my sis. I know you will do that. And you can tell her that I was decent with you, that'll help."

"Fine. I will do that."

"You have a nice heart." I meant that. She had been so considerate and composed during the whole episode. She was a really nice girl. Beautiful. Inside, as well as outside. I was gone for life.

"Thanks. Interesting meeting you anyway," she smiled after a long time. That brightened me up. It indeed wasn't all that bad now. In fact, I felt it had turned out brilliantly.

"Bang on, miss! It is always fun... being with me. I feel life should be a little adventurous. Normal is boring. What do you say?"

"Hmm, nice thought but I have a rather weak heart."

"Hmm, maybe you have the privilege of learning this from me too. Living life king size."

"Yes, *maybe*." She laid stress on that 'maybe'.

We reached the entrance of the theatre. I glanced at my watch. We were about twenty minutes late. We stopped before going in. "Don't worry ma'am, you wouldn't have missed much. The movie has just started," I said, putting on a sophisticated charm.

"I am not worrying, I have already seen it. It is you who should worry, sir." And she laughed. She was not very displeased with the developments, I supposed. In fact, she seemed pleased. Quite pleased.

"Eeeks," I uttered, laughing, "We better rush in then. A moment more though, ma'am. What happens to the guitar and dance lessons? Are they still on?"

"Hmm, I can't say, right now. I'll have to think about it, sir," she said playing around. That killed me again.

"Do tell me though. I hope to stay in touch. Shall I give my email contact?"

"Your wish."

I took that as a yes and gave her mine. I wrote it on a piece of paper I found in my pocket. Thank God, I was carrying a pen. She gave hers too. Not bad at all, Tejas; not bad at all, I said to myself. We moved in, finally. I hardly cared about the movie. I was in awe of her. I didn't know if it was love, but I could have done anything she asked for. These girls hypnotize you.

"By the way, happy birthday," she said so sweetly.

"Thanks, don't I get a gift?"

"No," she said cutely and just like a girl can. We parted finally saying bye and smiling.

I knew I had got the gift, though. The best I could ever get. It couldn't have been a better birthday. She had won my heart and I felt that I had made an impression too.

Such was the unique episode, then, my readers, an impeccable work of Mr. Fate, and I remember singing as I marched towards my seat.

> *Happy Birthday to you!*
> *Happy Birthday to you!*
> *Happy Birthday, dear T-e-j-a-a-a-s,*
> *H-a-p-p-y B-i-r-t-h-d-a-y, t-o y-o-u-u-u-u-u-u!!!!*

As I told you before, there is a song for every occasion!

September, the year before.

God! There isn't even one place where we can be alone. Why do people have to follow us everywhere we go?" I said in frustration. It was getting on to me. We had searched the entire hall, but there was someone everywhere.

"I know! I wonder... Everybody seems to be interested in us," she said, frustrated too.

"I know I am handsome. But that doesn't mean girls and, now, even boys will hound me!" I boasted jokingly.

"Yes, yes, why not! Everybody is after you, Mr. Tom Cruise!" she said bantering.

"*Please*! Don't compare *him* with me. I won't stand such ribaldry. Anyway, I think we should rent a room in this hotel only. There we can be absolutely alone. We can talk and do anything," I said jokingly.

"Wow! We two in one room when all our relatives are down here. What a brilliant idea! I am not your girlfriend, Tejas."

"If only you could be, *didi*."

"What about those two chairs? Pretty secluded, I guess," she said.

"I just hope nobody interrupts while I discourse or he'll be blasted!"

"What if it's a she?"

"Depends, *didi*, depends," I said, stumped and we both laughed.

"So tell the tale, Mr. Romeo."

"Right away, *didi*, right away."

And so I began to tell her the dilemmas that had been troubling me lately and who better to discuss them with, than her. Ria *didi*. The time to introduce her has come. Ria *didi*, my eldest sister, is the daughter of my youngest *tayaji* (uncle – father's elder brother). I have three *tayajis* and my father is the youngest brother. She has been my closest friend for years now. She has been my confidante and agony aunt, the one to whom I turn to in times of trouble, specifically, troubles concerning the devilish species of girls.

So I turned to her once again for her pearls of wisdom at that moment of distress. Thank God, I could do it in person this time; for she was luckily here in India. I have the fortune of seeing her only once a year during her annual summer trip; and now I was glad I did not have resort to the lovely but extremely slow correspondence through letters. In a world that has moved on from snail-mail to hotmail and what-not-mail we still prefer to compose long loving letters to each other. For it is joy to find her envelope with the unfamiliar but curious postage stamp nestling in my letter-box, bearing my name crafted in her hand. And, what joy it is, indeed, to tear open the envelope excitedly but carefully... taking out the letter... reading her lovely handwriting which brings with itself the fragrance of fond memories. She landed a couple of days back. I was there to receive her. We had hugged each other warmly and I had intimated her of my predicament while she was buying her safe mineral water from the IGI Airport lounge.

"*Didi!*" I had exclaimed, "Your brother is in a soup."

"Girls?" she had asked and I had nodded meekly.

"Tell me all, sweets," she had remarked and it was only now, in an obscure cousin's wedding, that we had found an opportunity to talk freely, without my dear sisters – Sneha and Palak – hovering around us. They had some exams.

"There's a problem, *didi*. I like a girl."

"I don't see any problem with that unless the girl thinks that you are a rotten egg."

"No, that's not the case, *didi*."

"Don't tell me you have finally managed to find a girl foolish enough to like you."

"Maybe."

"So that's the problem. You are not sure the traffic is two way?"

"That is just the tip of the iceberg, *didi*. Water's deeper, much deeper," I said, repeating like a philosopher.

"So will you fire away at once or continue to stare at the floor, Mr. Manoj Kumar?" I looked up.

"You remember Gayatri?"

"Of course, I do, the unfortunate girl of Verma uncle who lost her life in an accident? Extremely sad..." I must have leapt a foot or two on hearing that. After all, I had met her just the week before in the neighbourhood café. *Didi* said it in a manner so offhand that it took its toll on me. It seemed like a slap in the middle of a sound sleep. I had liked the girl, and she was a rather nice person. My mind went blank. I hardly noticed that the cutlet I had been chewing so meticulously, deriving joy from every bite, was no longer in my mouth. I had heard a thud, I thought.

"When did that happen?" was all I could utter.

"Why, you only told me last month?" she answered puzzled.

"I did?"

"Yes, when we talked on phone."

"Oh!" Then it dawned on me. It was a monumental communication error. "My God! I said Gayatri's dog lost its life!" I said with relief. And disbelief. A word out of place can cause havoc.

"Oh! The phone lines weren't clear. I am sorry. A gross mistake."

I let out a breath. Thank God, she was alive. There was *didi*, munching cutlets coolly, as if nothing at all had happened. As I regained my senses, now that the gentle soul was alive, I discovered my lost cutlet. There it was, perched comfortably at the bottom of my coke glass emitting bubbles. So that was what the thud was about.

I told her to be a little more considerate before uttering such shockers. She said she would be and told me, "But really, your voice wasn't clear and besides, you sounded pretty cool and happy that day. I myself was astounded by your attitude. Hence my casualness in mentioning the casualty."

"Oh, happy I was! Happy to be free after all, because that Rahul of hers had bitten my butt a hundred times and, in a benevolent mood, had licked my face like a mop on the floor."

"Rahul?"

"Yes, Rahul, the same grotesque dog."

"She named that dog Rahul!" she said, wondering at the ways of the world. Strange indeed, I agree.

"Yes, she did. Apparently Rahul had been Gayatri's crush since LKG who left the school one fine day."

"Sad!"

"Extremely sad! Hence the name Rahul. In memory of the departed."

"Change your name, Tejas!"

"Why?"

"She will be all yours!" she said and we laughed heartily.

"So, what about Gayatri?" she inquired.

"You know she is pretty, *didi*. She was shaken after the loss and found comfort in me..."

"Hmm, so you exploited the age old Rule One of the how-to-win-a-girl theory."

"Absolutely, hit the iron when it's hot. Wipe the girl's tears and she is all yours."

"Wow, brother! You too! All boys are the same!"

"No, *didi*, you know that I won't play with anyone's heart. Precisely the reason why I chat with you."

"Fine, go on."

"So... she has started liking me a lot and I am sure about it."

"Just a moment back you were not sure about it."

"Oh! That was not for her, *didi*. That's the whole problem. Where it gets a trifle too intricate for a nut like me."

She raised her eyebrows and said, "Why don't you say everything clearly, then? You tell it all with an unnecessary air of suspense. Now clear the muddle for me."

"I am trying, *didi*. But it is so damn heavy, too many details."

"I think you are compounding the situation yourself. As far as I remember you were nuts about this girl and when you have got the breakthrough... through a chance of, pardon me, funny misfortune, you behave queerly. And now if you are thinking about another girl, as I gather you are, you are just being stupid. The more you'll look, the prettier other girls will seem. Stop behaving like a child. You like her and she likes you. The case is dismissed. You guys are never satisfied," she thundered.

In wake of this attack, I lost completely what I had to tell *didi*. I began to appreciate the truth in her words and wondered why I was having this conference at all; when I realized that I had not yet completed the story. And suddenly it came back to me.

"No, the case has only just begun, *didi*; please show some patience. You draw conclusions so hastily," I thundered back, "Wait a while."

"Fine, sir," she surrendered.

"So where was I? Yes, true, that I used to like Gayatri, but I am not sure about her. The problem is that I really like another girl," I said in one breath.

"So what's the problem?"

"She is some two thousand kilometres away."

"What! How do you manage all this, Tejas? You can't do a normal thing in the world but pull off such unfathomable... You sure are amazing. Now who is she?"

"Shreya Bhargava."

"Wow, what a way to tell," she laughed. "Won't you add her dad's name too? I am not asking you for the name of the seventeenth president of Mozambique, idiot. Just say Shreya, dumbo," she continued to laugh. These sisters really pull your leg well.

"Yes, so Shreya she is."

"Who is she? Some school-mate?"

"No, Palak's friend." She was stunned.

"Way to go! That's something! Now eyeing your sister's friends... Not bad," she added teasingly.

"She is really great, *didi*."

"Now don't blush brother," she taunted and then suddenly as if stung by a bee added, "Wait a minute. How is she, then, two and a whatever kilometres away? How did you meet her?"

Well, it wouldn't be of use to add most of our subsequent conversation. I have already told you all that and in detail. Our first meeting. I told her everything gleefully and that solved some of her doubts. It would be convenient if you join the conference here. Right here.

"What guts, Tejas!" she said, shaking her head in disbelief. She had been fed a tad too much and I could see it was getting heavy for her. I allowed her a breath.

"Anyway, good move to obtain her mailing address. So did you use it?"

"Obviously. We started mailing each other once a week or so. Normal, friendly, harmless mails. Discussing the usual: movies, music, books... just the extension of our conversation that day. It took us no time to discover that we had similar tastes. Very similar."

"Cool! Go on."

"Yes, so... gradually the frequency of mails increased and so did the number of similarities. I mean, I was myself amazed. This is what drew me most towards her."

"Will you tell me some of them? Don't tell me something like... both of you realized that you had two ears, two eyes..." We both laughed again and I added:

"Of course, not. In fact, our anatomies are very different face down. Like I don't have..."

"Shut up," she intervened in time. Laughter, again. "Tell me something substantial," she asked, like the expert must.

"So yes, like... we both like similar kind of movies and music. Both not-partying types. Both love simple things; hate anything loud and cheap. And then, yes, she is pretty close to her family like me... a homely girl."

"Wow, my homely boy!" I blushed.

"Stop making fun, so yes... our outlook on most subjects is quite similar. Pretty conservative and sentimental."

"Don't tell me you discussed moral issues."

"We did, *didi*." She was impressed. "You'll say we are crazy if I tell you we discussed things like empowerment of women, role of women in our society, neglect of parents and the elderly, illiteracy and population, rapidly eroding traditional values, proliferation of drugs, confused, materialistic youth. We even planned to open a school for poor..."

"Enough. Fine, I get it," she hastily interrupted unable to tolerate anymore. "Seems pretty interesting. So the girl knows you are crazy and still bears you."

"Yes! And she is so nice. It is fascinating to discuss all this with someone. I mean... I have this habit of lecturing, you know, but nobody is ever interested, and here is a girl who is not just listening but complementing me so well. Of course, we have other trivial similarities like enjoying the same sort of movies – romantic and arty; ice creams –

chocolate and strawberry, chocolates – without nuts; pastries, popcorns, *bhutta*... But the thing that bowled me over was our similar emotional quotient. She is a very nice girl, the kind you rarely find nowadays. Simple. Not one who'll colour her hair or get funny piercings or get a tattoo or flaunt her legs or smoke or party... She is so different... I had to fall for her," I astounded myself by going on and on, "I was already smitten by her beauty and that she was so much like how I wanted my girl to be just finished me. She is like Sneha and Palak. Who'd be just the right blend of modern and traditional —who'd be dressed so gracefully and not follow the fashion trends blindly —who'd like to dance and all but prefer dinners by the candlelight— who'd be progressive, but would not hesitate to lend her mother a hand in the kitchen."

"Tejas, you are gone," *didi* interrupted again.

I knew I was gone. I couldn't believe that a girl could have that kind of effect. She was all I had thought for over a month now. I didn't know if it really was love or not but one thing was sure, I liked her, a lot. And I had never been so close to any girl, except, of course, my sisters.

My *didi* lovingly stroked my hair. And looked into my eyes and said, "So you are in love."

"So it seems."

"Hmm, so what is the problem now? Why are you thinking at all about Gayatri?"

"I told you, Shreya is so far away. Don't know when we'll meet if at all we do. It'll be really difficult. And besides, I am not sure she likes me."

"Hmm, of course she likes you. Otherwise you wouldn't have had such discussions. But the problem may be that she likes you purely as a friend. Girls do that often. Boys always look for the romantic angle though. But girls can just be very good friends. Boys take the wrong tip then."

"I know. That's another problem. So the dilemma is that I have a girl in the neighbourhood who likes me and I sort of like her. And then there's a girl, farther than most neighbouring nations, about whom I am absolutely crazy but don't know her position. And I have no one but you to solve it."

"What puzzle is being solved? Let me see too," said a heavy voice from behind. Dad was standing right there.

"Nothing, papa."

"So let's move home, did you have food?"

We replied in positive although *didi* had just had one cutlet and I couldn't even manage that. To hell with food, I thought. We'd go home and eat Maggi noodles at night. Lovely it is to stay up all night and talk, and visit the kitchen to cook Maggi together. We got up.

"Tejas, what's that cutlet doing in your Coke?"

"Nothing, dad... was just experimenting with new recipes."

<hr>

We reached home at about midnight. Sneha was already asleep. Thank God, I thought. Now *didi* and I could talk easily. The whole story had become so riveting that none of us wanted to sleep. I had no college the next day. We continued from where we had left. This time in whispers.

"You didn't tell me if you two exchanged mails only or started talking? I assume you talk a lot from the kind of discussions you have had."

"Yes, *didi*. We started talking gradually. I called her first time on her birthday, the seventh of February. In fact, that's the only reason why I bought a cell phone."

"So, bills must be burning your pocket, Romeo."

"Don't ask, *didi*. Most of my allowance goes there. But she is the one who calls for longer periods from her home."

"Okay! Great. If she talks to you so much on STD, one thing's for sure, she likes talking to you."

"I guess so!"

"See brother, all's pretty good and promising. But have you ever talked romantically?" she asked, examining each detail of her specimen.

"Yes, but very lightly."

"Like?"

"Like, discussing what qualities we would like in our partner, then jokingly calling each other perfect for each other as we have so many similarities. And yes, since nobody else in the world finds us tolerable, why destroy two innocents' lives, better marry each other. That'll be a humble social service."

"So, no boyfriend for her, too?"

"Luckily, no."

"Any previous relationships?"

"Luckily, no."

"Hmm, you'll have to be more romantic and direct."

"Okay. But it's been really good so far. And that's because my intention was never to woo her. It's true, I loved her the first time I saw her. But then the distance was a big deterrent. I had thought about her a lot initially but finally came to ground. I mean there was no way I thought we could be together. Practically impossible. And, then, it is lovely to be good friends with her. We gel so well. And it is really nice to talk clean all the time. And I like it this way."

"So... now the distance has reduced or what?"

"Well, I have been thinking..." In fact, that had been the only thing on my mind. "She comes here about twice a year. So... sometimes I feel... I like her so much and can wait for her but at other times I feel it will be a bit too much."

"Too much, as in?"

"As in, *didi*, my college years are racing past me and I haven't even dated a girl. Most distressing, *didi*. Sometimes I feel like a terminally ill man, with just two years of life left, who wants to make the most of them. Hence the quick need of a girl, who is nearby. It is a race against time."

I wonder, now, how immature and foolish I was to say all that. How ignorant I was of love — of its real meaning and power. Still, I mention it in hope that some of you will learn from what my *didi* said in response.

"Race against time! My foot! What do you want, brother; a time-pass?"

"Hmm, everyone around is happy doing it. But isn't it rotten to leave a girl once you are done?"

"I am proud of you, brother. We need more men like you."

"But *didi*... sometimes out of frustration... I do feel... what the heck! Why waste all these years? If time-pass is the only solution, so be it."

"What if someone does that with me or Sneha or Palak?"

Well, what could I say to that? The very question had kept me in check for so long. I knew the answer too well. I would kill that boy, better say bastard.

"I'd kill that bastard, *didi*. Sorry for the profanity."

"Now, what do you say?"

"Well, *didi*, I know that and would never fool a nice girl. But these days you do find girls who want no commitment... they are no less nowadays."

"You are incorrigible. I tell you what; call a call-girl if you are that frustrated."

I was speechless, again. And ashamed. What am I looking for? I thought. A nice girl who loves me. I knew that. I could never be happy with superficial relations.

"Why are you dumb? Look, I tell you what. You boys want girls for fun or maybe as a status symbol. It's like a banner announcing proudly 'Come, look, I have a girl. I am a stud.' You think we are something to be flaunted. But we are not things," *didi* roared, "You idiot, how can one be happy in a relationship if he is not in love? Time is not running past. Use your head. Dating is not the only thing. You don't meet everyday. You talk on phone too and most of the time that only. It is a form of intimacy. So if you really love Shreya, enjoy the times you talk to her. Wait for her. But only if you love her," she shot like an AK-47 and I could only stare blankly.

These womenfolk, I tell you, make one think a lot. Men would be nothing without them. Curious species, indeed! How they can think that much... all that pretty heavy stuff for us men. Some great man or, perhaps, woman has wisely said: "Women, the mysterious." And I don't have the audacity too, to find out what goes inside their head. So I just nodded appreciatively and said:

"True, *didi*, true. That means I should forget Gayatri?"

"What about the idea of spending a whole day with her, Tejas?" That hit me hard. I hadn't thought about it. I mean a date of one-two hours was fine, but a day with her! I'd rather sit the whole day in Prof. Chattopadhyaya's unbearable 'Evolution: How Monkey became Man' class than hobnob with a girl who names her dog after her crush. There are limits to insanity.

"Most disturbing, *didi*. We have nothing in common. It was just her pretty face I liked."

"So, I hope to have cleared all your doubts."

"Yes. Gayatri is out?"

"What about two days with her, alone?"

"Yes, yes, out she is, *didi*. But Shreya is so far."

"You have to wait for every good thing in life, child." Sometimes they do seem apt, these adages.

"But I don't even know her feelings for me."

"Leave that for the moment. First tell me, do you love her or not."

"Well, *didi*... All I can say is that I haven't found a better girl and she seems perfect for me. I like her very much and I think I love her too."

"So, idiot, forget about other girls."

"And what about... her liking me?"

54

"Ask her."

"What!"

"Yes, ask her. There's no point living in doubt. Ask her if she likes you or not."

"What if she says no?"

"She won't say no outright. She'll just say she never thought about you that way."

"Whatever, but that means no."

"That doesn't mean no, brother. That also doesn't mean she has never thought about you that way. That just means she is not that sure about you right now. We'll deal with that later, it won't be that bad. But you have to ask. Show some courage."

"But *didi*... she is very pretty and I..."

"You are smart, you idiot."

"Are you serious, *didi*? Can she like me, what about these pimples?"

"All I can say is, if I were the girl, I would never have said no."

Bringing back to the mind, my mishap ridden journey from childhood, I can fairly accurately say that save for an occasion when, still in half-pants, my molar had gone bad and had to be removed, courage has never failed me. I confess I have never been in the vicinity of a lion or within a gunshot, but I ask you all are these the only tests of pluck? Where my humble life has tested me, I have stood firm, and that alone brings gratification.

Yet I tottered when my moment of truth arrived and pleaded with my *didi* to change her mind. I grumbled a whole day but, "Be a man!" *didi* said in the end and that was that. It is compact dialogues like these, these pocket bombs, which, when delivered by army generals to shaky soldiers, change their fortunes forever. They march on to the battlefront.

As for us, we tip toed to the roof, quietly opening the creaking doors on the way. The night sky was clear, stars were twinkling and the air was refreshing. I have already mentioned numerous times the virtues of pleasant weather. It drives all your worries away. The scented air worked on me like a bottle of spirits.

Didi dialled her number and pressed the phone against my ear. I turned my face away from her. Ring. I started feeling weak on my knees and that strange sensation in the stomach which one feels when exam scripts are handed, surfaced.

Shreya picked up. "Hullo," she said sleepily.

"Hi! Sorry for disturbing you so late. Hope you were not asleep as yet." Of course, she was.

"I was!"

"Never mind... I wanted to... talk to you. So I called up," I said slowly.

"Alright! What happened that you wanted to talk to me in the middle of the night?"

"Nothing... was just thinking about us."

"About us?"

She sounded confused. I was at a loss for words. I couldn't think of anything to say. Nothing came to my mind. But, I knew if I had to tell her what I wanted to, I had to say it right away. It was unbearable to beat about the bush.

"Shreya, what do you think about me?"

"What sort of a question is that and in the middle of night?" she asked, obviously stumped. I was so afraid now. I was so nervous. I was almost certain she'd say, "I don't like you." And that would shatter me. I knew. It was better, not knowing her thoughts about me than her telling me off straight away. But I made myself strong.

"I mean, do you like me?"

There was a pause. She didn't say anything for what seemed like an eternity. I had shocked her, of course, with such an idiotic question. We had been great friends and now that would be off too. It was all ruined. She finally said with carefully chosen words.

"See, Tejas, I really like you. But as a friend. And you have been a great one."

There was silence again. I felt miserable, for I had thought she liked me. Not just as a friend. I honestly had.

"You too have been great, Shreya! But I thought I'd tell you my feelings. I really like you. And not just as a friend."

"But I have never thought of you that way, Tejas."

So finally the dreaded words that *didi* had spoken arrived, verbatim, "I have never thought of you that way." It irritated me no end. I wanted to ask her, "Why on earth haven't you thought of me that way? Am I that bad? I thought we got along really well and had so many similarities. What more do you want? All you girls know is how to trick guys." But I wisely skipped that part.

"So honestly... have you never thought about us being more than friends?"

"Tejas, I can't say anything right now. But yes, I have always thought of you as a good friend."

I was getting madder. I felt *didi's* hand on my shoulder. I looked into her eyes again. I found comfort. No, I didn't blame her for rushing me into this. Good that I came to know her feelings. I looked at the sky. It was still lovely. The world had not changed. I changed my tone to a more cheery one and asked her, "I hope the door is not closed for me?"

"See Tejas, let us continue to be friends and see how things move on."

"But please keep that door slightly ajar."

"It is!"

"By the way I have a habit of sneaking in from the windows. Good night!"

"Good night!"

I hung up. *Didi* took my hands in hers.

"She didn't close the door?"

"No," I smiled. One of those pensive ones.

"Don't you worry, she needs more time. She has to be sure before she commits. She is a good girl after all."

"Can we stay here and talk. The weather is not bad!"

"Sure, brother."

January, this year.

It was ten past three now. God, these girls should be on time at least sometime! I mean it's permissible if it's just another day and you haven't a thing to do except yawn. But certainly not now! You want to do away with these things quickly; you do not want to wait at a doctor's clinic knowing beforehand that a syringe is going to drill your butt. Idle mind is devil's workshop. Indeed! I couldn't sit, I couldn't stand. All I could do was fidget with my *hands*.

Her words kept echoing in my ears. I wouldn't take 'I haven't thought of you *that* way' this time. No sir, I wouldn't. She'd have to be clear as a crystal. No diplomatic dilly-dallying this time around! For heaven's sake, 'the bell must have rung', as the romanticists say, by now if there existed one. I had violins playing havoc in my mind! Tell me Shreya, if I am not *the one*. And I was afraid too. For a refusal this time could well mean the end of my innings. And I knew I could never be 'just her friend'.

Finally mademoiselle called. I got myself together.

"Hi"

"So, late again!"

"Sorry, but dad called up. So... what were you doing?"

59

"Nothing, just came down to the park, so that I could talk with you peacefully. To be more specific, I was staring at the grass."

"Alright! Are there no girls in your park today?"

"No, not at this hour. People prefer to stay indoors at this extremely lethargic time of the day."

"Right! Sad for you."

"Not at all, sometimes I prefer to be in solitude with nature."

"Sorry for disturbing you, sir."

"It's okay. Shreya, I want to talk to you about something," I came to the point straight away.

"Oh my God! What is it now?"

I wondered what to say and how to start.

"I don't know if I am rushing into this or not, but all I know is that it's very important for me to clear some things."

"Like?"

"You know like what, Shreya."

"Still tell me," she said slowly.

It was tough to say that again but she had forced me to say it, "About your feelings for me, Shreya."

There was that killing silence again. I closed my eyes and tried to cool myself. "Please Tejas; this will not be the end. There are other girls," I said to myself. "But no one will be like her," retorted another voice. "Please don't say no, Shreya. I know you like me," I finally prayed.

"What do you think, Tejas?"

"Please don't fool around, Shreya, I don't know anything. Please tell me."

"Okay, see you are a very good friend, Tejas..." I could see the axe coming in that so sweet and polite style. Sweet and polite, my foot! '...and I don't want to lose you."

"I get it, Shreya. I won't ever ask you again..."

"Let me finish what I have to say first. Promise me... you'll remain my best friend forever. Promise me, Tejas."

I tried to control my emotions. There was a lump in my throat. I could hold my tears as long as I didn't say a word. I was angry with myself for being so sentimental.

"Promise me!" she repeated again.

"I promise, bye for now," I managed to say and a tear slipped down my cheek. So that was it. It was all over. She didn't love me.

"Wait! Promise me another thing."

"What?" I asked, trying to sound normal.

"Promise me you will always remain my best friend if I tell you that I love you."

I don't know if I'll be able to put in words my feelings. It was so sudden and subtle, her declaration. Almost like a sudden shower on an oppressing day. And no, I did not smile for I wanted to be sure she had said that.

"What?"

"I love you, Tejas!"

"I love you, too."

"I know that."

Finally I wiped my eyes and decided to smile. An ever so small one.

"So... why didn't you tell me?"

"Boys ask first, you dumbo."

"But I did, last time."

"Then I wasn't sure but now that I was, I wanted you to ask me."

"Girls! A curious species indeed! I hope I understand you some day."

"Best of luck!" She giggled.

"Thanks! But do tell me, what made you decide on me this time? I'll try and remove the misconceptions."

"Shut up! You still haven't made the promise."

"Oh! I'll think about it."

"What do you mean *you'll think about it*?"

"I mean... it takes time to decide on matters of heart. Who knows better than you, Your Highness?"

It was nice to be on top, for once.

⁀

I took out my letter-pad and my pen. And I began...

"Hi Didi..."

I had to tell her.

Back to October, this year

So we are back here, again, after that little interval of nostalgia, and, though my heart yearns for more of it, we must move ahead. I had decided, more or less, if you recall, that I'd skip the Industrial Tour. I waited for the tour dates to be announced and one fine afternoon, I, having enjoyed my siesta in Pappi's 'Alternate Fuel' lecture, woke up to Khosla's voice. The fat Class Representative had his hands up, and valiantly attempted to control the menacing class.

"Yes, I will tell the dates if you all will allow me to."

"Who the hell has gagged you?" retorted a voice.

"Okay... We leave on the 10th for Pune. Reach Pune on 11th. Leave for Goa on 17th and start back for Delhi on 20th. We'll return here on the 22nd."

"Only three days in Goa! Damn the planning!"

The whole class broke into clamour. Groups of friends discussed among themselves what they'd do on the tour. Some darted weird questions at Mr. Khosla who being polite in demeanour could never satisfy the rascals. A friend of mine shouted, "Why don't we leave for Goa earlier?" and then suddenly the whole class invented a slogan: "We want Goa! We want Goa!"

For the first time I felt like an outsider. I wasn't party to their joys. I moved out quietly and no one noticed. They were lost in celebration. Now that I knew the tour dates, I could finalize my plan. I pictured Shreya waiting for me by the sea and felt no gloom on missing out on having fun with my friends.

I felt a pat on my shoulder. It was Sameer, our department topper and my very good friend.

"Tejas, don't you bunk the tour, as is your habit."

"No, no..." I smiled, faking excitement.

"Good, then we'll have a ball. There's no fun without you, *yaar*!"

I produce here, as an exhibit, the original specimen of my modus operandi. I would, no doubt, have loved to share with you the detailed discussions it required, but to make the novel lighter, we must avoid them.

1. **Departure**: 10th December, to Pune, Goa Express, with the rest of the class... as a simple precaution against the traditional habit of Indian families to see off their children at the stations... thus a direct train to Chennai should be avoided.

2. **Arrival**: Pune, 11th evening; call on dad's mobile showing Pune's code... thereafter every call on home landline – location concealed.

3. **While in Pune**: Click as many photographs, changing clothes as many times, at as many landmarks, changing the date fed in the camera each time... Visit – AFMC College, where dad studied and Kayani Bakery to buy Shrewsberry biscuits for home.

4. **Departure**: 11th midnight, to Chennai, Chennai Express: Alone.

5. **Arrival**: Chennai, 8 PM, 12th, 10 days stay.

6. **While in Chennai**: Call home at least twice everyday – give them no reason to call... keep in touch with friends for their whereabouts in Pune/Goa.

7. **Return Strategy**: Industrial Tour ends on 20th... but not satisfied

with so few a days with Shreya... so, tell at home that Pritish, Rishabh and me staying back to enjoy Goa for three more days... This gives me more time... Parents expect me back on 25th but instead I return on 24th itself, thus eliminating any possibility of them coming to receive me at the station. Thus, station problem at both ends solved.

I distinctly remember the thrill and satisfaction I experienced each time I went over the document. Imagining all that was so exciting... changing trains... travelling the length of the country... it was all extremely exhilarating. Wasn't DDLJ all about trains? I could hear the whistle of the engine... it beckoned me and the wheels were about to roll.

⌒

All the planning done, and, now, within an ace of action, I must tell you that although it all looks very easy, to my mind it was not. For days I lived in the fear of being caught by my parents. Though they are pretty understanding otherwise, I was certain they'd feel let down should my plan fail. My mind was disturbed by negative thoughts, helped in no way by my friends and kin in whom I confided, for they admitted frankly that they wouldn't have done it. And they were right too. After all, I was bunking a compulsory educational tour... lying to professors... changing trains... travelling the length of the country... meeting my love... about all of which they were unaware. I shuddered to contemplate the coming of it all out in the open together...

How, then, did I steel myself? True, I was madly in love and impelled by that mad drive only a lover knows. Yet, an incident from childhood played no small part in my determination.

Once during my exams in high school, I was caught with two answer sheets — one of them mine, of course, diligently copying a complex solution. There was a huge scandal. The teachers, one can still understand, treated me like the rotten fish that spoils the whole pond, but even my peers, who might not have been entirely scrupulous in their ways, looked down upon me.

Therefore you can imagine the heavy heart, the teary eye and the quivering body, with which I told my father about the summon orders. I felt that I was a stain on the blemish-less lineage. I expected a thrashing and had closed my eyes in anticipation when I heard my father say "You should always be careful, son!"

I prayed that he'd relate to my present mischief too in some strange way and be accommodating. He had told me only years later about his sheet-swapping exploits and I hoped there was still something in his closet, some such wild act, about which I was yet in the dark.

Still October, this year

Professor P.P. Sidhu, popular as Pappi among the students, is the head of the Industrial Tour Committee, to whom one must report in case one wishes to exempt himself from the compulsory tour. And so, it was required that I meet him. He is a Sikh, a jovial fellow as Punjabis usually are. One of the coolest professors in IIT Delhi, he doesn't mind students bunking or talking, as long as they don't interrupt him in his work. He has never failed anyone too, I guess. A pioneer in the field of research, he doesn't have much time to probe why bally fellows should go about bunking bally tours.

He taught us the fuels course in which I was supposed to make a 'Pneumatic Linear Double Sided Anti-Rotation Tubeless Air Transfer Cylinder', whatever that means. This was to be installed in a breakthrough bus being developed by my institute which was to run on bio-gas, and I hadn't even gone so far as to decipher the meaning of each term in the title of my project. This had not impressed Pappi, who, however jovial he might be on the subject of bally tours, is somewhat professional on the subject of projects. I tried telling him mildly that if making cylinders with such obnoxious names were child's play, India would be producing such buses like babies to which he replied, "That's exactly where I want to take India." He asked me if I

knew that in Japan, a seven-year old could make a computer, and I said
didn't know to which he replied that I better know. I had adroitly
delayed the project so far, but, now that the semester was coming to an
end, the going would be tough.

I saw him bending over a fat book, scribbling down notes with the
enthusiasm of a child who has just been gifted his first crayon-box. He
looked up at me for a fleeting second and bent down again.

"Sir," I began, "I am afraid it won't be possible for me to go on the
Industrial Tour."

"Ok-a-a-y," he said in a sort of tone which comes out when one has
cold. In his case the cold was perennial.

I didn't know what to do with this long 'Okay'. I found myself puzzled.
It couldn't have meant: "Don't be afraid, son, I am sure whatever that
prevents you must be a worthy cause, go home, son, go home and
celebrate!" I endeavoured to speak again, this time clearing my throat.
"Sir, I wanted to tell you that it is not possible for me to go on the
Industrial Tour."

"Okay," he said again as he continued to play with his crayon box.
The second nasal "Okay" was a tad too much. What on earth was that
supposed to mean? I felt increasingly that I spoke to a parrot that had
been taught extremely well to speak, the only problem being that the
classes had gone only so far as one word which happened to be 'Okay'.
I looked on while he played on. What else can a student do in front of
his professor, however jovial he might be, who has in his hands power,
which can be misused to stop him from meeting his darling?

It would, no doubt, be astonishing for you all this parrot-like conduct
of the professor but I knew better. The one adjective that immediately
comes to mind, the moment one talks about professors, however rare
that might be, is absent-minded. No other adjective described a thing
or a person better. Pappi was known to immerse himself some ten
thousand leagues under the sea, when in the midst of his research, so
that it took him jolly good time to come up to the sea-level. Presently

I waited for that very moment. But then I feared, perhaps he might have drowned. Thus, like a nimble lifeguard, I shot, this time coughing more and speaking louder, "Sir, does that mean I have got your permission?"

"Yes!" he shouted ecstatically and with ecstasy jumped my insides too. I had heard that it was all a cakewalk, this permission getting session, but what the hell, the professor hadn't even asked for the reason. I scarcely believed my good fortune. I admired the professor and his ways, what with the amount of ecstasy he showed, as if he was handing me his daughter's wedding card. Just when I was about to thank him, he shot out from his seat as if a pin had been poked and shouted, "Yes, yes, yes!" and then looked at me. I wondered what the next three yes's were about, just when he ran up to me as ecstatic as Archimedes must have been once out of his bath and said, "Tell me, what's five multiplied by six!"

One doesn't expect that. I wondered if it was a test one had to undergo to secure permission and I promptly replied thirty to which he said, "Thirty it is indeed then, you know what! We'll soon have a bus that runs on gas made from human wastes and gives an average of thirty kilometres per cubic..."

"Congratulations, sir," I hastened to add.

"Yes, yes, yes!" he added to the already confusing yes's. Listen! You wait right here and I'll be back!"

I wondered what I had to wait for, my work already over. Then it dawned to me, the mystery was solved, I had already placed what those three enigmatic yes's were about. Now, I knew the origin of the first ecstatic yes too. It was right there, right there with the next three yes's, like a bosom brother. They may better be called four yes's, four yes's of celebration, of finding that five into six was indeed thirty! What a fool I was to celebrate prematurely. Presently he entered with a pile of books and asked me, "What brings you here?"

"Sir?" I said, hardly believing that he had not heard a thing.

"What sir?"

"Sir, I told you that it is not possible for me to go on the tour."

"Tour? Ah yes, the tour, indeed, yes, yes, the tour, indeed. Okay!"

"Yes sir! I was asking for permission and you said yes."

"Did I? Okay! But why? What happened? Why are you not going on the tour? It is a privilege to go, isn't it?"

"Sir, it is my brother's marriage."

"So?"

"Sir, I must attend that!"

"Ah, yes, okay okay, I see, but you'll miss something; it'll be a landmark tour; not just for India but for the world. The first drive of the Biobull!"

"Sir, Biobull?"

"Yes, Biobull... isn't it a nice name for my bus?"

"Sir, bus?"

"What else?"

"Sir, the tour, the Industrial Tour to Pune this winter."

"Oh, that!"

"Yes sir!"

"You should have told me before."

"Sir, I did!"

"Okay, okay," his okays were driving me mad, "I must have been busy; you'll be required to write an application which'll require my signature. Now go, please go."

"Yes sir!"

"No, wait!"

"Yes sir!"

"Congratulations!"

"Sir?"

"Your brother's marriage!"

"Oh yes, thank you, sir, I'll write the application. Thank you, sir."

And with that I left his room. Never had I seen a man so absent minded. I worried about his wife who must have to remind him every dawn that she was indeed his wife. But then he was a gem and one doesn't mind much if gems are a little forgetful. Anyway, I had given him the application. He said gleefully that he would sign it and I could take it from him the next day, tomorrow that is.

How I wish, now, to go back in time and stop the clock here, right here!

I remember telling Rishabh, in his hostel room, about what a gem Pappi was, when a foot banged at the door and the weak bolt, not able to bear the shock, went flying in the air; and flying in came a colossus, evidently drunk, shouting, "Hello brothers!"

It was Tanker. You have met him before but, no doubt, forgotten about it. However, a moment's wait will make such a thing impossible. His parents had named him Bajrang, respectfully after Hanumanji, the most widely worshipped Indian God, in the innocent hope that the name would bless him with a great quality or two of the powerful God. He had acquired none save the size. He was as big as a bull and when drunk, which he often was, as mad as one too. But in our circles and many a circle before us he was called 'Tanker', for his capacity for any form of ethanol.

Rishabh called him names, obviously jolted having his door permanently dis-bolted and told him not to shout. "Okay, calm down, brother, I will not shout," bellowed Bajrang, "Anything for you, brothers. You both are gems, love you both, man, ask for anything and ... it will be yours, just ask!" he continued shouting, as was his habit when drunk. He couldn't talk softly and, yes, always spoke from his heart when drunk. Thus the stuff about us two being gems must be true. Anyway, he looks upon Rishabh and me as little brothers who must be protected and showered with affection.

"I will certainly tell you whenever I need anything; by the way, any special reason behind today's *daru* party?"

"As if they need a reason!" said Rishabh.

"Shut up, you sonovabitch! Of course, there are reasons you idiot, it is Murali's treat; he got a job with ITC," he said totally out of his senses, "And you both are coming with me. He has called you both; have a little beer, and we have ordered pizzas. Come, come, and, Tejas *bhai*, get your guitar."

"Oh, I am not in the mood... feeling rather tired."

"Come on, Tejas, you never come. Today, you have to come and play your guitar. What a night it is! We'll sing; we'll dance. Just play 'Purani Jeans' once. Please," he said like a child.

"Okay, we are coming, but no smoking..." said Rishabh.

"Oh, sure, sure, come, come. Ha ha ha ha ha ha... Lady in red is dancing..." Tanker sang in his hoarse voice, with a Haryanvi twang, spinning on his foot and draping his arm around an imaginary maiden.

I usually don't attend these booze sessions. Dark rooms filled with smoke and the smell of liquor depress me, an artist at heart; so I avoid these jamborees. But today I was in too good a mood to refuse. I felt like playing my guitar; and it feels good to have people around you when you play.

As we moved in the corridor, a frail *matka* stopped Bajrang in his way and told him to stop shouting. *Matka* is what we call the M.Tech's studying in IIT-D. We B.Techs generally do not get along with them. Bajrang clutched his collar and lifted him two feet in the air and roared, "Who are you to tell me what to do!" and then swung him in the air, resuming his "Lady in red is dancing..." and dropped him on the ground.

"Look what I do now!" cried the *matka* from the ground. Bajrang didn't even look back and kicked open the door in his usual style. I don't blame the *matka* for what he did. I myself find these binges too painful on the ear and have done my share of whining and complaining. I had seen this *matka* complaining for the whole semester and shouting his empty threats but no one bothered about him. He was the sole M.Tech in this wing of the most notorious B.Techs and thus had no say. We moved into the room where the aroma of hot pizzas had lost to the overwhelming reek of rum, whisky, vodka and what not.

We congratulated Murali, who was a teetotaller himself, and the topper of his Mechanical Engineering batch. There must have been ten or so packed in the room. Two or three were extremely drunk and the rest were on their way to glory. I took a customary sip or two of vodka and excused myself from more in spite of the pleadings. I threatened them that there would be no guitar. I began with 'Purani Jeans', moved on to 'Papa Kahte Hain' and then to 'Summer of '69' and so on, the usual popular campus songs, while all around me clapped and some sang in their trembling voices; and so we moved on into the wee hours of the morning. By then, some had retired to their rooms after puking, some had retired without puking but Bajrang was still alive, drinking as he usually does like a tanker but was much more composed now. Meanwhile we chatted on with Murali who proudly gave us tips on how to crack job interviews. There were just four of us left in the room, when we heard a knock on the door.

Bajrang shouted, "Which sonovabitch is it?"

"Radhaswamy," came the voice from the other side.

"Which Swami?" asked Tanker.

It was the unmistakable South Indian accent of the *matka*. I never knew he was called Radhaswamy. We all knew him as *matka* only.

"It is that *matka* again, Tanker," informed Rishabh.

"The bastard wouldn't listen. What does he want, now, when no one is making noise? It seems that the lesson was not enough for him!" Tanker took a bottle of soda, opened it with his teeth, shook it hard and then pressed his huge thumb against the hole, while the gas hissed out. "Open the door, Tejas," he told me. I did as directed, eagerly waiting to enjoy the fate that awaited the poor creature. The door opened and Bajrang sprayed around the contents of the bottle in wild frenzy. I stood laughing as I saw Radhaswamy drenched in soda with horror on his face but I stopped soon as I noticed that, for some reason, Murali and Rishabh had frozen in between. Bajrang continued and Murali rushed to stop him. I peeped out of the corner of the door which blocked my full view and I shudder to write what I saw.

To be honest, nothing comes to my mind, when I rack my brain to think of a thing that might have produced the same kind of horror, even in a life so full of mishaps. Once, yes, while playing a prank, I was bitten, out of the blue, by a female Doberman, which taught me that there were Dober-men who were not men, yet as dangerous... but never until this moment had I known anything to boomerang in this fashion, and this a prank, where my role was not more than of that hopeless extra who dances behind the hero.

Without stretching your patience and curiosity any further, I must tell you that I saw three portly gentlemen, standing upright, as wet as three towels, behind Radhaswamy, whom I didn't take more than a nanosecond, if that's the smallest second, to recognize and sport the same petrified look of my friends. Not to worry. This isn't a story about ghosts and spirits though now when I think of it, it'd have been better indeed if it were. I bet that one can't wet ghosts and spirits. I have it from reliable sources that you can't touch them and so logically can't wet them but here my friend had wetted two of the most important people in IIT, and third, the most important one for me, not with water but with soda and thank God soda, not champagne.

There they were and unmistakably so, as menacing as the three musketeers; Prof. P. K. Dhingra, Hon. Dean of Undergraduate Students; Prof. Keval Chadda, Hon. Warden, Karakoram House, my hostel that is; and Prof. P. P. Sidhu, Hon. Head, Industrial Tour Committee. I

couldn't believe that he was there too. You expect a Warden and a Dean
to be on a round to catch the defaulters but not Prof. Pappi. I couldn't
see any reason for his esteemed presence there; except that God had
finally decided to annihilate me and to do so in his most destructive
fashion. It would have taken a minute for a man of lesser intelligence,
but for me it hardly took seconds to realize that there went my chance
of skipping the Industrial Tour out of the window. I must say that a
man of lesser mental strength would have jumped out of the window
with it too, but not me. I stood my ground, injured, no doubt, but not
broken.

There was what one can call a killing silence for what one can call an
aeon after the last spoken words of wise Murali, who had wasted no
time in whispering loudly in the ears of Tanker (who had lost his sense
of distinction in the extreme state of inebriety) that it was none other
than the Dean on whom he had been lavishing the froth. It was broken
by none other than Tanker and in such frightful a fashion that I wonder,
still, what I had done so grossly wrong in this life or previous to land
myself in that hell. I'd like to reproduce the exact conversation or
monologue, to be precise, that ensued:

Tanker: Oh, hullo, old man! What brings you here?

(silence, spectators look on, incredulous)

Tanker: Why, of course, what a fool to have asked you that question!
You are here for the party, aren't you? Murali has got a top job sir, and
you, no doubt, want to congratulate this precious stone. Come in!
Come in! You two also! Everyone is welcome! This Murali is a generous
soul.

(silence)

Tanker: And who are these cute little old men with you? (Goes up
to the Warden, looks down at him with keen interest and points a
finger) I have seen you somewhere, haven't I? I fail to place you, but
you are most welcome too, what should I mix for you? Oh, I know,
TEJAS (he shouted), give soda and vodka to him!

76

(Why on earth should he have called me to do the honours, I fail to see, but blame it on my bad luck. Or Mr. Fate. There were two more students in the room and I was no expert barman, one of those who juggle with bottles and pour the drink from a mile above without sprinkling a drop, but still he called me and I felt like one of the arms, right or left, whichever is stronger, of an underworld don, who is about to get the same sentence as his boss. Meanwhile, I could see the disgust with which the three M. looked was intensifying and presently the Tour Head gave me an obnoxious stare while Tanker moved towards him. There was a card hanging from a chain which went around his neck and I knew like Holmes, that the inscription on the card held the clue to whatever he did in this room. I had desired to get a view of it, right from the beginning, but couldn't read more than SALAD, written in big, bold, capital letters with something small beneath, and that had left me more confused. What could salad mean? For a normal boy like me, it meant nothing more than those raw vegetables that doctors recommend for health. Why this Prof. was here and why he was publicizing salad, when I was sure he had nothing to do with chefs and butlers, was too maddening a mystery to me. Presently Tanker, in his third attempt, finally grabbed the card and tried to read.)

Tanker: You still wear I-cards, old man? Funny! (roars with laughter) You don't need it; you are not a kindergarten kiddy.

That was the final straw. What had so far been a monologue was interrupted by Pappi who could not take it any more. You don't expect professors, wet with soda, to like being addressed as kindergarten kiddies and neither did Pappi. He roared, "You bloody fool; do you not know what you are saying and where it'll land you? You will not be spared. As the head of 'Society Against Liquor And Drugs', (so that was what SALAD was) I assure you and your friends that I will not rest till I have you out of this college." This was the not-so-jovial side of the otherwise jovial Pappi that none of us had witnessed before.

We three were given summons and were to be court-martialled the following morning. The famous 'Disciplinary Committee' or the 'Disco' as it is famously known was to decide our fate, which indeed looked very bleak.

~

Though everyone will tell you that Disco is the worst thing that can happen to you at IIT, no matter how groovy it might sound, I wasn't much worried about its decision. I do not claim to be some super-cool toughie that can not be shimmied by the severest of storms. But here I was, a man confronted by two storms who has no option but to worry about the storm more lethal, which, here, undoubtedly was the one that threatened my union with my inamorata. It may sound a bit strange but that's how it is. A man in the throes of this queer thing called love doesn't worry about trifles such as suspensions. There are graver things in life to worry. He just waves his hand and says, "Ah, we'll deal with triflings later."

I had a vague feeling that we'd get away as we, from which I exclude Tanker, had really done nothing, save being present at the place of calamity; but how I would get away from Pappi was a question I didn't want to think about. Things definitely looked bleak. Pappi still had my application with him. It hadn't been signed and wouldn't be signed. I could scarcely believe my misfortune. How on earth could they convene a ridiculous body called SALAD and make the Industrial Tour Head its president! There were thousands of professors and even more butlers for this rummy thing called SALAD. And how on earth could I be caught for an offence of drinking when I had just wetted my lips. And how on earth could a guy go mad like that to bathe his teachers in soda and then go about offering them drinks! I had only heard that people lose their marbles on an overdose of hooch, but never had I expected to witness marbles so utterly lost.

I couldn't sleep the whole night thinking about the absurdity of it all. Once or twice, I thought of calling Shreya but did not. To worry a girl at three in the night with such ghastly shockers is not the conduct of gallant men. I reflected how sometimes one is just a spectator to his fate. I remembered a movie where Ram, as innocent a man as ever was born, goes to his friend Shyam's house early in the morning for their routine walk. He finds the house open and is surprised. He walks in as any close friend will and is shocked to see Shyam dead in a pool of blood. Scarcely does he turn in an effort to call the police that he finds it already there with Inspector Vijay merrily dangling the handcuffs in the air and muttering, "I knew you would return." I was feeling exactly how Ram must have felt about the whole damn business but what brought solace was that Ram was acquitted in the end.

While introducing Tanker I forgot to include a thing or two, which Who's Who(s) will not dare to forget in the years to come. I hasten to correct the error for it is vital to the story. Tanker or Bajrang, as Who's Who(s) should list him, is the absolute king of *jugaad*. *Jugaad*, as it is popularly known in these parts, is the art of getting things done in a way which is slightly deviant from how it should be done. Example, you can say, a backdoor entry. Coming back to our hero, Tanker has all the links in the world and seldom is a distressed soul disappointed when he comes for help to our Tanker. He is the undisputed king of politics that form a vital part of one's stay at IIT and has devoted his life to it and it seems that he would stay on here forever if there was not a clause in the IIT rule-book that states "...a student must not take more than six years to complete his degree..." It was Tanker's sixth year and the authorities were already fretting, faced with the task of dislodging the monster from his den. Reminds me of a story about Hanumanji, after whom Bajrang is named, when he blocked the path of Bhima who tried to lift the monkey-god's tail but even the mighty Pandava, with his infinite muscles, didn't succeed.

I mentioned above that I felt we'd get away, and specified strictly that 'we' excluded Tanker; but I was proved wrong and rightly so. I committed the folly of forgetting Tanker's talents and it was foolish. The gist of the story, without increasing the suspense or the length, is that Tanker got away and saved us unscathed, too. How he produced medical proof that his wild act was nothing but an epileptic seizure is an amusing story, but must be excluded here. Thus no real case could be formed against us and, in the comedy of errors that followed, we were warned that we were on probation for the rest of our stay at IIT, and any adverse report would most certainly result in an expulsion.

The recent developments – the DISCO meeting, and the sleepless night had left me weary. And I slept like a log. I remember my crazy dream in which the invading Pakistan army had come as far as my house and the entire mantle fell upon my heroic shoulders to save my colony. I was surprised to see that Pappi and the Dean were fighting for the Pakistan army, when I suddenly heard a bang... and again... and again. I feared that my house would be destroyed in that shelling when another bang woke me up and I jumped some feet in the air. Relief, which came to me on discovering that my house was safe, was momentary though as I noticed that some idiot was banging my door and calling out my name. I managed to get up. It was Khosla, my friend, the Class Representative. He had formed a habit of waking me up and I hated that. He was everywhere, it seemed. Whenever I slept, he came quickly, like a nightmare.

"What do you want at this unearthly hour?" I asked.

"It is noon, my friend, 12'o clock to be precise."

"Oh!"

"And get ready, Pappi has called you."

"Me?"

"And he is livid!"

"Oh!"

"Did you submit the interim project report?"

"No, when is the last date?"

"It was to be submitted in the morning class at nine for which you didn't appear. He was very cross at that."

I had forgotten the report. It only decreased my chances to meet Shreya. The professor who was to hand me my passport had been disgraced, or so he thought, by me and then I had not worked at all on the project. He would eat me up for sure. The fact that I had thought him a gem just a day ago brought no solace.

"How could I attend his class when he himself had caused me to land in front of the Disciplinary Committee?" I asked frustrated.

"Yes, I forgot! What happened there?" and on asking this his face beamed in anticipation. How people derive joy from such abominable happenings is beyond me. The world is full of sadists, I reflected. I didn't want to disappoint him by telling him I got away.

"Later, now, let me get ready!"

Life is not a bed of roses, someone has wisely said, but it wasn't supposed to be a bed wholly constructed of thorns either. Reflecting on these lines I moved on to his highness' room and he ushered me in after my polite, "Sir?"

He arose from the pile of books and looked at me like a dad eyeing the lover of his daughter.

"Mr. Tejas Narula," he started and I was startled to hear that, for not often am I addressed as mister and when I am, it indeed spells doom, "I did not get your interim report."

"Sir, I was at the disciplinary committee inquiry."

"Inquiry forsooth, we'll come to that farce later. How far have you reached in devising your cylinder?" he thundered.

"Sir, I am working on it..." I did not know what to say for I had nothing but fortunately or unfortunately he didn't let me speak and interrupted, "I'll tell you how far you have gone. You have gone as far as a deadbeat can go after bunking all the practical classes."

"Sir?" I wanted to say that I had not bunked all but wasn't given a chance.

"I know how to deal with rogues like you!"

"Sir?"

"Don't go on mumbling sir-sir, you think you are very smart? You will get away with anything? But I tell you what, you are wrong and you'll see when I fail you in this course. You were the one, if I remember correctly who sought permission for not going on the Industrial Tour. Right?"

I wished I could have said wrong but I was helpless. I just nodded in approval and tried to gulp in the shocker. I knew he would not exempt me from the Industrial Tour and that meant death.

"What did you say you had? Marriage of your brother? I am very sure that there is nothing like that and I am going to check it with your parents. You bunk classes and you think you can bunk anything?"

"Sir..."

Hell... I had not thought of that. I mean yes, I had thought, as a quick mind would, that due to the unfortunate events of the night my trip might be in danger but never had I thought that he would decide to call my parents to confirm the excuse. I was in hell and the deepest one. There was in front of me a different Pappi, a Pappi who was about to spoil his record of not failing a student ever, a Pappi who was mad, not the Pappi whom I had labelled a gem, not Pappi at all but Prof. P. P. Sidhu. The previous night's insults had been too much for him. I agreed, but felt unlucky to be singled out. Why hadn't I worked on my project? I thought. Again, because Pappi was known to be cool with grades. Rishabh had worked, and thus was seen as a conscientious student and I, a loafer whom he was about to destroy.

"I told you to shut up! What do you boys think of yourselves? It is a shame to have students like you in IIT. You are a disgrace! Utter disgrace! You were laughing while your friend was showering whisky on three professors. On three Gurus! You know who a Guru is? We used to touch our Gurus' feet everyday! Every single day, you buffoon and that is why we are blessed with such life and knowledge. I wonder if you respect even your own parents! I bet you wouldn't mind insulting your parents."

"Sorry sir but..." I wish I could have told him that it was soda, not whisky and that I had goodness in me.

"Sorry! Sorry for what? British left but left their legacy, sorry! Damned word... used anywhere and everywhere. You think I am friendly with students and so you can take any liberty? You fool! I have been such an understanding professor, all these years, ask your seniors and this is the way you treat me..." he had been hurt and all his anger was coming out, "And do you *feel* sorry? Not a bit! If you were sorry you would have apologized in front of the committee today but what do you do? You make such an insane tale of your friend being epileptic! I couldn't believe it when the committee told me. Epileptic! My foot! Never have I heard of such sacrilege! First you show the highest form of disrespect to your Gurus and then you choose to ridicule them again! You think it is all a joke? You might have been given a reprieve by the committee but there are other ways to punish and better ways. Take that in your head that I am not going to leave you like this. I will not rest till I have set you right! I have it from my sources that you are a good friend of Bajrang and you were a part of this derisive conspiracy."

"Sir, I did not know about it!" I said, defending myself. And I was honest. It was amazing the number of charges he had levelled against me when I hardly deserved any. "Honestly, sir, I was unaware!" I said, almost pleading and on the verge of breaking down.

"Honest! That will be confirmed soon. I know you are a liar, I have seen your conduct this semester... you attend classes as if you're doing a favour to me! Yet I give you one chance; I am going to call your father and check if your brother is indeed getting married. If this is a lie then God save you! Wait here, while I call the undergraduate office to get your phone number!"

He picked up the receiver of the phone and dialled the internal number for the UG section, the office where all the student records are kept. I felt what a victim when his head was stuck in a guillotine must have felt in those beastly times. Not many people witness death coming slowly to them but there I was, waiting every second for the blade to fall. The ground escaped from under my feet, it felt as if someone was churning my intestines determined to reduce them to pulp; my knees grew weaker as I waited for the call to be picked. Often in these situations one gives up and I gave up too. I could do nothing but stand and stare at my fate being altered right in front of my eyes. He would tell all to my dad, who would want a suitable explanation for my actions. He'd also tell dad how I had insulted my Gurus by spilling whisky on them and what a student I was. It was the end. But what hurt most of all was that I would not be able to meet Shreya. I had tried so hard, planned so well, taken so many risks only to meet her but this had to be the end... I started to wonder if ever I'd be able to meet her... that her dad was against me and would not allow her to come to Delhi. It looked so hopeless. Life had been so full of problems lately yet I had fought them all. I had loved honestly and devotedly. And this was my reward! I was moved to tears but didn't let them fall. My mind was full of thoughts. Why God was being so unjust, I did not know! Where I had gone wrong, I did not know. If trying to meet one's loved one against all odds was wrong then I did not agree with it. I believed that I had done nothing wrong. But the thing was, that my life was about to end and I was not going to meet Shreya. I closed my eyes as Pappi spoke,

"Hello UG section, Prof P. P. Sidhu here. Good morning, can I have the number of a student... Yes... Tejas Narula? ... Yes, Home Telephone number... He is not there? When will he be back? Okay, yes... Okay, yes, call me after lunch then... yes, after two, fine... I'll be in my room after one... thank you!"

I opened my eyes. He had replaced the receiver and looked at me. I had my eyes wide open in surprise and relief. I finally drew breath and a deep one that. I had got a lifejacket and I was not going to lose it. I thanked God silently while Pappi told me, "So two it will be then! The man who looks after the records is out and will be back then. He'll call me and give me the number. I don't want your number from you. Get out." I said sorry again and rushed off. There was no time to waste. It was twelve thirty, I had seen in professor's clock. I had ninety minutes to save my life, not a minute more, not a minute less.

Ninety Minutes

Iimmediately reached my hostel and woke up Rishabh, who was resting his drained, though considerably less than mine, nerves with a sound sleep. Then I told him and Pritish about my near death experience and that I had 80 minutes to prevent the catastrophe. They asked how and I told them how.

"We will have to prevent Pappi from taking the call."

"But how?"

"By keeping him out of his room when the call comes."

"But, won't the UG office guy call again?"

"No, he won't, because I will take the call as Pappi."

"What?" they both asked, puzzled.

I told them the plan, which had come to me in the ten minutes that had passed. There were risks, yes, but they *had* to be taken.

Pritish reached the UG office at one-fifty five and with his innate coolness asked for the official who kept the students' records. To him he hopped and informed that Prof. Sidhu had sent him to get the required phone number. "Tejas Narula, isn't it?" the official asked and started searching on his old computer. At that moment, Pritish gave me a missed call and, having got my signal, I reached Pappi's room and saw him lost as usual in a heap of books. Good signs, I thought. I stopped at his door and started wailing for pardon. As expected, Pappi told me that it'd be of no use and that he'd soon call my dad.

Meanwhile, the UG official had completed his search and as he started scribbling the number on a piece of torn paper, Pritish gave a missed call to Rishabh. Having got his signal, Rishabh dialled Pappi's mobile.

Pritish sat down in front of the official. He had to keep him engaged for some safe seconds. He began a cheery conversation with the official as he handed him the number. I waited there, each second killing me, anticipating nervously Rishabh's call on Pappi's cell and then it came. Pappi started at the ring as if woken from a deep slumber. He looked at the cell phone like he had looked at my friend Murali, the previous night, when he had compared him with some obnoxious pest.

"Mobiles! The ghastliest of man's inventions! They have eradicated all the peace from this world... worse than the nuclear weapons and yet one can't live without them in this age. Life is full of ironies. I hate to pick up unknown numbers!"

He kept staring at the mobile and a nervous thought crept into my head, what if the fool didn't pick the call! You could never be sure about their species, these professors, one could never predict with them. I prayed anxiously. But just at the moment his 'Jingle Bells' ring-tone was about to die, he received the call.

"Hullo," he said, "Hullo, who is calling? ... I see... yes... hullo... you can't hear me? ... hullo... yes, I am on the bio-bus project..."

Meanwhile, at the other end of the line, Rishabh played around coolly in an impeccable, business-like manner. He had called from a new sim-card we had bought the moment he had got Pritish's missed call and was playing his part to perfection.

"Yes sir, I can't hear you at all; I am Prashant Oberoi. I wanted to speak to you about the funding of the bus..." said Rishabh.

"Funding, oh yes..." replied Pappi ecstatically.

"Sir, I think you can hear me but I can't at all, could you move out?" asked Rishabh, according to the plan.

"Hullo... okay, let me move out... hullo... is it clear now... no?... hullo..." and with that Pappi moved farther away from the room into the open ground in front of his room. He didn't even look at me in his excitement as I had envisaged. His Biobull had saved me and it was only the beginning of our beautiful friendship as you'd see later. I gave Pritish a missed call.

That completed the missed call network. And so Pritish got his signal too. He had the paper with my home phone number in his hand and was biding the time by entertaining the UG official with some cricket talk. Just when he got my call, he got up abruptly and told the official that he had to go somewhere urgently; so couldn't give the message personally to Prof. Sidhu.

"Could you please call Prof. Sidhu and give him the number now, so that I can go, I have to meet another professor in a minute or he'll scold me badly. I got his call just now. I don't have time to visit Professor Sidhu," said Pritish, enacting his part to the T.

The official, who had been humoured adequately by Pritish so far, obliged and picked up the receiver to call Pappi's office through the internal telephone network. Meanwhile I waited anxiously for the UG guy's call. It is so strange how these nervous seconds seem like eternity. I had hardly waited for a minute when the call came but in that tension of what-if-the-call-doesn't-come it had seemed like an hour. With Pappi safely outside, I ran in, quickly picked up the call after half a ring, nimbler than any panther would dream to be.

"Professor Sidhu?" said the UG guy.

"Yes," I said in a low, nasal tone.

"Sir, your boy had come to me and asked for the number."

"Yes, yes, give me!"

"Sir, it is 0129 – 2284804 in the name of Dr. Narula."

"Okay, thank you," I rushed.

"Sir, anything else?"

"No, that will be it, thanks," and with that I quickly replaced the receiver and dashed out of his room to join Rishabh. I just about managed a glance at the professor. He had his back towards me and was still talking, with his right hand gesticulating as if cutting a water melon. I reached the Ex. Hall in a flash; Pritish was already there. I couldn't believe my eyes when I saw that Rishabh was still talking to Pappi about the Biobull. I signalled him to get over with it quickly and he did it by telling the professor that he would call later and that he had in his mind big things for the Biobull. As soon as he cut the call, he shouted "Cracked it! Did you intercept the call?" he asked and I merely gave him a high five and then to Pritish. I thanked God once again. In carrying out that extremely dangerous plan I had counted on the fact that God himself had given me those ninety minutes. And so I could not mess it up and I had not.

"Your turn to speak to Sir Sidhu, now, Mr. Pritish! Enjoy!" said Rishabh, laughing.

"Yes, yes but hope you are clear on what you have to talk!" I added cautiously.

"Chill, man!" he said and with that he picked up the receiver of the internal phone that lies in the Ex. Hall. He talked and talked well, changing his voice as far as he could.

"Professor Sidhu?" said Pritish, "Sir, you had asked for the number... yes sir... sir, there is no landline number in record but his father's mobile number... will that be fine, sir? ...very well, sir... 9899399772... Sir, anything else?"

"No, that will be it, thanks," replied Pappi as Pritish told me.

Pritish had given my mobile number to Pappi. I'd have to change my number but that was fine. Thus it was finally my chance to talk to the great man. In a second I got a call from Pappi which was short and sweet,

I changed my voice to an extremely gruff one as I have so often done in this life and maybe previous too.

"Hullo, is this Dr. Narula?" he asked in his irritating nasal tone.

I said I was and asked who he was. He said he was P. P. Sidhu, Professor, IIT Delhi.

"Good afternoon, doctor. I just wanted to speak to you about your son!"

"Hope he hasn't done anything wrong, professor! You worry me, professor, please tell it all soon and I will speak to him."

"No, no, no, no! I just wanted to inquire about your son's marriage."

"What! He is getting married? Didn't tell me! He is always full of surprises but this one comes as a shock! How can he do that? Isn't it too early? Tell me, professor. He is barely 21. What's the hurry? Do you know the girl? Is she also from IIT? This generation is too fast!"

"Oh! Not him, doctor. He told me his brother is getting married!"

"Oh! Why, of course, he is! On 14th Dec, engagement on 12th. Oh you scared me, Professor, I thought Tejas! Thank God, thank God, he is not getting married. Most distressing... this whole business of marriage! You agree professor?"

"Yes, yes! That is it, doctor, I just wanted to confirm, there are so many boys saying their brothers and sisters are getting married to bunk this Industrial Tour that I had to check. "

"You did the right thing, professor, these children; they lie so often these days. Distressing! But my son is a gem, sir. I hope he will get the permission, professor. Vineet is returning to India after two years... just to get married and Tejas must spend time with his brother, I hope you understand."

"Yes, yes, I do. I will grant him permission."

"Oh, thank you, sir, I am obliged, thank you!"

And so the doctor hung up and so did the professor, both satisfied, and thinking alike that the world wasn't that bad a place, after all, as they were making it out to be a few moments ago.

⌒

And so, finally, I got my much needed sleep which was interrupted, not before I had a livening chunk of it, not by Khosla this time, but by her call. She was naturally surprised to hear my sleepy voice at eight in the evening when most of the people in this time-zone are, no doubt, awake.

"Were you sleeping?" Miss Shreya asked.

"Yaaaa," I said and my yaaaa terminated into a yawn.

"At this hour?"

"Oh, I have been sleeping for the past five hours, I guess."

"Are you well?"

"Now, yes!"

"What do you mean, 'now yes'? What happened earlier?"

"That is a long story."

"And you are going to tell me."

"But of course!"

"Hope everything is alright!"

"Now, yes!"

"Stop saying 'now yes' and tell me what happened!"

"Tell me Shreya, have you read the Sherlock Holmes story, 'The Boscombe Valley Mystery'?"

"You know I haven't read Holmes!"

"And how many times have I told you to read him?"

"Will you tell me what happened?"

"Not until you read Holmes."

"Shut up and tell me. Have you gone mad?"

"Considering the amount of risks I am taking to meet you, yes, I have gone mad. Very much so! The road to Eldorado, I tell you, is full of mines, but let it be known that it doesn't bother me the least!"

"Tejas, I know all that... what happened today... that you are speaking like this? Tell me, please! I am scared."

"Hmm."

"What hmm?"

"Okay, okay I will tell you... but why I alluded to this 'Boscombe Valley Mystery' is that... if you had read it you would have understood my position in a much more complete manner, what with my situation being similar to that of the innocent young McCarthy except that he was charged with a much graver crime, that of murder..."

"Tejas, are you going to tell me?" she roared, evidently very irritated and rightly so, and that pleased me. There's nothing better than to get the better of these impish girls, who usually get the better of you.

"Wait a sec., darling. Sherlock Holmes quotes in this very story that 'Circumstantial evidence is a very tricky thing, it may seem to point very straight to one thing, but if you shift your point of view a little, you find it pointing in an equally uncompromising manner to something entirely different.'"

"Eeeee," she uttered, "I am hanging up, bye!" It is so funny how girls say bye at any and everything. The moment they find the situation not in their favour, they utter this callous bye and the guy, helpless, has to cry, "Wait!" as I did in this case, for he has lots of things to relate.

"Okay, now I'll be serious, senorita, you won't believe when I tell you all that happened after your call yesterday! I was merely quoting Holmes to tell you to etch in your mind those golden words before you brace up to listen to this most interesting narrative as Holmes himself calls his cases..."

And I told her all about the lavish bestow of soda, the three M., the invention of the Mesial Temporal Lobe Epilepsy, the Pappi outrage, the guillotine, the near death experience, the miracle, and the extremely well-crafted, ingenious and what-not plot that saved the day; and I did so, as methodically and meticulously as I have told you; employing all the liberty that a narrator has in his hands, or say mouth, to add as much spice as he can to extract as many whats, ohgods, eeees, and don't-tell-me's from a chicken-hearted lady listener.

"Tejas," she said at the end of it, "Are you sure it is safe to come?" and said so brimming with concern just like she had asked me a million times before.

"How many times do I have to answer that question?" I asked tenderly.

"Till I am sure it is absolutely safe!"

"Which it'll never be and which nothing can ever be! One cannot stop crossing roads thinking that the next truck will smash him to pulp. How many times do I tell you, one has to make up one's mind to do a thing and once one has, he cannot look left and right but stare straight into the eye of the tiger and finish his job!"

"Please don't come if you think there is risk involved!" she said, moved to tears and I could sense that.

"Are you crying?"

"No!"

"Yes, you are!" I said coolly.

"No, I am not!"

"Don't lie, as if I am deaf! Look at the way you are talking, like a small baby. I know you are crying."

"So what?"

"Why?"

"What why?"

"Why are you crying?"

"Just like that!"

"Ha ha ha ha, just like that!" I said imitating her tone.

"Don't copy me!" she said so cutely.

"Is there a copyright?"

"Yes there is!" she said cutely again, "But you can copy me. Special privilege," she said like a small child.

"Oh, thank you, ma'am, honoured indeed I am!"

"You should be," she continued in her three-year old tone.

"Now tell me why were you crying?"

"Is it necessary?"

"Absolutely!"

"Offo! Just like that, I was thinking... that you are taking so many risks to meet me... just me!"

"So?"

"What so?"

"What's there to cry about?"

"There is!"

"I can't see!"

"Because you are an idiot, dumbo!"

"That I know, you remind me regularly enough, but tell me, why were you crying?

"Offo! One gets sentimental thinking about how much you love me... that I am so lucky to have you and to think what all you have done for me!"

"Anything for you, ma'am! And, by the way, I am not doing all this only for you. Get that notion out of your head, I mean you can say 'For us' but not for you. And then I am selfish too. I am doing this for myself too, for I cannot go on living without seeing you for so long. And to think that your dad won't allow you within a light year of me for as long as he whims, drives me to despair. Thus I have to do something!"

"But... please make sure you come safely, there should be no problems at your home or college!" she resumed in her motherly concern tone.

"Oh, no problems, senorita! You are saying all this when the lord (read Prof. Sidhu) has himself descended to earth and given the go-ahead... not to me, but to my dad, no problems now! The going is as smooth as a baby's bottom!"

"As smooth as what?"

"Baby's bottom, baby!"

"Where do you get such phrases from?"

"Oh! This, unfortunately, is not one of my inventions; I read it in a waxing salon ad, get skin as smooth as a baby's..."

"Oh, my God!" And she giggled finally.

"Good to see the rose back on your cheek, and now keep it right there; laugh and celebr   , for I am coming and coming with a song on my lips and a bag on my hips!"

"Hips?"

"Oh, I had to rhyme it with lips, couldn't say bag on my back! This one's my invention! Nice?"

"Ghastly!"

"Hey, you know what?" I asked, suddenly getting an idea.

"What?"

"I have decided to write a book, a book about my voyage and what all I had to do to come to you. It is so exciting."

"It'll be a best-seller for sure!"

"You bet, but you know what, it has another advantage."

"What?"

"Like you are so worried, what if something goes wrong and all."

"So?"

"Now you needn't worry, whatever bad happens, only adds spice to the story!"

"Very funny!" It is her favourite phrase.

"Not funny, look, if I come there easily and nothing prevents me, it'll all be so bland and boring..."

"Wow!"

"Just think about it, if your dad spots us together there, and we run from him! Wow! Imagine! I run, you run with me, your dad runs after us and the book ends with us running from place to place and settling somewhere in Punjab, among the sparkling crops; I work all day on the farms, you bring me *garam-garam paranthas* in the afternoon and I eat from your soft-soft hands! Isn't it spectacular?

"Very!"

"So don't worry, and remember... if something wrong does happen, it just adds fun to the story, think about it that way. Okay?"

"Hmm, but... you know what? Seriously, you can write a book. The story is not bad and then you write well." She had heard a couple of songs I had written.

"I am serious, dearest Shreya, I intend to write soon, and these studies are so boring! It'll be a nice change. By the way, should I keep the same names in the story or change them?"

"Hmm, change them. At least ours. Otherwise we'll get so popular that people will hound us everywhere. After all, it'll be a bestseller."

"Point, so suggest the names, Madame!"

"Let us name them with T and S only!"

"Why?"

"Dumbo! Your name starts with T and mine with S!"

"Oh, yes, of course! So decided, I'll start from tomorrow, 'The Tale of S and T'!"

"Good! And write well!"

"Yes, and you know what? It has another benefit!"

"Now what?"

"When your dad will read it, he'll come to know how strongly and madly I love his daughter and that I can do anything for her! Maybe, he will change his opinion of me!"

"Yes! Don't worry; he'll change his opinion when he gets to know you better! He'd like you a lot."

"Hope so! And yes, one more benefit from the book!" I said.

"What now?"

"If someday you decide to leave me, for any reason, may be, after reading the book, wherever you are, you'll change your mind and come back to me; reading about how much I love you and once I did so much for you..." I said laughing.

"Shut up, just shut up, I can never leave you, Tejas, never!"

"Don't, I'll surely die!" I said laughing again, but I was dead serious.

"Shut up, why do you have to talk about dying? Idiot. And I am the one who should say all this... maybe, if one day you decide to leave me for another girl, like so many guys do, you'd be reminded about our love after seeing your own book. Boys need reminders, not girls! So now write, *pakka*!"

"Sure, ma'am, anyway, I was thinking... if I should bring my guitar along!"

"Not a bad idea, if it is not cumbersome!"

"A little yes, but, wouldn't it be lovely to play it on the beach, jamming with the waves?"

"It will be! I'll love it!"

"Remember the last time I played it for you?"

"As if I can forget!"

"You looked like a Goddess!"

"And you were 'not bad'!"

"The terrace!"

"The beautiful night!"

"Your lovely black dress!"

"Your 'not so bad' white shirt!"

"Sweet smell of the wet sand!"

"Lovely candles!"

"Dancing with you! Oooh!"

"And your guitar and the song!"

"Magical night, surely!"

"Don't forget the best part!"

"Which one?"

"Orange Juice!"

"Yaaaa..."

And we went on talking about that night...

Monsoons, this year.

The monsoons had arrived and this time 'on time' betraying the unpredictability one associates with them. They have this habit of embarrassing the meteorologists, year after year, by rubbishing unabashedly all the forecasts, from the time of their arrival to the time of their departure and everything that happens in between.

If there is one season that lies right up there with the winters, or probably a shade above, is the monsoons and blessed are we all to live in this part of the world and witness its beauty.

Never is a season more welcome. The first drops washing away the fire of the earth and bringing with them the most pleasant fragrance. Never are the colours of the trees and mud so brilliant! Never is the breeze so intoxicating! Never is the poet so inspired! Never is romance so much in the air!

I welcomed the monsoons as I always do but this time not just for the lovely showers, that rejuvenating bath in the rains, the picturesque boat in the puddle, the ideal temperature, the wet fragrance and the joyous, riotous football match in rain. The monsoons this time had brought with them much more, the love of my life.

Shreya had arrived in Delhi with the monsoons on the 28th of June as if they had had a secret pact. And therefore the romantic weather had a never-before effect on me. You could see Tejas with a subtle smile on his lips; only when he was not singing songs; joy on his face, playfulness in his heart and a trot in his step. Life had never been better. After all, seldom does it happen that two beauties descend from heaven on the same day. The effect was so profound that even though acknowledged as the most cheerful of souls otherwise, I surprised my peers and parents with that extra dose of mirth. Time and again they would stare at me agape and utter, "What's the matter with you, Tejas? Won a lottery lately?" and I would answer them all with a wave of my hand, "No, no, nothing of that sort, one should stay happy and cheerful and in this weather it's the easiest of tasks!" I remember I composed ten songs during those monsoons, all dealing with nature and love and was playing guitar all the time I was not with her.

But what those divine monsoons must be remembered for is a single evening, a celebrated one. A magical evening it was...

I had long wished to have a candlelight dinner with her, and I knew she would love it. I am a romantic at heart, which you must have discovered by now, and girls, you know, love these mushy things. But for all the loveliness and the romance of candlelight dinners, there is a drawback and a big one at that. One needs darkness for the candlelight to have a visible effect on the surroundings; one cannot just light candles on a bright day and feel happy that he's had a candlelight dinner just for the record. I bet you understand what I say. I just want to express the non-feasibility of such dinners with lighted candles in this part of the world, for girls, in this otherwise lovely part of the world, are not allowed out after the sun has set. The girl's parents would say, "The roads are not safe." It was, therefore, with considerable astonishment, that she exclaimed when I suggested this rare type of dinner:

"Are you serious!"

I said I was and she asked me if I was drunk to which I replied that I was not.

"Then, how come, you are getting such insane ideas?"

"It is not insane, it is lovely!"

"Lovely, I know, but impractical!"

"You only talk about candlelight so much... and when I think about making it a reality, you shudder. Girls are dumb," I shot back.

"Tejas, do you think I'll get the permission to stay out after six or seven in the evening?"

"No!" I replied coolly.

"Then?"

"What then? You don't need any permission! When did I say you need it?"

"Of course, I need it. Now, don't suggest that I should sneak out of my window at night..."

"Shut up! You don't even listen to the plan and go on and on," I interrupted her.

"What's the plan, now?"

"I don't want to tell you, I can see that you are not interested, do what you wish to do!"

"Offo, sorry! You know I am interested. Tell me! Quick!"

"Hmm! When is your friend's sister's wedding?"

"Fourth of July."

"And... you have got the permission to attend it. Right?"

"Yes!"

"Then we don't need any other permission."

I explained the plan to her and she assented on my insistence that it would all be alright. I booked a place called 'Rendezvous' for the dinner. I should rather say that Bajrang booked it for me. We once had a party on the terrace of that place and I had been smitten by the ambience. I thought that the place was fabulous if less noise was made, and I wanted to suggest to the owner to lend the place to lovers, rather than waste the space on loud binges.

The terrace was usually reserved for parties and called for a hefty sum but the owner was Tanker's pal. I don't know how and I don't wish to know; he found out that there was no party on the fourth and got the entire terrace for me at no extra charge. I couldn't believe it when he told me, but, then, Tanker has his own impeccable style. "Both of you must be alone, brother; why should morons interrupt you. I would hate that myself," he had said to me and I was extremely pleased to have a pal like him. I had wanted open air for dinner, not one of those stifling five stars where one longed for breath and the shattering of the sickening decorum. Besides, I couldn't afford them.

Her friends smuggled her out from the wedding and dropped her at eight as promised and were to pick her up at nine thirty. They were hugely cooperative. All her friends wore colourful *lahengas*, and were a bit extra giggly and chirpy. I could only blush and smile at their teasing remarks as they called me '*Jeejaji*'.

"We'll be there at nine thirty sharp, *jeeju*," said one and then added teasingly, "So be done with *all* you have to do by then; after all, she has to change back to her *lahenga* and that takes time."

I thanked them, promised them a treat, bade them goodbye and then turned to look at Shreya, who, all this while, had been concealed by the giggling girls. I would not waste much space in describing her beauty. But she had stunned me once again. I just gaped at her, as though petrified. She smiled, knowing that I had been knocked out by her spell and whispered, "Where shall we proceed?" and I mumbled something like, "Upstairs." But I kept looking at her and she crossed her slender arms, pursed her lips, raised her eyebrows and shook her head at my behaviour. "Come on, now, Tejas, I am not looking that good." But she was and she knew it fully.

She wore a black dress that ended just above her knees and had thin straps. It was not revealing, or provocative but extremely graceful. The dress had settled on her curves beautifully, highlighting her slender figure, making her look like a Goddess. The black of the dress matched with the colour of the night and contrasted beautifully with her fair arms and neck that glistened in the moon light. She wore her usual make up that consisted of a line of *kajal* and a touch of gloss on her lips. That was it. Her face didn't need any more. Her silk-like tresses were open as usual, thrown back, shining silver at places. And she wore the silver ear rings that I had gifted her just the day before. For the first time with me, she wore heels and that brought her almost to my level — thankfully, not above it. She was lissom, lithe, elegant and all that.

I took her burning hand in mine and led her up the stairs, and she was surprised to see the setting. She pressed my hand, looked into my eyes and said that it was beautiful. I was glad that she approved of the place.

It was beautiful indeed, and no other word could have described it better, just like no other word could describe her better. It was a terrace and idyllic – no roof on the top, just the sky studded with diamonds. It had rained in the evening but the rain had stopped, the heavy clouds gone, to display a spectacular star-studded sky. Thin foam like clouds still spattered here and there added to the beauty. Though the clouds had made way for the stars, the beautiful smell of wet earth lingered on, wafted by a brilliant, cool breeze — the hallmark of monsoons. The moon was out too and bathed the night with its silver splendour.

There was a criss-cross bamboo fence on the border that acted like a trellis for the creepers which I thought were ivy. Entwined with the ivy were small, vivid flowers that added a splash of colour to the whole fence. The arrangement was splendid. The rest of the terrace was outlined with beautiful hedges from which purple flowers peered lovingly. I noticed how lovely purple looked with green. Love makes you love nature as well!

Out in the left corner, near the fence, were two wooden chairs with a wooden table in between. On the table, two long candles illuminated the setting, and the silverware cast their light and the moon's. I had chosen the corner as it was the most exquisite one, overlooked by a Gulmohar tree which had gained sufficient height over the years to provide a friendly shade to this corner on sunnier days. Neither was it day, nor had the sun come out for two days, yet I had chosen this nook for the beauty that the tree with its ready-to-bloom orange flowers lent to it.

There was a fountain too, on the far right hand corner, and it sparkled, too, in the silver of the moon. Nothing could be better, I reflected, and led her to the chairs. I pulled a chair for her, bowed with one hand on my middle and the other drawn out, gesturing her to sit, and said, "Muh-daam, have a seat," and she obliged by saying a 'Thank you, sir.'

I took my seat and looked into her eyes. Lately, I had realized, she allowed me do so and her eyes smiled when I did that. Earlier she would feel shy when I tried to concentrate on her eyes and would laugh and say, "What are you doing, Tejas?" But, now, we both loved it.

"Hope the place is not bad, Muh-daam! This is all this humble bloke could manage!" I said.

"Not bad? Shut up, Tejas! It is lovely, I told you. Like a dream," she replied sincerely.

"See, I could not afford a five-star for you," I said. That had sometimes bothered me, the money issue.

She came from a much richer family and was a habitual diner at the hotels with her family. I was from a good family but we couldn't afford five-stars, and didn't like them either. So this money problem bothered me. I always felt I couldn't treat her lavishly, couldn't give her expensive gifts, couldn't get a car to go on a drive with her, couldn't afford balcony tickets for movies as rates had soared to a hundred and a fifty each now; in short couldn't do anything that a modern girl would expect from her boy and she knew that. Time and again, we would have conversations about this paucity of money, and she didn't like them. She would always say, "Who said I want expensive dinners and gifts?"

"But all girls do!" I would reply.

"Well, I am different and we won't have this type of talk again. If you want to gift diamonds, go, and get a new girl... You talk like this, once more, and I will stop talking to you," and with that, the topic would be closed.

And, that is why I loved her... because she was different...because she was not materialistic... because she loved me and just me. But, in spite of her sweetness and understanding, sometimes this problem did trouble me and I had once gotten so sentimental that I wrote a song about my love for her and I intended to play it that night.

"Who said I like five star hotels?" she asked irritated.

"You go there so often..." I had touched an exposed nerve, but she interrupted me, and how!

"How many times do I tell you, not to talk about five-stars and all those idiotic things, but you wouldn't understand. How many times have I told you, I am a normal girl, who likes simple things in life? I am an average girl who likes to eat her five rupees orange bar, who likes her artificial, junk jewellery over gold and diamond. Please Tejas, understand... that I am NORMAL. N-O-R-M-A-L," she spelled it for me, "let me enjoy these things, and stop worrying about treating me like a queen. I know how much you love me and that is it. That is all I want. And I know how much you have sacrificed for me already... to foot your mobile bills and give me such lovely dinners. I won't embarrass you by asking how much this place has cost you but I know you have sacrificed for it. Tell me, how many weeks since you saw any movie?" she roared.

"Leave that!"

"Now, why should we leave *that*? When I say leave all your insane gibberish about money, you don't!"

"Okay, sorry, *baba*, I won't mention it again!"

"You dare do it and I'll not meet you again. Already you insist on paying the bills every time. Can't we go Dutch, once?"

"No, I think we have talked about that enough, too. So leave it right here," this time I roared. I was very clear on that. That was the least I could do for my princess, I thought. I belong to the school that believes in thorough gallantry. I wonder how guys can go half-half with their girls on dates. They have lost all shame nowadays. They don't make gentlemen these days. All they make is chicken shit. Some ridiculous movement called metro-shetro-whatever-sexuality was sweeping the town and guys were doing all sorts of insane stuff like getting facials and manicures, and asking their girls to give their share of the check. The roles were shifting in this modern society and it sent in old hats like me a shiver down the spine. Whatever happened to the roughness and toughness that separated a boy from a man and, more disturbingly, to the chivalry and courtesies that we had been taught, with which a woman ought to be treated. Anyway, I was completely an antique and had made it clear to Shreya, and in no uncertain terms, that, "We might have to live like squirrels and nibble at five rupee sweet buns if I don't have adequate money, but *no way*, mind you, *no way*, will *you* poke your hand in your bally purse or pocket. Do you get me?" I had asked and she had got it. She didn't bother carrying her purse after that and thanked me for that. It was a lot of hassle, she said.

"Anyway, leave all that, but nice place, yes?" I resumed.

"Yaaa... lovely sky, candles, fresh air, lovely flowers and you. All my favourites! What else do I need? Paradise. To think of a five-star cluttered with old people who would die than raise their voice! One can't even breathe there!"

"Exactly. Better a *dhaba*!"

"I swear!"

"Where one can breathe, yawn, sing or dance and even pick one's nose!"

"Yuck, shut up!"

"And what a vulgar price to pay for a *dal* that my mom cooks better!"

"Exactly!"

"But to think of it, they are not that bad too and sometimes a whole lot of fun! I clearly remember a most entertaining evening at a five-star."

"Why? What happened?" she asked raising her brows.

"Oh, that is an amusing story, but a long one!"

"You have a story for every occasion."

"That's why they call me a raconteur."

"What's that?" she asked cutely.

"A teller of anecdotes."

"So tell me what happened."

"Okay, let us order first, we hardly have one and a half hours and there are so many *things* to do. While the food comes, I'll tell my five-star tale."

"What all *things*?" she asked suspiciously.

"Surprise!" I said and, with that, called for Michael, the waiter, who was told to wait downstairs until called for. He had helped a lot to make this tryst a dream and I liked him. We ordered the lip smacking *dal makhani*, *shahi paneer* for me (she doesn't eat *paneer*) and *malai kofta* for her (I don't fancy koftas) and some *lachha paranthas*.

And then I told her the amusing incident, of the times when I was an impish school kid, when my *tayaji* had taken me and my elder brother, Vineet; both of us naughty rascals, for a dinner with a haughty old man, one of those who have in their hands power to award those mysterious tenders. And one of those idiots who are inordinately fussy about trifles like table manners. He told my uncle, who is a thorough gentleman himself, to make less sound with his spoons and in not so polite a manner. That was the last straw. Seeing that he was not going to grant the contract to my uncle, Vineet and I saw no point in extending any further civility. Both of us dipped our hands in the gravy and started licking our fingers one by one, and flashed a smile at the old man who looked at us as if we were dirty, overflowing garbage bins. I concluded the ceremony with a – "Ma'am, your father is a real gentleman," to his third wife, as had been conveyed to us by *tayaji* and at that she uttered a cry and I immediately apologized, "Oh! I am sorry, I did not know. Pardon me, I meant your grandfather," and she eyed me like a basilisk and screeched in a rat like tone, "Heee is myyy *husband!*"

That was so funny that we had to laugh and we did unabashedly while *tayaji* looked on dazed, not entirely unhappy with the proceedings, I guess. Mr. Gobardhan, as he was called, decided that he had had enough and shouted at us, getting up, "You rascals," and at that my brother threw a fake lizard that he used to carry in his young days at the lady at which she uttered a howl and jumped on to the table.

Shreya was literally on the floor laughing and told me that it was enough for the day. There is a limit to everything, she said. It is special making girls laugh and to make her laugh, a lot more. Dinner arrived and we started, being as informal as we could. It was heavenly to eat together as the two candles lent our corner a gorgeous golden glow. I tell all lovers from personal experience, "You must go for candlelight dinners!"

"What would you like to drink?" I asked.

"Water!" she replied.

"Wine?"

"Shut up!"

"Michael!" I shouted.

"You shout for Michael as if he is your younger brother."

"Oh he is, sort of," I said, as he hurried up the steps and arrived with a skid.

"Michael, there is a little problem," I said.

"What would that be, sir? I hope the food is alright!"

"There is a fly in the *dal!*" I said.

"Sir?"

"Joking, *yaar*, not this sort of problem. The problem is that Muh-daam doesn't see anything on your card worth sipping!" and when I uttered that, Shreya eyed me.

"Ma'am, there are cold drinks and juices and even *lassi*."

"Juices there are but not fresh!"

"Sir, we serve Tropicana!"

"But ma'am doesn't like canned juices, that's precisely the problem," and with that I motioned to Shreya to keep quiet as she was beginning to say something, "This can be solved easily if you run down and get two glasses of orange juice from the Rambharose Juice shop. Here's the money," and with that I turned to Shreya and said, "They offer excellent juices. Your favourite."

"What was the need for all this?" Shreya asked.

"Don't ask questions, senorita. Just enjoy the weather and the orange juice. You'll love it." And she loved it. Then we ordered our common favourite chocolate truffle pastry and as we were eating it, I said, "You look beautiful, Shreya."

"How many times will you tell me that?"

"Till you tell me how I look. You haven't even said one word in praise of this handsome young man!"

She took a bite from the pastry and said, "One shouldn't speak when one's mouth is full," and started smiling. Then she finished it and eyed me from top to the bottom of what was over the table and said, "Stand up first!"

"Why?"

"I should get a full view," and I stood up. One has to agree with girls.

"Hmm," she said sinking back into her chair, "Not bad!"

"Not bad?"

"Yes!"

"Great, thanks," I said sarcastically.

"What do you want to hear?" she played around.

"Nothing!" I said.

"Offo, don't make faces like girls. Okay, you would have looked handsome if you were tall. Say six feet."

"Oh?" I said, "If height is such a problem, get yourself a basket ball player," I said peevishly. I always got irritated when people talked about heights. I was just five feet, six and a half inches at maximum stretch, no impressive height and everyone teased me about it.

"But I don't like tall guys; after all, I am just five feet three."

"Two and a half at full stretch!"

"Whatever, so five feet six is perfect for me."

"Six and a half inches!" I corrected her.

"Whatever," she said.

"No whatever, you borrow half an inch from me and add that to your own height. Wow!"

"You look so cute when you are irritated. God! How much I love irritating you!"

"Oh! Now I am cute. Not 'not bad'?"

"You are cute and good you are not very tall. That would have diluted your cuteness. Now, you look perfect, like a small baby, my cute little baby! And you look cute in my favourite white shirt and blue jeans. Happy?" she said so sweetly that one had to be happy. I had bought the white shirt at her request. She loves white.

We finished our meal and I looked at my watch. It was quarter to nine. Forty five minutes had passed just like that. And the next forty five would fly the same way. I wished time would stop. I moved my chair next to Shreya and told her to listen to the rustle of the leaves of the Gulmohar tree as the breeze sifted through them. I took her delicate hand in mine and looked into her eyes, and we both enjoyed the silence as she gently placed her head on my shoulder and nestled close. Her perfume was beautiful. I could feel her breath on my neck. I wanted to kiss her on her lips but had promised her I would not, until she asked me to. She looked lovely as I observed her features in the moon light. I kissed her forehead and then her soft hair and she kept still. Her fresh hair was between my lips, and I was lost in their fragrance. Those were blissful moments. I wished we could sit that way forever. The lovely breeze, the lovely scent and the lovelier Shreya... But I knew I had to do other things as well and we had hardly any time left. I gently removed from my pocket the ear rings that I had brought for her today. One pair of ear rings a day she had demanded. I showed them to her as they glinted in the moon. "Are they nice?" I asked.

"Yes!" she said.

"Now get up, time for some surprises."

"Can't we just sit like this for some more time?" she asked in a subdued voice.

"I wish we could, for the rest of our lives, Shreya! But then you have to leave in some time and I have something planned."

"What?"

"Wait," I said and called for Michael.

She lifted her head from my shoulder slowly and got up.

"Do you remember, by any chance, the deal we made when we first met?"

"That guitar and dance one?"

"Yes, time to complete it."

"But where is the guitar?"

"Here it comes," and Michael entered with my favourite, black guitar that I had borrowed from a friend. "Look, I'll teach you in a while, but, first, here's a song I composed... you might like it... then your classes, and after that you teach me how to dance."

"Okay," she said surprised.

"Now don't laugh when I play. It may not be good"

"Shut up!"

"Michael, have you brought your harmonica?"

"Yes sir!"

"Tuned with the guitar?"

"Perfectly, sir!"

"Then let us start," I said, as I slung the belt of the guitar over my shoulder and plucked a few strings. Michael put the harmonica to his lips and Shreya was bewildered to see all that.

"Ladies and gentleman, wherever you are hiding but listening," I started, "Here's a song written especially for this girl sitting right there, yes, that one who is giggling. Let me introduce my band. This is Michael, on harmonica and Tejas, on guitar and vocals, the drummer was sleeping, so couldn't come and we are a little short on funds, so couldn't arrange mikes; I hope that is okay." Shreya said yes and I began plucking the strings of my guitar softly and listened to the rhythm as Michael started playing his harmonica. It was perfect, and after the intro I began to sing as the chords changed from D to G to A to D again, and I sang thus:

I am no rich kid, just a poor nerd,
I've got no money, my pocket's full of mud.
Faded jeans and ragged shirts, thank God, they are in,
For those are the only things, I have to fit in.
If you're the kind of girl, who just goes for money.
You can check out Harry, he's got a big limousine.

All I have got is unconditional love.
All I can promise you is
I'll be there when the things are tough.

No, I can't promise you dinner on golden plates.
No, I can't promise you disco nights so late.
We can get a candle or two and light up my place.
Maybe wash some crockery, order pizzas at low rates.
No lousy music, my guitar gently plays
A song, written, especially for you, babe.

All I have got is unconditional love.

111

All I can promise you is
I'll be there when the sea is rough.
All I have got is unconditional love.
All I can promise you is
I'll be there when the things are tough.

The soft plucking of the guitar notes blended beautifully with the rich sound of the harmonica and my serenade was a success. We both bowed after the performance while Shreya looked on overawed. Then she smiled and said that it was lovely. Michael knew it was time to leave and I told him to put on the music. Then Shreya got up from her chair and gently kissed me on my cheek. She whispered she loved me and I told her too. "You can be a song-writer, Tejas! That was so beautiful," she said. I merely smiled. I really wanted to kiss her then.

"So, you want to learn guitar?"

"No, not today, but I will teach you dance," she said.

"Hmm, not bad an idea considering we have just twenty five minutes left."

I had prepared a play-list of some soft instrumentals, mostly in four by four beat, which I thought would be just right for a dancing couple. There were some solos on guitar, some on piano and violin. Presently the music began to resonate in the magical aura. The first tune was 'Ave Maria' by Johann Sebastian Bach, one of my favourites, and one on which I had always dreamt of dancing with a girl. Shreya closed her eyes, listened to the beat, and then looked at me.

"It is lovely," she said, "Now, you don't have to do anything, just follow my feet. When I go right, you go right, when I go left, you go left. We'll start with these basic steps. Okay?"

"Yes," I said, lost in her eyes and perfume.

She took my hands and placed them on her waist, then she placed her hands on my shoulders and we kept looking into each other's eyes. She moved gracefully, three steps to the right, and then three steps to the left, and I hopelessly followed, not caring anything about my feet, but just about her eyes. She patiently kept along with my clumsy movements and said that I would learn in a while. It took me quite a while to get those six steps right, after a lot of tripping, falling and balancing, but once I got them right it was joy to move with her. It was effortless and we both had drowned in one another's eyes. She came closer and closer it seemed and I smouldered in the warmth of her body. Time and again, I'd caress her hair; time and again, we'd talk in soft whispers and enjoy as our breaths got lost in each other's. Time and again, my hands brushed against her slender arms; time and again, I thought I would have no sadness if I were to die thus, in her arms.

The music changed and it was a bit faster now; it was the instrumental version of La Bamba.

"Time for some new steps," she said as we both emerged from the trance, "This is a salsa beat. Give me your left hand," and with that she held it with her right and adjusted the bend of my left arm to ninety degree. "Now, you are the leader and I am the follower, and I just obey you in this dance... Got it?" I merely nodded. I followed some steps, could not follow some and we danced on. She taught me how to spin her and that was the best part of salsa or whatever it's called. It was beautiful to watch her spin so elegantly, as her hair brushed against my face again and again and immersed me in their perfume.

Soon the music changed and was slow once again and we resumed the six basic steps she had taught me. It was easy. It was heavenly. It was Bach again and once again she was nestled in my arms and we resumed our soft whispering.

"Let's continue this only, it is lovely!" she whispered.

"Michael," I shouted, "Play track one and repeat it till the end," and with that 'Ave Maria' was on again.

Once again I was lost in her eyes and her warmth.

"Can I kiss you?" I whispered.

She merely swayed her head to signal a no. I was not disappointed but I really wanted to kiss her.

"We are dancing, Tejas, maintain the sanctity of the art, just enjoy the dance," she whispered back.

"Hardly five minutes left, your friends must be about to reach."

"Yes," and with that she drew me closer and we were lost in the embrace. It felt then, I distinctly remember, that our souls were one.

November, this year.

I was fast asleep, curled up like a dog, on the concrete bench installed magnanimously outside my classroom, to provide, one assumes, rest and air to tired students in between lectures. And rest it surely did provide. It is a lovely bench for the sun shines generously on it throughout the day, providing the much needed snugness on cool winter mornings. It was November already; the temperature was falling like a child who has tripped off his balcony. And the sun-bathed bench was just the thing one needed.

It was seven forty-five in the morning to be precise. The class started at eight and I had no business to be there fifteen minutes before, nor did I intend to, yet there I was, as unmistakable as the remarkable sun of that very morn. Attending the first class is a rarity in comfortable weather, and to be there a good fifteen minutes early in such chilly weather, was a feat I should have been proud of. But I was hardly alive to such emotions of pride and achievement.

I must disclaim, right away, all responsibility for reaching there in such a fashion, for I am not the one to claim false credits, which in this case must go to my sister Palak, and so should the blame for my half dead state. She kept me awake till four in the morning, listening eagerly to and commenting expertly and worriedly about my plans to visit her best friend in Chennai. She was aware of the developments that had taken place, between her brother and her best friend since that movie-mishap, for a long time now. She had been shocked when she had come to know of it but, like all shocks, it had subsided.

I was at her place on Sunday, and she was supposed to drop me at my college the following morning. But, unfortunately, it turned out that her class that day began half an hour early, at eight due to some absurd reason, and so she *had* to be there at eight. As a result we had to leave home at seven thirty sharp, and I was dropped off like a sack of rotten potatoes at IIT Delhi, which is half way down to her college; at seven forty! I couldn't have been sorer with her, what with her denying me sleep, and then slapping me in the morning at seven, telling me sharply to brush my teeth. Grossly unfair, I tell you, but that is life! And that is life with sisters!

Somebody patted me on my back. Maybe his intention was to pat; I perceived it more as a punch. I opened my eyes with great effort and saw the haze clear gradually. Even if the haze had persisted it would not have been too difficult to deduce who that colossal figure was. It was Khosla who, I told you, had made it a hobby of his to wake me up. His eyes were wide in disbelief; he pinched his cheek and presently he uttered a howl. It had hurt. The pinch had hurt. It was all for real.

"Say man, has the sun risen from the west or what?"

"Why?" I asked, annoyed that I had to be woken up to answer such a dumb question.

"Have you seen the time? Still ten minutes to go, man."

"The very thing I should say to you. Ten minutes to go, you fat fool, and you wake me up! Every time I sleep you are there to do the honours!"

"Sorry, *yaar*, but I found it amazing that you should be here when there are ten minutes to go for the class!"

"I was here when there were twenty minutes to go!"

116

"So you have finally decided to listen to my advice, and are mending your ways. It'll pay you, friend, and pay you well. You will see your grades soar."

"I have not decided on any such stupid thing. It is a mere accident that I am here and I hope life doesn't play such a sinister trick again."

"Hmm, so you'll never reform?"

"Not in this life!"

"God only help you!"

"I tell you, Khosla, just once, only once, I ask of you, cast all your fears aside and lie cosily curled up in your blanket and savour the joy that comes from it. Then, only then, will you relate to my philosophy. You will see this world with new eyes, my friend. You'll be a changed man! And trust me, it'll all be for the better," I lectured my friend who had a habit of arriving for class at such unearthly hours, and that too after a bath, as if they were giving gold medals for the first arrival. The clash of our philosophies went on for a few minutes when, suddenly, I remembered. I had to ask the fatty a question that had been slipping from my mind in that state of half-sleep.

"So have you decided on the professor?"

"Which one?"

"Idiot, the one who'll be with us on the Industrial Tour!"

"Oh yes, don't you know?"

"No, tell me!"

"I didn't decide, *yaar*; Pappi called me himself and said that he would go with us on the tour."

That hit me. As if a sock had been soaked with water, whirled in the air and hurled straight at me, between the eyes. Those were ominous beginnings. I could sense something fishy. Stinking fishy. Why would that professor want to accompany us on the tour when he was known to be indifferent to such things? I wondered if it had got anything to do with me. I then remembered his words, his evil words as they echoed in my ears: "Take that in your head that I am not going to leave you like this. I will not rest till I have set you right!"

I wondered what he was up to, now. He had granted me permission to miss the Industrial Tour. Now what did he want to do by assigning himself as our guide on the tour? It was all a big mystery to me. But something told me that all was not well and the words of Pappi, that I had forgotten, came back to me, in a more threatening tone.

"What happened? Why are you so stunned? You have got your permission. Right? So you needn't worry!" said Khosla, naively, but I knew better. I knew these professors, being involved in a few scrapes earlier. They didn't let you off so easily. Not even jovial ones like Pappi, who, it seemed, had given up his joviality once and for all.

"When did he tell you?" I inquired.

"Friday only!"

It was almost eight by then and my class mates had started coming in and presently a circle of bewildered souls surrounded me; some slapping, some pinching, some even pulling at their hair in order to make sure that it was not a dream. Was it Tejas Narula there, for real? At eight? Some pinched me to make sure that it was not a ghost who lay there. I was thinking on the same lines too, though the ghost in my story was someone else. I wondered how life could change within just a weekend and wondered what it had in store for me.

The class came to an end and the next two hours were free. I wearily got up and followed my friends out. I just needed my bed badly. Rishabh stopped outside the Mechanical Engineering Department office.

"Wait a second; have to meet Sandhu for my project. I'll be back soon," he said.

Meanwhile I leaned against the wall and talked to Pritish. We both had not dared to take up any extra projects. Compulsory courses were already too much of a burden. Rishabh had take up a project in a state of infant zeal that so often fizzles out, and was suffering at the hands of Prof. Sandhu, who was a thorough professional and didn't tolerate any laxity. Pritish and I made fun of his desolate state when suddenly I heard Rishabh shout for me. It sounded out of place. I thought may be Sandhu had finally decided to strangle my friend's neck for lack of discipline, and he had cried out for help but I saw him well outside the professor's room before the department notice board.

"Look," he said, staring grimly at the board.

"You know I don't bother about notices talking about deadlines and..."

"But it doesn't deal with that," he said, and I must say there was a distinct chill in his voice which made me uneasy.

I went closer to the notice board, half expecting to see words written in blood. It was nothing of that sort. It was a simple printout on a plain letter sized paper.

DEPARTMENT OF MECHANICAL ENGINEERING
NOTICE – By the order of Dean, UG

1. All students are hereby informed that they must produce documented proofs if they wish exemption from the Industrial Tour. In case of a marriage ceremony, the wedding card must be produced and likewise for other reasons.

2. The documents must first be submitted to the Tour Guide, Professor P.P. Sidhu, who, after his approval, will forward the application to the Dean, UG for his validation.

3. The leave will be granted only for the days of ceremonies and one day extra for travelling purposes after which the student must report to the tour. Under no circumstances the student will be allowed to miss

the whole tour. The tour is a part of the curriculum and thus a prerequisite for the B. Tech. Degree.

Prof. P. P. Sidhu – Tour Committee Head and Tour Guide

Prof. P. K. Dhingra – Dean, Under Graduate Students

"Damn the fools!" came a voice from somewhere, and I discovered that the speaker was a boy standing next to me. I recognized him, he was my department-mate but one of those who sat in the first three rows, and thus I had not had the occasion to hobnob with him before. One cannot be chummy with all the class when it has about a hundred potential candidates. "Damn the fools!" he cried again, "Don't they have any common sense? How can one report to the tour immediately after his sister's wedding? Insane. Damn the fools!" He looked at me and said, "You look horrified too, friend, someone getting married?"

"Yes," I said deeply shaken but presently relieved a little to find a friend, "My brother!"

"Brothers are still fine, brother. But sisters! One has to do so much work in a sister's wedding. There are endless arrangements and then the sentimental parting. How can they issue such a foolish and callous notice?"

"Don't know, *yaar*!" I said, though I knew the answer.

"Damn the fools!"

I withdrew from the cluster that had formed around the green notice board. I was gripped by a strange feeling. I was not depressed. It was a setback, no doubt. My suspicion, after all, had not been baseless. It had been vindicated by this notice. And that made me a little happy. I had been right. I gazed at the notice again, so simple in its black ink but so sinister in its content. There it was, pinned innocuously on the green board – my missing link. It completed the picture. It justified the professor volunteering himself for the tour. The notice was not there for the Mechanical Department. It was there for me. Just me. I knew others would be granted permission in the end but not me.

120

To anyone else, I guess, it might have seemed the end. But not to me. It was not the end, I told myself, but just the beginning. Beginning of the battle between men who had all the power and a boy who had nothing but the fire to do anything, anything to meet his love. There had to be a way out of it all, as there always is, but where, that was the question.

D eserving or not being kept aside, if ever a historian was asked to put together a chronicle of my life, he would jump at the offer. For seldom does a life have its moments so distinguished and worth recording. Not a year has passed since my birth that doesn't stand for something special. Therefore, mine would make a trim chronicle, with the years arranged neatly on the left, followed by a hyphen, and then the mishaps, listed year by year, in the column to the right. And the historian will find at least one satisfactory imbroglio for each year, thus not facing the predicament, that the historians inevitably face in putting together annals like these, of researching madly only to draw a blank. To illustrate the simplicity of the task, here it is, briefly, and a historian may be allowed to use it:

1984 – Born amidst utter confusion... Lost in an ocean of babies in the hospital by a careless nurse... Finally identified... After referring to the records... He was the only boy born in that week. The rest were all girls! What company! Phew!

1985 – Speaks his first word. Not common for a baby though. 'Darling!' Psychologists postulate the overdose of western content on television as the reason. Nevertheless, they add, it shows early signs of a budding Casanova.

1986 – Takes his first steps... when everybody had given up hope... surprises everybody by standing suddenly, walking and attempting to cross the road on his very first move. How daring! But the attempt is cut short by a speeding car which hits him; he flies up in the air, lands on his head, bounces a couple of times and comes to rest... Doctors attribute mental instability to this very incident.

1987 – Shows early promise again, this time of becoming a boxer... Knocks his classmate down after a fight over the ownership of a pencil... Suspended for fifteen days... Parents call the Guinness Book of World Records... But he misses the world record of the earliest suspension by three days... Tragic! India misses another world record!

And so the chronicle will proceed effortlessly to arrive at this year, and go beyond, no doubt. You can gauge very well from the early years, what a life it has been! Thus you'll expect in me nerves of steel and muscles of iron and you'll not be wrong either. Therefore, the present imbroglio, however distressing, could not shake me and I took it as casually as just another entry in the chronicle. Something had to be written against this year and this was it. The fact that I had sailed through all the earlier predicaments, gave me immense relief and encouragement. The only thing that I said to myself in the followin days was, "Think, Tejas, think!" I had a particularly favourite teac r in high school, Mrs Bhatia, a delightful lady who showered me with favours, who had this favourite line ready, whenever we failed to answer her questions, "Put on your thinking caps, children!"

Whether I found my thinking cap or not, I would certainly have made Bhatia ma'am proud, for I did arrive at a solution. I decided against mentioning all this to Shreya or else she'd tell me, again, not to come But, having come so far, I was not going to retreat.

⤝

Tanker lit a cigarette and sank back into his chair. Smoke rings appeare out of his nose and mouth. He flicked off ash and looked at m disappointed. Then he spoke:

"You have let me down, brother... after all that I have done for you!"

Elder brother was unhappy that he had been kept in the dark and was not a part of the planning commission. But today, I had to tell him, as I needed his help. I honestly considered him a good friend but hadn't told him because there was every chance that he might blabber something out while on drinks.

"You really love her, bro!" he said, smiling.

"Leave all that, *yaar*," I said, avoiding such remarks as a rule.

"But you do... taking so many risks... must say, listening to your tale, I want to love someone too," he said and we were surprised. The tough Bajrang was talking about love.

"So... what do you want me to do, brother?" he said, tapping at his cigarette again.

I told him the plan. I needed a wedding card, as the documented proof, reading 'Vineet weds Preeti' or any other lady, 14th December, which excused me till the 16th, after which I needed to hop to the Inter-IIT sports meet. There was nothing else that could ambush me. And, for that, it required, that I be a part of some team. But then, teams are not as readily available as the Haryana State Lottery tickets, and that too at the crunch; unless, of course, you have Tanker as your guardian angel.

"So... it is imperative that I go to Inter-IIT after marriage. Any team for me?" I asked Bajrang.

"Shot-put," he said coolly and there was a funny silence. Then Rishabh started laughing, clutching his tummy and looking at me, the subject of the joke. I weighed a mere sixty kg.

"Shot-put?" I asked, unbelieving, "The game in which you have to throw a ball weighing a ton, as far as possible?"

"Yes," he said coolly again.

"Do you realize that the ball is heavier than me?" I asked wisely.

"Don't you worry about the technical details!"

"Do you realize that the authorities won't allow you to take a handicapped with you?" I tried to reason.

"Don't you worry about the authorities!"

"I don't believe they will allow him for shot-put," interjected Rishabh.

"I don't say things just like that, you buffoons. When I say, he is in the team, I mean, he is in the team. No one can throw the put better than me. I can safely go alone and they will not complain. They know that all the medals will be ours. But rules say a five member battalion must be sent, and so it'll be. Thus even if I take, with me, four paralysed chaps, it wouldn't make a difference. Don't you worry, it'll all be done."

Rishabh and I looked at him, amazed. A man of resource, if ever there was one. A gem of a friend. Other people would have laughed at me, if ever they saw me in the shot-put quarters, and mistaken me for the chap who draws the chalk-lines. But here was a man who saw potential in me, a mere duckling. I was not weak but certainly not strong enough for shot-put. Once, in school days, I had tried my hand at it, this whole business of shot-putting, and I had putted the shot with full force, and expected it to land out of the school, but my expectations were short lived: the put landed right on my foot. Never in my life, did I try juggling with puts again. The pleasant thought was that, of course, that I won't have to do it this time. It was all just a cover up.

"So happy, now?" inquired Bajrang, "You attend the marriage and then hop off straight to the sports meet. And the tour is killed, nothing of it remains," and at that he chuckled.

"There is still a problem," I said prolonging the grimness, "I haven't yet told you about the main course of plan."

"What is it now," both my friends asked in unison. For them the battle had been won, the enemy trampled and the flag unfurled. But I knew better. It was alright, this whole combo plan of wedding and sports, brimming with *masala* and thrill, still it left my enemy with plenty of room. It foiled the enemy's current strategy, but didn't eliminate the enemy, and I knew, until that was done, the battle was not won.

"Pappi has to be removed," I said and a deafening silence ensued. Both my friends looked at each other and then at me stupefied, with bulging eyes, as if a dragonfly had landed on my shoulder, which must be squashed, but with caution. I looked over my shoulder, first right and then left. There was nothing, save my blue shirt.

"Come on, my brother, it isn't that big a reason too, to start removing professors," Tanker replied shocked.

"But he has to be removed."

"He has kids, goddamit!" cried Rishabh.

"Where do the kids come in now?" I asked innocently.

"You idiot, who'll take care of them if he is removed?"

And then I followed their train of thought. In the grim aura that had been created, they had started to think like mafia. One couldn't blame them.

"I meant, removed from the position of Tour Guide," I replied.

"Oh," said Tanker and "Oh," said Rishabh.

"How will you do that?" asked both.

"He'll be forced not to come."

"How?"

"I'll make him an offer he can not refuse."

"What offer?"

"Biobull!" I stated and laughed sinisterly. They both looked at me and joined in too. The laughs dissolved in the grim silence. I picked up my guitar and started playing the immortal tune of Godfather. It felt nice to be able to play with the mood. The professors had dared to displease the Godfather, I told myself, and they must not be spared.

Still November, this year

I waited at the airport lounge. I leaned against the barriers and craned my neck to see if he was there. All I saw was three beautiful girls, part of the Lufthansa crew, as was written on their badges, but there was no sign of him yet. I tell you, it is a most fascinating place, this airport lounge. You get to see some stunningly pretty girls and, besides, it is a nice feeling, waiting keenly for your near and dear ones to emerge out of the crowd.

Don't imagine too much, I warn you all, if you are suspecting what I should be doing at an airport, and whom I should be waiting for. To disappoint you all, eager beavers, whose minds have been corrupted by an overdose of thrillers, nothing's fishy here. I was just waiting for Vineet, my brother, who, I promised you all, has no small role in these memoirs. He is a real chum. I was there to receive him at the airport in absolute secrecy. It was supposed to be a surprise for the whole family, his arrival, and only I was let in on the secret, partly because we two are really close, but mainly because somebody needed to arrange a taxi.

Presently I saw his head appear, his body hidden behind two beautiful girls. I was sure he was following them. Some people never change. Then I saw his neck emerge, then the belly and I could see him wholly now shoving his trolley as the two girls turned left. I could see a tint of disappointment in his face. He had grown a little fat.

"You saw those two girls?" he asked me, his eyes opened wide. No hi, no hello!

"Yaaaaa," I said.

"Stunners they were, bloody, turned left!" he said frustrated, "Anyway, wassup, brother?" and with that hugged me.

"I am fine, you say!"

"I am cool as usual, how's Shreya?"

"Fine too!" I said.

"All well?" he asked.

"We'll talk about that in the taxi," I said as I took his trolley and directed it towards the taxi stand. With the luggage shoved in the dicky, and both of us settled snug, I ventured to explain to him the situation.

"My dearest, respected, elder brother," I began, as was my wont, whenever I wanted anything from him, and he interrupted, as was his wont, understanding that it was indeed something that his younger imp of a brother wanted him to do. And past experiences had taught him to keep a mile from me, when I was in such a mood.

"I have just landed, brother!" he said, giving me one of his looks of suspicion.

"I'd be the first to wish you rest, brother, but, I am afraid, this thing needs to be done quickly, or I'll be damned," I tried to explain to him the gravity of the situation.

"You'll never change, will you? I was so happy... living a life of ease and peace... continents away from you... and a minute with you..." my brother said dreamily.

"Don't begin, brother. It is just a tiny task and you are just the man for it. What a deuce of a situation I would be in, had you not come!"

"I hope I had not!" he said.

"Most disgraceful of you to say that! Now listen, don't make a mountain out of a molehill. It is child's play, this task; yet, it needs a man and so we need you."

"Which man?" he asked suspiciously.

"Oh, I'll come to that."

"Tell me all," he finally said, yielding.

He knew, of course, that I was going to meet Shreya but nothing beyond that. Nothing about my tête-à-tête's with eminent professors, and all the planning done, thereafter. I narrated it all with the required stresses, and saw the effect I wished to see.

"Damned unlucky of you, to land yourself in such a soup," he said commiseratively.

"Don't call it a petty soup, brother, call it an ocean... an ocean full of alligators," I corrected him.

"Whatever... but this time I have to admit that it is not your fault. You haven't hit your foot with an axe and my heart goes out for you!"

"You have heart of gold, brother. Twenty four carat if there is no carat above it. Help me; you are the only one who can!" I looked at him with melancholic eyes and he melted.

"Alright, what is it?"

"We have to remove the professor."

"Hmm, well thought, but how do you go about it?"

"I don't go about it, big brother; it is you who go about it!"

"Oh!"

"Yes!"

"How?" he asked, nervous like a man about to jump in an ocean of alligators to save a drowning friend.

"The professor is hell bent on going on the tour and there's just one thing that can prevent him."

"What?" he asked with an air of a man about to be told the darkest of secrets, not sure if his heart would cope with it.

"Biobull," I said with an air of a man telling that secret.

"Biobull?" he asked, not knowing what to do with it.

And I hastened to clear the haze. Biobull – the pride of the professor, the bus that will rock the world... Biobull – the bus that runs on a gas made from human wastes and gives an average of... Biobull – the professor's dream... Biobull – the thing that the professor will do anything for!

I gave my brother all the definitions that the lexicons would supply in the centuries to come.

"Biobull!" he said with a sigh, as if it was his lover's name.

"Yes, Biobull," I asserted again, "Biobull, the future of locomotion!"

"Biobull," he repeated, not able to get over the repulsive word, "What a frightful name!"

"I know, but that's what it is, Biobull, and we needn't worry about it. All we should worry about is... what all can be done with the Biobull!"

"What all?" asked my brother, innocently.

"You should ask what cannot be done with the Biobull. We can have an alternate fuel, we can save the humanity, counter global warming, we may never have to worry about saving power; all that'll be required from us, is what we presently do, shit! And the rest will be done by the Biobull. Imagine serving the world by sitting on the potty. You'd be a millionaire, brother, with your current excreting abilities," he eyed me; but I resumed, "What can't the Biobull do, brother! It can bring about a revolution and, more importantly, for us, brother, it can prevent Pappi from embarking on the tour!"

"How?" he asked again, piqued to the extreme after listening to such drivel.

"Ah," I said, "Your focus impresses me, never the one to stray, here's how! You just need to go to him, and tell him that you are an NRI entrepreneur, who is interested in putting all his life's savings, which incidentally run into millions, into this gold mine of a project, the famous Biobull! And that you'd be coming to India again in December, December 13th to be precise, and will be here till the 20th; those are the industrial tour dates; and thus both of you can work together during that period. If he asks you whether you can meet him some other time, give him a flat no for an answer. Convince him to meet you in December. This, for you, Mr. CEO, will be nice experience, considering you intend to do such idiotic things for the rest of your life. Thus he will be prevented from going to Pune! He won't risk losing out on such support for his dream project! Isn't it a peach of an idea?"

I must say that I wished to see, in my dearest brother's eyes, a spark, a relief that the world, after all, wasn't a boring place, and it still offered us, albeit occasionally, moments worth remembering. I aspired to see the zeal of his younger days, those wonderful days, when we went from place to place, shattering many a windowpane and lamp-shade. However, I was shattered to see his eyes. In place of glint, there was gloom. His look was of a man who had finally decided that it wasn't wise to jump in the alligator-ocean. Touched he was, to see his friend drown, but could not risk alligators.

"Sorry, brother," he said plaintively, "I cannot do that."

"Why?" I asked.

"I won't advise that, brother, I don't want you to get into any trouble. I tell you, these professors are merciless. They will ruin you if they find out."

"How the hell will he find out? It is perfect, my friend, this plan, and you are the man for the job."

"You always say so, brother!"

"And I am right, am I not?"

"Not always!"

"Always," I asserted.

"Remember... when in class six your father was summoned, by your moral science teacher, to complain to him that you had hit her with a piece of chalk..."

"I had not *hit* her with any chalk. She had hit the chalk instead. I had merely thrown it in the air, it was a bloody coincidence that she appeared out of nowhere and collided with the missile. Most unfortunate that was." I corrected him again.

"Whatever, but *chacha* was summoned, and you did the same, then, what you intend to do now!"

"Come on, not that brother!"

"Why not? It is exactly the same. You made me appear, before that brute of a lady, as your dad and it was all a dud. She saw through it all and in three seconds…"

"She had to see through it all, brother! How on earth was she to believe you are my father? You are hardly four years older to me, and, I remember, your front two teeth were missing, then. It was an error, brother, and I admit it! Ingenious though the plan was, of replacing my dad, it was also immature. It had a fundamental flaw. I chose the wrong man for the job. But then I had no option, then, brother. Now, I am in third year of college. I have grown up and there is maturity in my plans! You should be proud of me, and look at you, you shudder like a rabbit! Whatever happened to the spirit of Narulas?" I asked, appealing to his self pride.

"My only concern, brother, is that it shouldn't harm your career in any way!"

"It will not, don't you see the ingenuity of the plan?"

"Brother, I see it, but I see the risk, too; we shouldn't do it!"

"Fine, let your brother drown," I said.

"It is not that, brother."

"I know it is not that, it is much more than that. I see my brother of the yonder years, one whose eyes shone at the hint of mischief, is dead," I began my emotional blackmail.

"Not the case," he waved it off.

"That's the case. You are a coward now, with no sense of adventure."

"That won't work, brother."

"Please, brother, please," I pleaded, "Just once… remember our days of glory. When we walked arm in arm, shattering windows, flowerpots... whatever that came in our way. Just once... let us relive them brother... You come here only once a year! And I miss all our adventures," I said. I meant that. "I miss all the time we spent together. I miss you, man," I bellowed. I could see his eyes get dreamy and misty. After all, how could he forget them? "Remember those golden days, brother. The teasing of girls, the shoplifting, the thrashing I once got for puncturing Mr. Dhanpat's car tyre, the way we used to run away after ringing doorbells, and the five-star incident when we demolished that... what's his name..."

"Gobardhan!" my brother replied eagerly, clearly transported to the era gone by.

"Remember that lizard you flung on that rat of a girl, 'Heee is myyy HUSBAND!' Remember, brother? How can you forget all that? Where's that spirit?"

He came closer to me and put his arm around me.

"I can't forget, brother, I can't. I miss those days too, damn it, I miss those days too. And here, your plan is a good one, and just the one for a soul like me. Reminds me of our favourite Fatty of Enid Blyton, the one who used to disguise, impersonate and what not..."

"And you are fat!"

He gave me one of his looks and then laughed.

"And I am fat. I wanna do it, bro, but are you sure it's safe? I'd love to help you and Shreya. But it should be safe..."

"Have you lost your famous vision, brother? You should have analysed the situation yourself and declared it as safe as a Swiss bank locker. You let me down. You want me to explain all to you. Spoon-feeding, that's the phrase. I see all these years out of India have taken a toll on you, and all that astuteness of yours has eroded. But this plan will reactivate it all, brother. It'll be an elixir for you."

"Fine, I'll do it; after all, the professor doesn't know I am related to you..."

"You are the man for the job. You fit like T into the image one needs. It is like this role was written for you, brother. You don't look like my father, still, but you look like a young corporate investor, one of those who make millions before they are thirty!" I saw him dream again, "I can see you wrapped impeccably, in a tuxedo, and boy, don't you mean business!"

"Make that a black tux!" he added.

"Perfect, the man in the black tux, stepping out of his black Jaguar, with his black briefcase, going to the professor and telling him, 'I want to invest a few millions in your bus.' Isn't it chic?"

"I wish he was building a jet."

"One cannot have it all, brother, bus it is, for now," I added with empathy.

"When do I meet my client?" he asked.

"Tomorrow, after we discuss at night what all you have to tell him. You are the man, brother. And the best thing is that you have done your courses in entrepreneurship. You know all that crap about venture capital, angel capital..."

"Don't worry about all that, brother, it'll be done."

"I knew you would do it. Thanks."

"Mention not," he said, and with that I slipped in his hand, his new visiting card.

'**Prashant Oberoi**,' it announced in impeccable black over a smooth white,

'**Venture Capitalist,**

Make Millions Bake Billions Inc., Austin, Texas.' I had ordered ten of those a couple of days back, and it had cost me just hundred rupees. A man in black tux, black Jaguar, with a black briefcase, was definitely not complete without those. My brother looked at it, felt it and flashed a smile of well done!

I waited for him at the Holistic Food Centre along with Pritish and Rishabh. He had taken a long time. I was nervous. What if he couldn't pull it through! It was a winner, the idea, yet the way Mr. Fate had taken a dislike to me lately, anything could be expected to happen. Presently he called on my cell; I nervously pressed the button to receive his call, praying silently that all was well.

"Hullo," Vineet said.

"Hullo, what happened?" said my voice, shaking.

"Come out of the campus to Barista, now!"

"What are you doing there?"

"Will you come?"

"But tell me what happened or my heart will fail."

"It's a long story."

"Alright, will be there in five minutes."

He was acting like a brute. Prolonging the agony and making me miss classes. All along the way I prayed for his victory over Pappi. I could see his colossal figure through the glass. He was dressed in a formal shirt and trousers. He sipped cold coffee and eyed a girl as usual. We entered, took our chairs, and I hoped the introductions would be short and sweet. But my brother has no sense of timing. There I was, under such enormous strain, and he talked about girls. It is all very well to talk about girls, pleasure always, but there are times one wishes to talk business.

"Isn't she hot?" he said, rolling his eyes in the direction of a pretty lass.

"Will you tell me, what happened?" I asked, trying to be cool.

"She has been looking at me for so long," he chuckled.

"She *has* to look for *so* long; it does take an hour or two to look at you fully, from the right end to the left! You fat rascal. Creating unnecessary suspense. Calling us all the way to Barista! Will you tell me, what happened?" I said, this time bringing my fist upon the table.

Heads turned and so did the head of the girl who was 'eyeing' my brother. She was pretty.

"You call me rascal? I am not delaying, you knucklehead! I called you here because it was not safe to meet inside the campus; your Prof. Pappi walked with me to that food centre where you wanted to meet me. It would have been cataclysmic had he seen us! You are a complete jackass!"

"But, please tell me what happened; I can't take any more, brother!"

"He isn't going on the Industrial Tour..."

"You did it, brother?"

"No, you don't understand, he wasn't, anyhow, going on the tour..."

"What?"

"You are saved..."

"How do you know?"

"Because he refused outright to meet me in December, and I saw our plan failing..."

"Then? Didn't you entice him with the two million dollars investment?"

"Didn't work..."

"A production capacity of hundred buses a day?"

"Didn't work..."

"Selling the technology to the US and EU?"

"Didn't work..."

"That it would be India's biggest achievement since the discovery of zero?"

"A zero effect..."

"That scientists from Germany and Japan were working on the same lines and their patents must be beaten..."

"Nothing worked..."

"What is he doing in December?"

"Turns out his partner's daughter is getting married in December. He got to know about the dates only now..."

"His partner?"

"Yes, his partner on the Biobull project..."

"That's great..."

"Wait..."

"What now?"

"You'll faint when I tell you where he is headed to..."

"Where?" I asked quickly, before my mind could run amok.

"Chennai..." he said, and I fainted.

But I wasn't allowed to enjoy my unconsciousness. My mobile howled. I clumsily took it out of my jeans pocket. It was Bajrang's call. I wondered why he called... perhaps about the shot-put training!

"Hullo, Tejas?"

"Yes, say, brother!"

"Bad news, *yaar*!"

"What?"

"The wedding card can't be printed!"

"Why?"

"It is damn expensive."

"How much?"

"Minimum two thousand rupees!"

"I just want one, *yaar*, I heard it costs about fifteen a card!"

"Yes, but the template of the card costs two thousand! They don't care if you want one card or a million; they take separate money for the template formation!"

"Okay!" I said dejected.

"Don't worry, man, we'll find a way, and then you are on the team. Don't worry!"

"Yes, thanks, bye!"

"Bye!"

Brace yourself for life, I often say, for nothing is more unpredictable. However, I couldn't help but droop like a withered flower after the twin shock. News of the wedding card was, no doubt, unfortunate, but one didn't know what to do with Pappi's news.

"What happened?" was the natural question that came from all corners.

And I told them. Obviously, I couldn't churn out a princely sum of two thousand rupees for one card. I wished I was one of those spoilt sons of a rich millionaire, who threw money as if dealing cards. Already, I just about managed to make both ends meet with my allowance, and then, there was the forthcoming trip itself, where money would be needed for lodging and food, and regaling her highness. My brother, as I had foreseen, put his arm around me and said, "I'll give you two thousand bucks, don't worry."

"Shut up!"

"If that smoothens out things, why not? After all, it is hardly fifty dollars!" he said after his brief calculation.

I told him to shut up once again. Money wasn't the solution.

"Hey listen," Rishabh said, "Now... Pappi personally gave permission to your father... that you may skip the Industrial Tour. He doesn't think that you are bluffing... so... I don't think a wedding card is necessary. After that you go to Inter-IIT, which is within rules... I think you can take a chance by skipping the Industrial Tour without any formal, written permission."

Pritish concurred. My brother played with his hair. I thought.

"But there *might* be a problem, and then, if, by chance, my family is contacted by these professors, I'll be dead. You see, I can't always intercept calls," I said.

"As far as everything is done within the rules, there is no problem," contradicted my brother, "But there is the chance that professors *might* cause a problem, if you don't show the card, and decide to skip the entire tour. I mean... the way you have told me, their dislike for you... And they are mad after being drenched in soda... Most insulting! So... you shouldn't take any more liberties with these professors. Think of something within the rules," he added wisely.

"And this Industrial Tour is a degree requirement. If they decide to go to the extremes, Pappi and the Dean, they may invalidate your tour, thus extending your degree! And they are pretty hot with you," commented Pritish.

That hit me hard. Degree extension! It was a thing that should not be mentioned, just like Voldemort's name in Potter books, as it has the same horror attached to it. Presently an ugly scene conjured up in my mind. I was wishing my friends, clad smartly in black graduation robes, with a wry sombre smile, wearing torn and tattered clothes myself. There was Pritish, smiling and saying, "Don't worry. You'll get it too *someday*!" and Khosla saying, with his head swaying, "I told you to mend your ways." People turned up their noses at my sight and talked among each other, "He is the one! He brought shame to his family. Disgraceful! Spoilt his parent's life for a girl! Better not have a son at all!" And this scene took a heavy toll on me! I drank two glasses of water, and then became aware of the conversation going on.

"Why don't you go on the tour and leave for the Inter-IIT sports meet on 15th, and then be with Shreya?" Rishabh asked.

"How many times have I told you, I want at least ten days there! See... she is a girl and may not be able to meet me every day, and if that happens, I would hardly be able to meet her. I am not going to reduce the length of the trip! No way! There must be a way!" I said.

"There is," said Pritish, who was staring at the ceiling blankly.

"What?" I asked.

"Attend the tour with us!"

"How is *that* a way? I told you I am not wasting any days!"

"You won't!"

"How the hell?"

"Break your leg!"

"Break my leg?"

"Yes, break it. Reach Pune with us, and break it! Then, obviously, you won't be in a position to accompany us on our Industrial visits... The doctor would have strongly advised fifteen days strict bed rest! If you get up you may risk losing your leg forever. Thus you must rest and not move around," he said.

"Genius!" I remarked, "And the best part is that Pappi will not be with us. I wish he was not even in Chennai, but I don't think there's any chance of us bumping into each other. Now, Khosla will have to choose the professor who goes with us, and we'll help him to decide. We'll choose the kindest of professors who would not see anything fishy and allow me my sweet and deserving rest. And then I'll sneak off to Chennai!"

"But how will you go to Chennai with a broken leg, you moron?" asked Rishabh.

I could only smile at that. I saw that Pritish was smiling too; so was my brother, and, slow that he might be, my friend is certainly not dim, and, eventually, he smiled too, and remarked before any other could.

"Of course, you do not need to break your leg!"

The winter sun shone outside, and my life was trouble free once again. I could see Shreya, clearer than ever, waiting for me, by the sea side. My hands automatically started playing bongo on the table, and a song came to my lips – Louis Armstrong's 'What a wonderful world!'

> *I see skies of blue.....clouds of white,*
> *Bright blessed days....dark sacred nights,*
> *And I think to myself.....what a wonderful world!*

November end, this year

The days were getting colder and colder as we moved closer and closer towards what promised to be a chilly December. Jumpers and jackets were out, and it had just gotten cold enough to allow me the pleasure of breathing out white frost in the morning. The final semester exams were perilously close and most of the students had got down to serious studying. The Major Tests, as they are called, were to commence from the third of December and go on till the eighth. I had calculated that I could not afford to give less than five days for preparation. It was the last week of November, already, and the date when I was to resume my romance with studies was quickly approaching. I had to work for long hours on my project too, that enigmatic cylinder and Professor P. P. was keeping a close eye on its development. The professor had calmed down a bit after watching me sweat (only if one can in winters), in the workshop. The cylinder was shaping out almost satisfactorily. It was official now that the reverend professor was not accompanying the students on the tour. My friends were also busy in putting finishing touches to their projects and poring over the deep books. And well, I was busier than ever, in putting the finishing touches to my plan, and, of course, dealing with the cylinder. Life was travelling at a breathtaking pace

Few days were left and there was much to do still. That the plan was changed at such a late stage did not help either. The last minute exigencies manifested themselves much like a flood. The new professor had to be chosen, a plan had to be made to 'break' my foot and, would you believe, I still hadn't arranged for my accommodation in Chennai! I decided that this problem needed to be dealt with first. I had always been preoccupied in planning how to reach Chennai. Where to live and how to, were questions that came way down in the priority list, and rightly so. But now the matter could not be delayed.

I had a friend studying in IIT Madras. Nitin and I had been coached for the IIT entrance, by an act of providence or of Mr. Fate, as I now saw, by the same institute and had become friends. Though we hadn't talked for long, I had a feeling that he would help me. I had written to him that there was something important that needed to be discussed. His reply was a curious one. He told me to call him right away, and I did just that. We talked just as long lost friends do, when he came to the nub.

"So what is the problem, Tejas?" he said excitedly.

"I feel bad... You'll say this guy only remembered me when he was in trouble. No phone, nothing earlier, and when he needs me, he calls me!"

"Come on, Tejas," he added sarcastically, "How can you forget me? I know you never sleep without taking my name?"

I laughed and he laughed too. Then he said, "Chuck these formalities, man! Say, what happened?"

"See, I'll be in Chennai from the 12th to the 22nd."

"Great, for the sports meet?"

"No, *yaar*!"

"Taken any project? Don't do that, *yaar*; enjoy in Delhi, you'll die here, it is hot!"

"No, no... I haven't changed a bit from the good old days. No projects for me!"

"Good! Then?"

"How do I say?" I felt shy telling these things. But I had to. So I shot, and quickly, to spare the blushes and told him about her, her dad and our problems. "I have to come to Chennai or else I'll die!" I summarized the situation for him.

He took his own sweet time to gulp all that. Then he said, "Lovely, beautiful!"

"Don't make fun, *yaar*. I am serious; it is a little difficult to stay apart!"

He laughed as if he understood everything and then replied, "I am not making fun, *yaar*, and I know how hard it is! My girlfriend's in Delhi!"

Mr. Fate, I don't know why, plays such strange games with us. I mean, how preposterous the whole thing was! It was an error, a gross error on his part. One can only laugh at such anomalies. Everything could have been perfect, if we had swapped our positions, me and my friend. But Mr. Fate had to intervene and play his cruel games for pleasure. He had to show his might. Extremely sadist, this approach, I tell you. After we both had blamed this bally thing called fate, and all adjectives had been exhausted, we resumed our chat.

"So now, I have to help you, my friend; it is a matter of love, and who can understand it better than one, who himself is in its clutches," he said, understanding my pain and longing, like only a fellow lover can.

"Exactly," I said.

"You really love her!" he remarked after a brief pause.

"Hmm, you can say," I said shyly. I loved her madly. I could do anything for her.

"Heartening to see true love in these times! It is guys like you, who restore faith in love in this otherwise materialistic world! Don't worry, friend, I am here in Chennai till the 20th for my project. And you are going to stay in my room!"

"I hope that is not a problem!" I added.

"Told you, man, no formalities with me; I hope you don't have a problem in sharing the room with me!"

"No way, just ensure we have separate beds," I said, laughing and he laughed too.

"Now don't worry about anything, and come down here!"

"Thanks, *yaar*, you are God's messiah! Just pray everything goes fine!"

"It will be fine, don't worry. Even God appreciates how much you love her! So don't worry, he'll put everything in place!"

"Thanks, *yaar*!"

"Best of luck, see you soon!"

"Bye!"

"Bye!"

He was really a nice chap back then, I reflected, and he hadn't changed. I could never thank him enough for helping me. Or, for that matter, anyone who had helped me in my endeavour.

"This is the man I want!" I burst out on seeing his photo on the computer, "He is the one!" His face was one of the most amiable ones. He smiled out of his photograph harmlessly, and gave an impression of a man who'd have nothing to do with canes and cudgels.

"He is the same man," I excitedly remarked, remembering an old incident, "He is the man who saved the life of a young kitten!"

"What?" asked my friends, Rishabh and Khosla, confounded.

"Yes, you should have seen him make a dash for it?"

"Dash for what?"

"The kitten!"

"Where?"

"On the road!"

"What was the kitten doing on the road?"

"I don't know. Immaterial. But a car was speeding, and our kitten was in the middle of the road, sure to be trampled by it."

"Why did the kitten not run?"

"I don't know, you idiots, and, besides, it is immaterial!"

"Then what happened?"

"Our man happened to pass by, saw the young cat in danger, immediately dived, grabbed it, and rolled off to the other end of the road, just like they show in movies!"

"Wow! He is a hero!" remarked Khosla.

"That I don't know, all I know is that he is a gentle soul, and perfect to act as our guide on the tour. And add to my knowledge of this man, your piece of information, and he is the man we want!"

Khosla was showing us the photos and profiles of the professors on the college website for selection of the Tour Guide. I had told him to do research and find out the coolest of professors. He had found three. The first two still had mean faces, and, besides, they had never saved the life of a kitten, at least not to my knowledge. Khosla had added this caption to our man's photo: He had joined only a year back and thus was not much aware of rules and regulations at IIT. Reliable sources said that once, a boy hit him with a chalk on his nose; he didn't rebuke him at all and, instead, gave him a discourse on non-violence. Add to this, the kitten saving incident, and his friendly face, and you had just the man you were looking for – one who would look tenderly at a boy with broken foot, may be shed a tear, pat him lovingly, and order him to rest for a month.

Mr. Uttam Trivedi was our man.

'Uttam Trivedi', announced the door-plate in black on gold, 'Asst. Professor'. I knocked at the door. "Come in," came the call and in went me and Khosla. I must say photographs lie a lot but not this man's. In fact, it had understated the amiability of the face. The man, even with his moustache, looked the most harmless I had seen. I hoped he'd prove to be as friendly, and remembered the adage about appearances being deceptive.

"Yes?" he said cordially.

"Sir," said Khosla, "I am Anand, the Class Representative of the Industrial and Production Department..." and, after telling him about the tour, he asked, "I'd like to know if you could accompany us on the tour." He was damn courteous.

"Where do we go?" asked our man.

"Sir, Pune and Goa," I replied, adding as much courtesy to my tone as I could.

"Why me?" he asked laughing.

"Sir," I said, "I happened to see you, once, saving the life of a kitten. Ever since, I have yearned to be associated with you. You won't teach us any course, I guess; so this is the only chance we have to spend quality time with such a noble soul!"

"Oh," he said, blushing, "Don't embarrass me. So you saw me save that poor thing's life. I love animals, you see."

"Me too, sir," I smiled back at him, "Sir, it will be great if you can come with us. Students will learn a lot."

"Yes, sir!" added Khosla.

"Oh, yes, I would love to, tell me the dates."

"Sir, 10th we leave and return on the 22nd," said Khosla.

"Okay," he said, thinking.

"Sir," I added, "Goa is a nice place and you can take along your wife and kids too. It'll be enjoyable."

"Yes, yes," he said, "It'll be a nice surprise for Kittu!"

"Yes, sir, ma'am will be delighted."

"Oh, no, Kittu is my son, eight years old!"

"Kittu, of course, will be delighted too, sir!"

I almost danced with joy that moment. Things were finally falling into place. Good omen, I thought. Khosla produced a sheet in front of the professor and told him to sign somewhere. He did that happily.

"I love students," he said, smiling one of his best ones, "I never miss any chance of interacting with them."

"Thank you, sir," we both said.

"Just a minute," he stopped us, as we were about to leave, "What is your name?" he asked me.

"Sir, I am Tejas. I am helping Anand with the arrangements for the tour. There is so much work to do. I thought I'd lend a hand."

"Oh, a gem of a thought. Always help others."

"Yes, sir, one strives to," I replied, and we moved out. I shook Khosla's hands. The work was done. Our man was in. Thankfully, appearances aren't always deceptive. I wondered, in amazement, at the existence of such professors in IIT. And the fact brought solace to the heart. Not all professors were brutal; some had their heart in place. I moved along happily, but a small thing troubled me, I'd have to lie to that gem of a man. But then, I was lying to my parents too. It didn't make me happy but it had to be done. I sought forgiveness from God.

You could quite say that I was on a roll. Things were finally falling neatly into their respective places. You are, I am sure, familiar – if you have not been too bored with these memoirs of mine, and dozed off, and the pages have been fluttered by a passing wind, and, waking up, you assume that this is where you left off, for the number on the page tells you that the torture won't last for long – with the latest happenings, the withdrawal of Professor P.P. Sidhu and the adroit appointment of a befitting proxy. And I am sure, in the wake of these extremely desirable developments, you are saying to yourself again, "Ah! He has done it again; he is a man with the *strongest* of will and the *strangest* of brains! God bless him!"

I take these compliments with a humble bow. To find me hence, with my head in my hands, a deep furrow in my brow and a brooding look in my eyes, you will, no doubt, be appalled. You will hasten, like a true friend, to tell me that the sun is out, and I should be swaying to salsa than sit sadly on my sofa. But I will tell you the reason, and right away.

It is dashed difficult, I tell you, this bloody business of getting one's foot broken. It seems simple, but, going a little deep into the whole matter, you find it a muddle of the first degree. It is not the breaking of the foot, but the events that should follow the damage, which are extremely murky.

If you are not as dim, if I may use the reference again, as the bulb of

148

my room, you would have gathered that I don't actually need to break my foot. I mean, I don't need to undergo the extreme test of valour, of sticking out my leg at a speeding truck, or smashing a mixer-grinder on my tender toe. I am lucky, and I mean it. I have been spared that test. I saw a movie, once, in which a dude was in much the same fix as I am now. The only way he could get away from some disaster, of considerably lesser scale than mine, was to break his foot. He was advised by one nincompoop to drop a typewriter on his foot. I was prevented from seeing the rest of the movie due to a power-cut but, now, my heart went out for him. He was not blessed with the company of my friends, or he would have been wisely counselled. He would need to do, exactly what I was going to, except that I did not yet know, how?

Broken feet, for all their disadvantages – the pain, and that it is most inconvenient to romance a girl – have a distinct advantage. One doesn't need to find a doctor. I mean, of course, one needs a doctor to repair the damn thing but one doesn't need to *find* that doctor. Any doctor will do — anyone who knows his bit about the bones and the marrow. One need not organize a special search for that doctor. He could be any of the friendly neighbourhood faces we see, with a stethoscope hanging down his neck. But the doctor one needs, when one doesn't have a broken foot, and wants it to be proven broken still, is of a special kind. Our doctor may still be lurking in the neighbourhood but we can't be so sure as to be able to point to one and say he is our man!

I hope my problem manifests its impressive magnitude before you. And I would be greatly impressed by those, who have, by the skilful use of that brilliant theorem of equivalence, replaced the problem of breaking a foot by the problem of finding a suitable doctor. Keep it up, you all, you need to put in a thought or two about making mathematics your career. The problem that presented itself before me was a monumental one. I had to find a doctor, and of a special kind, who could lay his scruples aside, and plaster an unbroken foot, and produce a brilliant medical certificate that strictly recommended bed rest.

You could, of course, find such doctors; I knew some personally, but the sad thing was that they were all cooped up in this part of the country while I needed someone in that part of the country. I wished I was a mafia don, who had his left and right arms scattered all over the country, and just a phone call would ensure that the work was done.

What rendered the dilemma even more complicated, was the fact that I had just an evening for myself in Pune. We reached Pune at about five, and I had about four hours, to conjure up a doctor, a medical certificate, and then convince the professor that I was practically out of the tour. It could all go horribly wrong, for it was entirely possible that I may not find an unscrupulous doctor. And the distinct possibility that a doctor could eventually be found, who would melt at my love story, and help me, was extremely distinct. I might find a doctor, but the professor might not release me, he might want to watch over me caringly for at least a day, as he was a gracious fellow. The problems seemed to be endless and hit me like a hurricane.

But I was not daunted. I had to act and I realized that two things needed to be done quickly. The first I did right away, for I could not afford to lose even a single moment. I took my hands off my head and used them judiciously to call my travel agent. I asked him about the availability of tickets on the train from Pune to Chennai, one day later than I had booked. He said there were tickets, and I told him to cancel my present one and book for the next day. I needed that extra day and badly too. One day less with my darling was better than not staying with her at all.

I got down to the second task in a second. I had to find a doctor in Pune, not when I was in Pune, but now. I had one and a half days now, still it was wise to play safe. It was an infinitely better feeling, I thought, to have a doctor or two tucked in my armpit, than to search like a sniffer dog on the very last day. Hitherto, I had always been a man of the last moment, but now, I had to depart from my habit.

I was not a mafia don but I had my share of contacts. I listed the names of all my near and dear ones, who were even vaguely linked with Pune. The list stopped at five names. I called them one by one, hoping at least one would yield a doctor.

December, this year

The list was not a bad one and I had hopes of drawing, not one, but two-three medicos. But there I was, bankrupt when it came to doctors. The first four in the list, if I may divulge them, in priority order, were:

1. A very close friend, whom I refrain from naming, whose brother himself was a doctor in Pune.

2. Ria *didi*, who had studied engineering in Pune and had friends there.

3. My brother Vineet, whose best friend had studied engineering in Pune and had friends there.

4. Rishabh, who had a friend there.

As I stared at the list, a fruitless enterprise, I saw the designs of Mr. Fate again. I was plunged into the deepest of despairs. After two days of contacting the listed people, I had drawn a blank. I must say, though, that the last three tried earnestly but were unfortunate. My friend's brother, however, let me down.

Anyhow, these ups and downs of life were becoming a bit too much for me. Only the last name remained on the list made according to priority. I had not much hope left. The task was destined to go into the

151

final day. But then I remembered that thing about sticking to the guns. Wait, till fate becomes your mate.

I turned to the last name. I prayed that this link, the least powerful though it seemed to me, would be the dark horse. I called her, though I did not want to involve her in all this, as she worried a bit too much. Yet, she was the last hope.

"Hi!" I said.

"Hi!" she said.

"I want you to call your friend in Pune, and ask her if she knows a doctor!" I said businesslike.

"What?" she asked perplexed.

And I had to tell her everything – the change in the dates, the new plan of finding a doctor, and how she was the last hope. And then I just sat back and listened patiently to Miss Shreya's 'don't comes'. I assured her all would be safe, a million times, and only then she agreed to call her friend.

"Now explain to her the situation, as I have told you, and tell her I'll call her in the evening. Okay?" I said.

"Yes, take care."

"I will, you too."

"And one thing…"

"Don't have time, *yaar*, call her now, and let me know."

"Offo, just a minute."

"What?"

"I would have kissed you, were you in front of me, now!"

"My beautiful luck, or call it the game of fate again; you only feel like kissing me, when I am a million miles away!"

She tut-tutted and said, "My poor baby!" and giggled.

"Bye, presently, and save this kiss for future."

"That, unfortunately, cannot be done; your bad luck that you are never at the right place at the right time!" she said, teasing me.

"Wish they had a bank account for kisses, one could deposit them for later use..."

"But there are none! Sad!"

"I know, now call Shraddha and get back to me."

"Bye, unlucky prince of a lucky princess!"

"Lucky, you are surely, what all I have to do for you! But as I say time and again, anything for you, ma'am!"

"That is how things are with princesses, darling! But don't worry; you'll too get lucky soon!"

"How?"

"No how, just bye, time is less, as you said!"

"Will you kiss me?"

"Bye!"

"Will you?"

"Love you, and a final bye!"

I called Shraddha at nine in the night, as directed by Shreya, and prayed that she would help.

"Hi Shraddha!" I greeted her.

"Hi Tejas! So finally I get to speak to Miss Shreya's boyfriend."

Boyfriend, did I hear? Works me up, this word; better call me a cockroach, but boyfriend? One loves with all his heart to be called that! No true lover would take that. I would have loved to correct Shraddha that Shreya was not my girlfriend, but my love, my life, but I merely said:

"Well yes, you finally have the honour!"

"Hmm, I can't believe how secretive she is! *Chhupe Rustam* you both are! When she needs me, she calls me, and tells all about your fascinating tale. But she didn't have the courtesy to tell her friend before."

"Oh, I am extremely sorry on her behalf, ma'am!"

"Oh, by the way, how is Palak? I never knew she had a brother."

"She is fine... Actually not... She is kind of afraid about my safety. She prays day and night that her brother reaches the shores of Chennai safely, and, for that, we all need your help, Shraddha!"

"Great! Both of them hide such an interesting love story from me all this while, and now they want my help! What has this world come to?"

"I know, extremely materialistic, but I assure you, I have a heart of gold. Had I known that your friends haven't told you about my most fascinating story, I would have phoned you personally. But those two hid from me too, the fact that they hid my story from you! So we both are on the same ship, dear! I was livid, of course, when I came to know that you do not know, but now one can't help it..."

"Oh stop it, Tejas!"

"Yes, of course! I have this habit of speaking a tad too much and especially with girls! Forgive me!"

"Man! You seriously go on and on; how does Shreya bear your incessant nonsense?"

"That question can be better answered by the victim herself. I think, however... I have a theory that...."

"Shut up!"

"Oh yes, of course!"

"Listen, I am in no way pleased by the way I have been neglected! I mean... we were a trio in school... me, Palak and Shreya, and they desert me like this..."

"I strongly agree; my heart goes out for you!"

"So I think, if they don't bother to tell me, why should I bother to help them?"

"Oh, don't say that! There is an innocent life at stake too, Shraddha. What about me?"

"I am talking to you for the first time, mister, why should I help you?"

"Oh, for humanity, Shraddha, for restoring our faith in those virtues of benevolence, philanthropy and altruism that this world seems to have forgotten. Your act, Shraddha, will make this world stand and introspect, and shudder in shame. They will say to themselves, 'Where was my conscience all this while?' The world will see you as a beacon of....."

"Oh God! Where do you get all that crap from? Got a dictionary or something in your hand?"

"Oh no! Even if I had, I have not the adroitness of flipping the pages so quickly and find words that fit!"

"Hmm, you impress me, mister. I see, poor Shreya cannot be blamed for falling for a fool like you. I always thought her to be a little crack, but now it is confirmed; so many handsome guys proposed to her in school, but she wouldn't even look at them. And now, she is in love with you..."

"Life is full of anomalies, ma'am!"

"Okay listen, let's get to the point and you stop speaking so much. I'll help you."

I uttered a cry of joy, at which she shouted back, and told me to be softer.

"Can you?" I asked timidly.

"Of course, I can, Shreya told me all. You need a doctor, right? Who'll plaster your leg and make certificates?"

"The very man!" I exclaimed.

"It'll be done!"

"Are you sure?" I asked, stumped by her confidence.

"Yes mister! It is a common thing!"

"You mean this breaking of feet? Is it so common in Pune? Slippery roads, I guess!"

"I mean false certificates, you fool. Students need them often for various reasons. I know a couple of doctors who do such stuff!"

"Wow! You, sure, are an angel! But at least talk to the doctor, first, and confirm it."

"Don't bother about all that. The moment Shreya told me, I talked to this friend of mine; he is a real resourceful guy, *pukka jugaadoo*; gets all kinds of things done," I conjured an image of Tanker in my mind, "He said there was nothing to worry about, and it'll be done, and when he says don't worry..."

"One should not worry!" I emphatically completed the sentence, "You see, I am much the same type of guy, but my network ends in Delhi, I have been thinking of expanding my operations for long. I think your friend can be my aide-de-camp in Pune, what say?"

"I say, shut up, and I have to go now. And, yes, an important thing, I am busy on 11th, when you come, so call me when you reach, I'll give you this friend's number and he'll help you. But I should get a grand treat on 12th. Let me also meet my friend's love. Is it fine?"

"Absolutely fine, miss! I'll have cakes and chocolates lined for you. I cannot express in words the gratitude I feel towards your esteemed..."

"Cut the crap!"

"Thank you!"

"That will be enough, bye!"

"Bye, see you soon!"

❦

That put a seal to the phase of planning. Just as I put the phone down, I felt a surge of relief, of work well done. What had I not done to meet Shreya! I moved to the window in my room, and saw the sky, full of stars. Life was indeed beautiful with her in my life. Love, I reflected, changes one's life forever, and embellishes it with joy. The joy of knowing, that no matter where you are, what you do, someone, somewhere, is thinking of you. The joy of realizing, that you can do anything for that someone. It is an extremely special feeling, I tell you all.

Delhi Station. December 10, this year.

Nizamuddin Station,' said the blue board installed outside the station. Our car braked in front of it, amidst an ocean of humanity. There were people here; people there; people, confusion everywhere. Some were loaded with luggage, some with children and others were just idling away, enjoying the ebullience of the station. Dad told us to get off, and said he'd join us at the platform after parking the car. I took my rucksack out of the dicky and flung it over my shoulders, while Sneha handled my guitar and laughed at me.

"What is it?" I asked.

"Nothing, just looking a bit funny. The bag is taller than you!" she giggled as girls do. At least all girls I know giggle.

"Shut up!" I said.

"Don't use such words," said *dadima* politely, "It is not auspicious."

"Come here, here's the way!" guided my mom.

"I have eyes, mummy, I can see!" I retorted.

My whole platoon had landed at the station to bid me adieu, as had been foreseen, but I didn't mind that. I was going with the other boys, on the tour. Only my *dadaji* was not there, his health didn't permit him. We passed the hall, where black screens depicted various train names and departure times in red. I looked up and saw that mine was leaving on time. We climbed the stairs slowly, keeping pace with mom and *dadima*, and descended to reach platform number two.

Trains and stations always fascinate me. It had been more than five years since I'd been on a train, and my heart brimmed with joy at the prospect of the journey. Nothing matches the colourful canvas of a station. And the romance of trains! Red bogeys of my train shone majestically in the brilliant sun. On the red of the bogey, 'Goa Express' was written in yellow. The sight of the train, up close, after such a long time, filled me with childlike excitement. The carriage rested royally; went on and on, into the eternity. My fingers, merrily, touched its metal, as I walked on.

The station was all chaos. Coolies, dressed in red, appeared out of nowhere to snatch your luggage. "Why do you labour, sir? Give the bag to me," I heard over the lady announcer's '... train will arrive shortly on platform number...' Tea sellers rattled their spoons against the glasses, and shouted, in their shrill voices, the famous station slogan of '*Chai-Chai*'. The vendors cried themselves hoarse to attract customers to their stalls that served every Indian snack you could imagine – *Bhelpuri, tikki, aloo chaat, samosas, gol gappe*... There were book-stalls, phone-booths, shops of every possible knick-knack. It was hardly a station, more of a bazaar, with all its hustle-bustle. There were people in all shapes and sizes, from different backgrounds. Different languages were heard, as I surged through the crowd. Punjabi, English, Hindi, Urdu, Marathi, Bengali, Kannadda (or, it may be, Tamil or Telugu)...

Nothing, I reflected, unites India the way the trains do. People from every part of the country are brought to the same bogey... from every stratum of the society to the same platform.

Never does chaos, the hallmark of our nation, look so picturesque. Never is it more colourful. Never does noise, a blend of the train's snort, the engine's whistle, the *chai-walah*'s rattle, the vendor's cry, the traveller's murmur, bring such brightness to the heart.

With the whole atmosphere glistening in the sun, the sight of my friends took my spirit to an all time high. I saw Rishabh, Pritish, Jasdeep, Manpreet, Sameer, Khosla, all chatting gleefully. They hushed on seeing that I had brought my family along, lest their expletives be heard. There were other parents too, but no one had brought a battalion like me. Papa arrived and pleasantries were exchanged. The ambience was electric and the air was full of gaiety. A lot of bantering went on. My friends laughed madly, clapping excitedly, my mom smiled, so did my dad and Sneha. *Dadima*, not used to such fast pace of humour, understood little, but flashed all her teeth in her trademark smile.

My mom decided to conduct an inquiry with my friends, "How many shirts are you carrying?" Some said nine, some eight and none below seven. Her eyes directed themselves at me, "See, I told you," and then she told my friends, how I insisted on taking only four shirts, and how she had managed to convince me for eight. They all laughed. Suddenly the professor appeared, with his wife and Kittu, I guess, smiling as ever, adding to the happiness. He wished all of us cordially and we responded in a chorus. He got busy with Khosla.

Just about five minutes remained for the departure. People started climbing into the train. My friends withdrew too after greeting my family. I looked at the four of them. Sudden emotion hit me – "How much I loved them!" A foolish thought crept into my mind – "What if something goes wrong... and this is the last time I see them all?" I shoved it away taking God's name. "Don't be foolish", I told myself.

"So... bye," I said to them, hesitantly. My eyes were becoming moist. Not because I was going to miss them; it was hardly a ten day trip. It was just that I was keeping them in the dark... lying to all of them who had so much faith in me, and loved me so much. I didn't like it at all. I felt guilty. I wanted to tell them, "I am not doing anything wrong, I really love Shreya..." but would they understand? My head was clogged. All sort of thoughts came into my mind. I didn't want to leave them. I wanted to meet Shreya, but didn't want to leave in this manner. I prayed to God again to set everything right, and told myself that I was just following my heart. I was not doing anything wrong, I repeated. Love could never be wrong.

I touched *dadima's* feet and she gave me her blessings. She thrust, into my hands, two white plastic boxes. "*Amla* and *Chooran*! Keep them. Your tummy is so sensitive! Eat carefully!" I nodded and smiled. I looked at her. She had not changed at all since my birth. Her silver hair, simple *sari*, big glasses, her love and concern were a few constants in my life. I would know, only in time to come, their real value, the comfort that their presence brought to me. She took out some sugar from her little box, and distributed some among all. It is a custom at our home. Eating something sweet before leaving is considered auspicious. I always enjoy sugar and chewed it happily.

I hugged mummy and papa. Mom was sentimental as usual, "I am not going to Kargil, mumma!" I told her. "If only you were not so naughty, I would have sent you happily. Please don't get into any mischief," she said, and I wondered, if what I was about to do, qualified as mischief, "Walk carefully on roads, and don't play pranks on people," and as I saw her eyes watering, I hugged her again. I tried not to speak for it would make me cry. "And you haven't even brought a blanket, *everyone* else has," she said worryingly. "I'll share, mummy," I managed to say.

Dad was cool. He is never demonstrative. But he loves me no less. I am his pride. "Enjoy yourself, son!" he told me, "Have fun, but remember – everything in limits, and I know you'll bunk industrial visits, but go to two-three industries, at least, and bunk carefully!" He knew me well. It was no use telling me to be diligent. He himself was the fun type. But he didn't know that I was going to bunk the entire tour.

My darling sister stood with her hands crossed, with tension all over her face. Only she knew where I was going. She had tried to stop me, but I had not relented. "What if something goes wrong?" she had asked again and again, but I had waved off the question. She was not cross with me for going, just worried. "Take care," she said, "Please be careful, *bhai!*" and pushed into my hand a folded paper unobtrusively. I looked into her eyes and gave a look of assurance. I kissed her on her forehead, took my guitar and went into the train. I took my seat and the train started to move, slowly. There was so much noise in our bogey already. I went to the window and waved out to my battalion. I could hear mom shouting, "Don't get off the train on the stations in between! Remember when you..." A tear of guilt trickled down my cheek, and I quickly wiped it off. My friends surrounded me. The fun had begun.

I excused myself from the celebrations, and quietly went to the end of the bogey. I opened the folded letter that Sneha had given me.

Dearest Goon, (She calls me that and whatnot)

I couldn't say all this as mom and dad were there. Don't think that I didn't want you to go to Chennai; it was just that I was extremely worried about you. I still am and will be till you return safely. Please be very careful! Don't take any risks. I know you live life 'king-size' but once there, in Chennai, with Shreya, maintain a low profile. It is not only about you, but also about her well being. Meet her very discreetly; her dad shouldn't come to know.

Now remember to message me at least five times a day telling me what you are doing. Give my 'Hi' to Shreya. She is a nice girl and I really like her.

And ya don't get off at the stations. Remember once when the train had started and you were idiotically buying magazines! How you managed to get on the train! Don't do that. Remember Mr. SRK your Kajol is not at the station, she is in Chennai waiting for you. So stay on in the train.

And don't forget to bring me something from there.

Love,

Take care,

Your Muniya (I call her that)

Just then, Shreya called. I wiped my tears and drew a deep breath.

"Yes Miss Shreya, the train is on its way, I am on my way, Chennai beckons me, you beckon me and I'll be there soon, clutching you in my arms tightly and..."

I looked out of the open door. Vast open spaces rushed past. Trees, lamp posts, men, women glided away. I sensed how every second brought me closer and closer to her.

Often a problem with writing novels is that one has to follow a theme. Each incident in a novel must be linked to the central theme of the novel. One can't stray here and there too much, or else he'll be called directionless, incoherent and all those adjectives that only critics have knowledge of. Therefore one has to painfully delete incidents, no matter how interesting, which though occurred in progress to the climax, are essentially irrelevant to the theme, viz. the train incidents: 'When Rishabh rubbed oil on an uncle's back', 'The journey of the stinking socks (of Jasdeep)', 'The Adventure of the Missing Blanket', but they have to be excluded presently. They can, of course, be produced separately as 'A Treasure Trove of Train Tales', as I am wisely advised by a friend.

However, at this point in the narrative, it will suffice to say that the train rattled and swayed all the way, and rattled and swayed to a halt at the Pune station at about five next evening.

Thus I completed what can be called the first leg of my voyage. I was some thousand kilometers closer to my love and that brought to my heart a buoyant feeling. A small step it may be for others, it was a giant leap indeed for me.

Pune. December 11, this year.

Doctor Prabhakar, our man, was not in. He was out on an emergency. It had been an hour since I left Ram Lodge, our residence, with Rishabh and Pritish. Every minute added to the tension. I moved restlessly outside the clinic, while Pritish and Rishabh chatted on. Peela, the person commissioned by Shraddha to help us, smoked nonchalantly.

"Man," he said in a *tapori Mumbaiya* accent, "You should smoke!"

"Should?" I asked, puzzled. Made it sound like a motherly advice.

"I should say you must!"

"Must?" Now it sounded like a thing that ought to be done. I wondered if I had always been kept in the dark about all the vitamins and minerals that filled the cigarette stick.

"Yes, must! Look at you, man, moving about like a chicken. This," he said, pointing towards his cigarette, "Cures it all. You feel low, you feel aglow, you feel crappy, you feel happy, howsoever you feel, this is your best friend; loyalest, I should say, if there is such a word."

"There is no such word, and, besides, what about the damage..."

I was about to begin a didactic discourse on the damages of the damn thing when a handsome man in late forties, dressed neatly in

165

blue, rushed past me into the clinic. He had a stethoscope around his neck and thus had to be the missing doctor. I must say that the sight of the physician didn't do anything to alleviate the tension that was crushing me. The fact that he was so well dressed and looked like a proper doctor didn't go down well with me at all. I had expected the man to be like the amoral ones they show in the movies – shabby-clothed ones, who peer crookedly from the corner of their narrow eyes, probably have a nasty scar or two, or, at least, a big black mole somewhere on the chin. But he had none of these features that a man, if he churns out false certificates, ought to have. And that made me quiver. I hadn't the time to look at his shoes and that bothered me. If only I had looked at his shoes. Shoes give away the scruples, I have heard, and I prayed presently for dirt on the doctor's boots. And then I had a brainwave, what if I hadn't seen the shoes, may be one of the other three had.

"Did you see his shoes?" I asked.

"Why the hell, man? Why should I look at his shoes?"

"Did you or did you not, just tell this."

"No, man," he said, and resumed blowing smoke rings.

"No," said Rishabh and Pritish on my questioning glances, thinking I was out of my mind. I pursed my lips.

So the mystery remained a mystery. With each passing second, I grew more and more jittery. What if the doctor didn't agree to do the job!

"Are you sure he will do the job?" I asked Peela, again.

"Man, you need a smoke!"

"Are you sure?"

"Man, how many times I tell you?"

"He doesn't look the sort who'll do unethical work. And besides, you didn't even see his shoes."

"What about the shoes, man? Screw the shoes. And, man, I tell you, he is a damn good person to do unethical work. He doesn't do it."

"Then?"

166

"Then, what man, he is a friend. I told him you had a severe family crisis and thus..."

"Family crisis?" I shot out loudly, with a look as if I had been punched in my belly.

"Yeah, family crisis" he said coolly, as if my family didn't matter to him.

"What family crisis?" I demanded, indignant that I had been kept unaware of any crisis, real or fake, which concerned my family. What if the idiot had drivelled about death or something; I had often seen it happen in movies, and especially detested such shameful, morbid excuses.

"I just told him, it is one of those things that you wouldn't like to talk about. You know, one of those things that one can't talk about openly, and he understood. He said he understood what it could be and that he'd help you," and at that I cooled down.

"Great, man," I told him borrowing his 'man'. He was an intelligent guy. I was relieved. A nice excuse – a thing that cannot be talked about!

"So even if he asks, which, I am sure he is understanding enough not to, just tell him you are not comfortable discussing it. Fine, man?"

"Yes," I said and Peela was called in by the doctor. He emerged out in about a minute and winked at me. He patted my back and told me to go in. "It'll be done," he said. I entered a little nervously. There was a look of condolence on the doctor's face. His eyes told me that they sympathized with my grief.

He told me to sit and asked me, "Are you fine, son?"

"Yes," I said hesitantly.

"You should be brave, son, the night will pass and the day will dawn," he said. He thought of me as one of those unlucky sons of misfortune.

"Yes, sir, I am trying my best," I continued in my mournful tone.

"Listen, now; you want a broken leg, don't you?"

"Sir, only a certificate!"

"Yes, of course!"

"Yes, sir!"

"See... plastering your leg is not required. I'll write such a thing on your medical certificate that no one will question. You'll only require a crepe bandage."

"Sir, but it won't produce the same effect. A plaster is much more profound."

"I'll handle if your 'Sir' questions. Don't worry, son. I'll write a ligament tear. You say you tripped on a stone while walking. Even if one does an X-ray, a ligament tear doesn't show, and, so, it is the safest. You don't worry about all that. Fine?"

"Thank you, doctor."

"Oh, don't say that. I am pleased to help you. Now tell me your name and college," he said and tore off a sheet from his pad.

"Sir, Tejas Narula, IIT Delhi."

He stopped in between. He had lowered his pen to the paper but he stopped. He looked up at me and there was astonishment in his eyes. I wondered what it might be. He studied me, and his mouth opened wider with each passing second, like an inflating balloon.

"Oh-my-g-a-w-d, this cannot be possible!" he uttered and shook his head.

"Huh!" I uttered, almost involuntarily.

"Tell me, aren't you Ravi's son?"

I jumped from my chair and sprang a good metre or two in the air, narrowly missing the ceiling. If ever there was a line that could induce more horror in a human, I hadn't heard it – "tell me, aren't you Ravi's son"... hell, that is precisely who I am – Ravi's son, Dr. Ravi and Dr. Madhu Narula's proud son. How on earth did he know my dad's name? He wasn't an astrologer or something. My eyes bulged. It was evident that something in my name had struck a chord, and it had to be my surname. He knew my father and I was shaken to my foundations. I kept staring at him, wondering what to say.

"Tell me, boy, aren't you the son of Ravi Narula, J Batch, AFMC, Pune? You resemble him so much."

I was speechless. I congratulated Mr. Fate. If you put a black ball in a bag full of nine-ninety-nine red balls, your probability of drawing the black one is still higher than mine drawing a doctor who was my father's classmate. Mr. Fate had switched sides again. Little use cursing fate, I thought, for I realized that I had been staring at the doctor for too long. What to say though was another question that perplexed me. I could tell him he was mistaken. That it would have been nice and merry, if I was indeed his pal's son, but I hated to break the news that I was not. But then he, in his suspicion, may decide to call my dad and tell him, "Tell me, Narula, was your son in Pune?" To which my father will reply, "Yes!" "He was up to something. Something dubious, I tell you," this doctor would say and all hell will break loose.

"Yes, sir, I am his son," I said, hoping I'd be able to persuade him not to bother my dad.

"Oh, I knew it. But tell me, what happened? Is all well at home? Your friend told me that there was a severe family crisis. Is my friend fine?"

I had forgotten all about that rotten excuse. Family crisis, forsooth. What was to be done now? I kept on gaping at the doctor stupidly. What was to be done? That was the only question that rang loud and clear in my ears.

"You can tell me, son, he was a great friend at college. I feel bad that we are not in touch, and that I couldn't help him, when he was in trouble. But it seems God has sent you to bring us back together. These ways of providence! Strange, but wonderful!"

The ways of providence, indeed! Strange and loathsome! There was no escaping now. There was only one way out. To tell the truth and hope for sympathy. I couldn't conjure a family problem, and assure my dad's friend that it was alright, and that he shouldn't bother. I know how these old chums are. The moment they hear that an old crony is in a soup, they waste no time in picking up the phone and dialling the-pal-in-soup's number.

"Uncle," I began, "My friend has lied to you. There is no family trouble. I wanted an excuse out of this tour for a different reason, and I am not sure if you will agree with it. But I beg you, not to tell my father because then, surely there'll be a family problem."

"What is it?" he asked suspiciously, and I told him all, like the way I have been forced to tell all, to so many for so many reasons. He stood up and came to my side of the table and looked at me with fatherly eyes. I saw his shoes, finally. They were shining black. And so shining were his scruples.

He looked at me dreamily and said, "Do you really love the girl or just want to have fun?"

"Come on, uncle, I won't risk so much, just to have fun."

"True! You know, if you love her so much, you should have told your father."

"Uncle, I didn't know how he'd take it. You know how it is with parents. I am really friendly with my dad, but..."

"He would have been proud of you, son!"

"What?" I uttered.

"Yes, it would've reminded him of his days, and he would have helped you to go and meet your love. That is how he is, your dad."

"Really?" I asked surprised. I knew my dad was a playful lad in his days, but this was a bit too playful.

"You know what, if this helps you, your dad would have done the very thing if he were in your place," he said, smiling.

It did help me. The man was indeed a person with a golden heart. But then, a curious question came to my mind.

"Uncle, did my father ever do such a thing?"

He smiled. His eyes lit up and he said, "I have told you enough, my friend. Let secrets remain buried between old timers." I understood. I had got it. My father *had* done something in his heydays. Not may be spanning the country to meet his love, but something crazy, something that couldn't be told to all. I was relieved.

"So will you help me, uncle?"

"Of course," he said smiling, "But don't you cheat a girl, I tell you. At your age, one does want to do it all, but be good, you, okay?"

"Yes, uncle, I will be."

"You know, you resemble your dad in looks, and even more in disposition; I am proud of you, son. Always follow your heart." And with that he went back to his desk, and resumed writing the medical certificate.

It made me so happy to see the doctor, a gem if ever there was one, writing the false certificate. It made him glad to help his friend's son, and he didn't find anything wrong with what I was doing. I had always known it, but it was extremely pleasant and comforting to know that someone, so much like my father, approved of my ways. There were people in this world who understood love, and that made me happy. I always salute these people who have their heart in the right place, and will do anything to help others, as long as their heart says, it is right. I presently saluted the doctor, my father's friend.

He tied the crepe bandage neatly and firmly on my ankle, and taught me how to limp, laughing all along, and reliving his youth. At the end of it, he said, "Come, son; let us go to the professor."

"You will come?" I asked surprised.

"Of course, I have to. Nothing must go wrong. I'll drop you personally in my car and no one will ever suspect."

I looked at him appreciatively, silently. I could never thank him enough. Here was a man I always aspired to be. He had taught me so much in that brief meeting. Now, I wished I had told my dad too.

"You are the best, uncle," I said, smiling.

"No flattery here, and, remember, whenever you tell your dad, one day you will, of course... tell him, to give me a call. I'll call him in a couple of days, oh don't worry, I'll mention nothing of this, just a li'l catching up, son. So, yes, tell him to give me a call then, he owes me one, now."

"Sure," I said and he put his arm around my shoulder.

"Now, let us move and tell the professor what happened," he said with childlike enthusiasm.

"Thanks a lot, uncle. I can't believe any one can be so helpful."

"Oh, I should thank you, son... thank you for letting me relive my college days. Oh, what crazy, fun-filled days those were," he said dreamily, "And after such a long time, I am back to doing what I enjoyed most – playing around with prickly professors," he laughed at that, and added as I walked, "Remember, son, you have a ligament tear, and a man with ligament tear should limp," and we both emerged out of his clinic laughing, much to the surprise of my three friends who stood outside, waiting.

Mr. Fate had switched sides, yet again.

A crowd had gathered around Ram Lodge, 6, Junglee Maharaj Road, Pune in a vague semicircle. At the centre of it, stood seven people – a boy with a bandaged foot, supported by his two loyal friends, a doctor, as was evident by the stethoscope hanging from his neck, and three others; a man, a woman and a child. The inner crust of this conglomeration looked on with frank astonishment and the outer crust just looked on to see what had happened that so many people were looking on. There were two short men in this outer crust who, despite being on their toes and craning their necks, were not able to see the hot scene at the centre.

"What happened?" asked the short man A to short man B, thinking the other may be able to help him.

"They say, there has been an accident," replied B, giving up his struggle to watch the proceedings live.

"Was there blood?" asked A.

"Oh yes! A lot of it, they say a truck hit him," said B.

"A truck, it must have been a painful sight!" said A.

"Very!" said B.

"Did you see the victim?" asked A enthusiastically.

"Yes, a young boy," bragged B, obviously lying.

"Is he alive?" asked A.

"Probably not!" said B coldly and moved off, while A got on his toes again, trying to catch a glimpse, moping about the growing callousness in the world.

Meanwhile, unaware of this obituary given by the short man, I stood before the professor, his wife and Kittu, as Dr. Prabhakar spoke on, "He must have strict bed rest for at least fifteen days or it can be serious."

The professor looked on in a condoling manner, just as the doctor had looked at me, when I had entered his clinic. His look was even more profound and touched, more like of a mother whose child had fallen off a bicycle.

"He must have rest then," he declared.

"It is vital," added the doctor.

"Tejas, I know you were so enthusiastic about the tour, you arranged it all and God decides to injure you out of everybody," he said, wondering at the ways of Providence. 'Strange and wonderful!' as Dr. Prabhakar would say.

"Unfair," added Dr. Prabhakar.

"Most!" said the professor, "I know you will not like this, Tejas, but you must not visit any industries," and, then, looking at the doctor said, "He must be sad, you don't know how he helped arranging this tour. He is a fine boy."

"I have gathered as much from the short acquaintance I have had with him, professor," said the doctor. I looked on as if the world had ended. 'No tour, no life' was the message that my face flashed.

Meanwhile, the astonishment of the inner crust, which consisted of my peers, had increased to a bursting point and there was absolute mayhem. The students were obviously amazed at what was happening, refusing to believe the genuineness of it all, for it was none other than Tejas, the king of frauds, at the helm of affairs.

"What on earth is happening here?" inquired a fresh spectator, who happened to be Khosla. Quickly, seeing the scene, he kept quiet and looked on with that 'in vogue' astonished look. He knew about my plans to skip the tour, and was bowled over by the way that had been chosen to do that.

"Sir, it is okay; I will rest. I will talk to my father and ask him what to do," I said, hanging on to the branches that my friends offered.

"If you want to go home, do that, but make sure you are comfortable," said the professor.

I wanted to dance but I didn't. I wanted to smile but I didn't. I just thanked God. The final frontier had been conquered. There was no stopping me now. I looked at my friends and then at the doctor, thanking them with my eyes. I could see that they could scarcely suppress their happiness too. The time had come to walk off from the scene, or rather say limp off, for, how long can mirth be muffled.

"Sir, I'd do that," I said, "I'd like to rest now."

"By all means," said the professor, "And thanks a lot, doctor. Really nice of you to bring him here personally. You two, take good care of him."

"Yes, sir," added my friends.

"We will miss you, Tejas," said the professor.

"I'll miss you too, *bhaiya*," said Kittu, who had become a friend during the train journey, looking sad.

"I'll miss you all too," I said and limped off, wondering if it was correct what I had said. I thought it was.

The professor withdrew into his quarters. The crowd started to disperse. The whole class of Industrial and Production Engineering surrounded the three of us as we made our way.

174

Voices could be heard, "What the hell is this?" "This is fraud!" "Is this genuine, Tejas?" I remained silent, while my two friends did their best in answering.

I had never felt better before.

⌒

The short man A, as we have been told, finally got his chance. The coast was clear. "Ah!" he said to himself, "Finally, I'll get to see." He looked keenly but saw no blood, none whatsoever on the road. He looked around for a corpse or a bloody face, but there was none. Finally, he saw a boy with a bandaged foot, ably supported by his friends. He thought, may be, they have the answer.

"Did you see the victim?" asked A.

"Which victim?" asked the boy with the broken foot.

"They say there was a terrible accident, a truck hit a young boy..." said A.

"Oh!" said the boy.

"You didn't see it either?" asked A.

"Oh, no, no, I saw it," said the boy.

"Was he serious?" asked A.

"Yes, he was. Very serious, we thought he'd never make it," said the boy.

"Is he fine now?" asked A, concerned.

"Oh yes," replied the boy, "He is out of danger. Almost ready to fly..." he added and couldn't control smiling.

"What! You shouldn't make fun, young man. No wonder, God has punished you with that broken foot!" said A and walked off cursing the world, which, he thought, was certainly devoid, now, of those splendid virtues of humaneness and feeling for a fellow creature.

Pune Station. December 13, this year.

I sat on a bench on platform number three, all by myself. It was one forty five in the night and my train was two hours late. The station was a lonely place at that hour, lacking all the effervescence of the day. A few shops were still open and a few passengers still there, but to me they were all non-existent. I was in the strangest of moods, one of those that people often term philosophical, and my mind was a gamut of emotions. In my hands was a copy of 'Carry on Jeeves' but even its brilliantly humorous prose had ceased to have an effect. I was supposed to be happy but I was not, not entirely.

I was supposed to have a sparkle in my eyes, but, instead there was just a brooding look. I was just a train journey away from the love of my life with nothing to stop me, surely, but I did not give it a thought. Often, I have experienced, when victory is so near in sight and a tough, thorny journey about to come to a close, the eye is pensive and the heart sentimental. And, so was my case.

One thinks at such junctures, not about the awaiting trophy, but about the journey to it all. The resulting prizes, that, once, solely occupied the mind, fade at this junction before the journey to the prize itself. One feels nostalgic about the path that has been travelled, and is sad to think that it will all be over soon. One has, subconsciously,

176

fallen in love with the path, and yearns for it. No matter how difficult the path was, it had become a way of life, and one knows one will miss it.

Ironical, I reflected, as I thought about all the chapters that had brought me hither, to the penultimate stop in this entertaining expedition. All along, there had been so many ups and downs. Yet, I had enjoyed them all, deriving thrill out of the many adventures, treating each hurdle as just another challenge, another test of my will and love. But all along the journey, I had wished to see the end of it; I had waited, all along, for the day when I'd meet my love and, now, when the day was nearer than ever, I hesitated to move ahead. I'd miss those times, I knew. Right from the night she told me she could not come, to this night, I'd miss it all: The planning, the plotting, the discussions with friends... those treasured conversations with Shreya... deciding the trip dates and the route to take... booking the tickets... that shower of soda and the tussle with the professor... that phone-call to professor as my dad... the expensive wedding card... almost being included in the shot-put team... the exploitation of the Biobull... the search for the doctor... the broken foot... finally, it was all going to end. I felt sad.

I had met so many wonderful people, those who had helped me arrive here, and I was thankful to them. The world had good hearts, still; Vineet, Rishabh, Pritish, Ria *didi*, Bajrang, my sisters, Nitin, Shraddha, Peela, Dr. Prabhakar, Shreya... it was a gladdening thought.

My journey had been all about love. I had discovered more and more, along the journey, how strongly and sincerely I loved Shreya. And it gave me a feeling of goodness and gladness. The journey had been about discovering what love actually was, and understanding that it went much deeper than holding hands and talking romantically... understanding that love may be in the longing, the missing, but more in the waiting. That it may be in passion, in desire, but more in the desire, the passion to do anything for someone. That love was about facing thousands of storms with a smile, knowing that just one sight of her in the end will make it all worth it. The journey, for me, was all about love.

Sitting there, I couldn't help thinking about my mother, father, sister and everybody back home. I missed them. Words of Sneha, Palak and Ria *didi* kept coming back to me. They had all advised me not to go in such a fashion, changing trains and fooling professors. "What if something happens?" they had all asked me. "If by chance, God forbidding, I don't even know how to say it, some accident..." Sneha had said. It all came back to me. I prayed that all should go well with my train. I couldn't dare to imagine how unforgivable a deed it would be, and what would happen to them all, if something wrong happened. I prayed, trying to shut out all negative thoughts.

Just as so many emotions played around in my mind, the train entered the station, and, for some moments, I got busy in transferring my belongings and my own self.

I often say,

"A change of place

Does a change of face," and my saying certainly reinforced itself presently. The brooding look slowly made way for the sparkle. The train brought with itself fresh excitement and energy. I, cheerfully, sat down on my seat, and looked out of the window at the starlit sky as the train started to move. The breeze was cool and it flirted with my face, stirring in me, once again, bright emotions of love and victory. Gone were the philosophical tones; it was not a time to brood, I told myself, but a time to remember forever.

Nothing could stop me now, I was on my way.

I woke up with a start. I was in the deepest of slumbers on the top berth, when, all of a sudden, I heard an explosion. Sleepily, I looked right and left from my base, and everything seemed alright in the compartment. I closed my eyes, trying to go back to my sleep, cursing whoever had made the noise. I strictly disapprove of such ghastly acts; they shake one to his core. I have a small, impish cousin, who has this habit of going around bursting balloons in the ears of sleeping beauties, and I tell you, having been a victim, it is a shock like no other. One jumps, at once, almost hits the ceiling, and shudders while coming down. These sudden blasts come like death knells, and one takes his own sweet time to recover.

Thankfully, this time the sound seemed to have come from somewhere far off, like a fat man falling from the top berth to the floor. And, being in the middle of the deepest of slumbers, I slept again quickly. These unwarned blasts are no good to the nervous system, and I tremble to tell you that another one, several decibels louder than my brother's balloons, went off soon after. This time, I went off too like a rocket, and in the process hit the low ceiling with a clang. I could feel my heart throbbing in my mouth. I am not shaken that easily, I must say, but this sound would have shaken the stoutest of soldiers, who sit calmly on our border, used to treating bombs as flimsy fire crackers. It seemed that a bomb had gone off right underneath my berth, if not closer, and I was dizzy from the impact with the ceiling. The only comforting fact was that I wasn't the only one shaken; it had not been a bad dream after all – I had heard some hundred other distinct clangs; my fellow top berth brothers had broken their skulls too.

Suddenly, the train stopped and people started talking anxiously among themselves. I had no one to turn to and remained in my berth, stiffer than ever, keenly keeping an eye on the corridor. Something was wrong, for sure. A wise man in our bogey announced weakly, "There are ghosts in these parts. An army of ghosts has infested the train... make no sound... I am from these parts and I know. A similar incident had happened a long time ago." Nobody dared to ask him what the outcome had been then. I wanted to talk to someone. It was bugging to remain as stiff as an over-baked cake, and have no one to talk to. I stretched myself and peeped below cautiously, half expecting to find a ghost, except that I didn't know how they looked. Instead, I saw a man crouched in fear. I couldn't see his face. It hid hauntingly in a shadow.

"Hello," I said in a whisper, hanging my head down, and at that, our friend crouched more and suppressed a cry. "Don't worry, I am not the ghost," I resumed, clearing my credentials. It was essential for further conversation.

"Then, don't hang like that, like a bat, you almost killed me," he said, relieved.

"Fine," I said, and removed my head, "Can we talk?"

"Yes," he hissed, "But quietly!"

"Do you believe in ghosts?" I asked.

"No, no way..." he replied.

"Good, nor do I, let us tell these idiots that the man is bullshitting."

"Are you mad?"

"Why, you only said you don't believe in ghosts," I said, bantering.

"Still, why take a chance?"

"True," I said.

There was a silence. A pin-drop one, as it is sometimes defined. People had stopped whispering fearing that any sound might wake up the sleeping monster.

"At least, turn on the light!" I said, feeling it would be safer. Ghosts like it dark, I had heard.

"Are you mad?"

"No, I have heard ghosts are afraid of light!"

"Still, why take a chance?"

It seemed the man only knew two sentences.

"Can you say anything else? You keep mumbling 'are you mad' and 'why take a chance'."

"Will you shut up?" he whispered, as loud as he could in a whisper, and that made me happy. His language was not as limited as I had thought.

"Good, you can speak! But, I tell you, ghosts are afraid of light."

"So, I have heard too!"

"Or, was it fire?"

"Yes, it was!"

"We can't be sure, I wish mom was here. She knows about it exactly."

"Mine too, I guess!"

"Hey, you know what? My *dadi* has always told me that all ghosts and monsters were killed by Ram."

"Who is Ram?"

"Rama, the God!"

"Oh..."

"Don't be so afraid, *yaar*, one should enjoy adventures. Anyway, if she is right, then there are no ghosts..."

"So, I have heard too!"

"Then, why be afraid?"

"And, why take a chance?"

The man was incorrigible. He seemed to me one of those plump *baniyas* who wouldn't take a chance anywhere. I don't like such people. Life is all about risks, I always say. Realizing the man won't budge from his point of not taking chances, I decided to give in.

"You are right, why take a chance? May be one, just one monster had escaped, somehow, from the arrows of Lord Rama, and my *dadima* might not be aware of him. So... why take a chance, may be, he is the same demon, or possibly he has multiplied... but how..."

"Will you shut up?" he beat his old loudest whisper record.

"Yes, I will," I said, and we were immersed in silence again, a deafening one, let us say this time.

The deafening silence was shattered in a manner so majestic that it would have embarrassed the storm of the sea that breaks the calm. It seemed that a herd of wild bulls had broken loose, after days of torture. The sound of their hooves increased more and more, till it threatened to demolish the entire mechanism of the ear. Remembering Doppler Effect, which spoke about the characters of the approaching and the receding sound waves, I derived that the present wave had to be the former, and, therefore, I stiffened a little more and lay still, waiting for the bulls to arrive.

The sounds kept their promise as a barrage of men, not bulls, as it had seemed, stormed into our bogey, and threatened to take it apart. They whizzed past me like a train within a train, and only after they had gone past me completely, did I dare to look up and out of my berth.

I must clear a thing or two, here, though I think you'd have it figured out already. I never, at any time, believed in the ghost story. Which you can gather from my frivolity. I firmly believed my *dadima's* story. I remember saying 'something was wrong', when the train halted, but in the interval between the second explosion and the wild bull race, my mind had made up that it was nothing to be worried about. Perhaps, a nut or bolt in the train had loosened, thus causing some part, vital to train's motion, to creak and stop. Or, perhaps, a fat man, after all, had slipped down his berth, this time, with his trunk.

But what met the eye was not a good sight at all. I was right. There were no ghosts, no bulls either, but policemen, as lavishly decorated with guns as an Indian bride with jewellery. I craned my neck and saw that they were running after two short, bald men, whose oily heads shone in the dim light of the bogey. It was apparent that they were on the other side of law, but the fact that almost ten policemen chased them with so many guns and rifles made it all look a bit grim. And grim became my mood.

Hadn't I passed enough exams, I asked God, that he had to spring up rogues and cops out of nowhere, to test my will this time? Weren't professors enough? I was cross. It wouldn't have surprised me, if a gunman was to emerge out of the dark, and take me as a hostage. Mr. Fate's game was getting dirtier. Of all the million trains in this country with the second largest rail network in the world, the criminals had to choose this train! And why? Because, the one and only Tejas Narula was on this very one. Damn it all!

My mind was busy in cursing the latest developments that threatened my reaching the destination, and calculating the zeroes after the decimal in the probability of this happening with an unbiased traveller (unbiased as mathematicians say in an unbiased coin). What if the entire train was blown up? My sister-trio's comments came back to haunt me, and I heard several thuds and explosions. The explosions that had interrupted my siesta, I now understood, were sounds of firing. The present explosions came from outside the train, and I was relieved to realize that the battle scene had shifted to the open. I tried to resume my talk with the lower berth man, and manage a laugh in the trying times.

"I told you, there were no ghosts. Didn't I?" I whispered.

"Shhh... there were crooks and bullets..." he whispered.

183

"Want to have a peep outside?" I joked.

"Are you mad?"

"They must be dead!"

"Still, why take a..."

He was about to say, no doubt, the word chance, but it so happened that the lights were switched on suddenly. I stiffened again and he crouched, as we waited for hell to break loose. A stick banged against metal and a gruff voice started shouting.

"Don't worry, now," it said in a coarse Bihari accent, "All is safe. The bandits have been killed. The train will start soon..."

I stuck my head out, this time without any hesitation, and saw a policeman in khaki, rubbing his thumb on his palm, evidently preparing snuff, as he spoke on coolly.

It was four in the morning and the nerve-shattering episode had, in addition, shattered any hopes of getting sleep. The train had begun to rattle and sway again, and after about a hundredth attempt to sleep again, I gave it up. I cooed to my friend on the berth beneath, "Are you asleep?"

"Yes, I am!" he said, and I appreciated his sense of humour. The guy had earlier seemed to me hopeless.

"Mind some *gupshup*?"

"Not a bad idea, sleep is off on a holiday, it seems," he replied. I was surprised. I had expected a why-take-a-chance.

I hopped down while he put the light on. I must say, I expected to see a fat, droopy-eyed *seth*; after all, he had behaved in such a chicken-hearted manner. Practical, some of you might say, but to me chicken-hearted. But what I saw was a pleasant surprise. Here was a man, smart and sophisticated, dressed in impeccable clothes. He seemed to be in his late twenties, and had an air of being well-read. We shook hands. He was surprised to see me too. Perhaps, he had expected a man, by which I mean somebody older, but what greeted him, was a boy.

"Hi," I said.

"Hi," he said.

"Hope I didn't bother you much! I have this habit of speaking, bordering on the excessive, but it helps one to keep smiling..."

"Hmm, you are quite a talker. You had the nerve to joke around in those tense moments..."

"Oh, well, I also believe in always keeping others smiling. Humour is important; besides, it was essential to joke then, or the nerves would have burst!"

"But it could have attracted danger, my friend."

"You really believe in ghosts?"

"Attracted danger, as in any one, those outlaws for instance. Better safe than sorry!"

"True," I said, "But what is gone is gone. Now, all's well with the world."

"By the way, I am Rajit, Rajit Ahuja!"

"I am Bond," I laughed, "No, no poor jokes, I am Tejas Narula."

"So what are you doing... as in studies... college?"

"I am doing engineering from IIT Delhi," I said proudly.

Suddenly his eyes lit up and his face beamed. I had known the effect of the name of my college, but never had it made someone so plump with joy. His face gave a look of a proud father, whose son had just got into IIT.

"Unbelievable," he said, excited and that disappointed me. I mean, I know I don't have a studious face, nor do I sport thick spectacles. Yet, one ought not to mock right on face. But I took it sportingly.

"I know, I don't look like one from the prestigious institute..."

"Oh, no, it is not that, *yaar*," he was opening up. This was the first time he had said *yaar* and his forthcoming words told why. "I too am from IIT," he said, and looked at me like a long lost brother.

It is a thing well documented about IITians, that when two of the same species meet, no matter in which year they passed out, or from which of the seven great institutions, they look upon each other as long lost brothers. The eye is one of affection and heart of warmth. Our fraternity is a cohesive one, it is said, and it can't be truer.

Presently my eyes lit up, and my face beamed. I looked at the other with new found fondness. He told me he was from IIT Bombay, passed out a good four years back, then enriched his curriculum vitae with a degree from IIM Bangalore, as so many IITians do, and was now employed with Daimler Chrysler, the Mercedes Company, in Pune.

"So what are your career plans," he asked, "MBA?"

"The last thing I want to do, no offence, but I find it boring and too damn trivial," I said with the air of a CEO.

"Oh! You are right in a way, but one needs it for the brand name!"

"I know! Too sad that time has come to this, when humans are branded, labelled, tagged... feels like one is talking about underwears!"

"Underwears?"

"Say jeans..."

"Better! True, but one can't help it," he said smiling.

"You know what, there are so few people in IIT itself, the greatest institution supposedly, who study for knowledge, or get happiness out of it; most are just biding their time, waiting for their label, so that they can move on to the next one!"

"Which was true in our time too; to each his own though!" he said.

"Anyway, enough about boring careers, what takes you to Chennai?"

He smiled slightly. He blushed a little. There was an unmistakable glimmer in his eyes and I got it. Something to do with love. These are unmistakable signs. And I was not wrong.

"I'm getting married, *yaar*."

"Well, congrats!" I said sincerely, "Love or arranged?" I asked – the first question that pops into the mind, when one talks about marriage.

"You won't believe it, *yaar*, my story! It is a one in a million case." I frowned.

"Don't tell me you are marrying a boy!"

"No, come on!"

"Thank God, I just asked. You said one in a million, these days such things happen, you see."

"No, no, I said in relation to love and arranged."

"Then, tell all."

"You know what; Nivedita and I were at school together. Nivedita, that's her."

"I thought as much, go on."

"My dad got transferred to Chennai, when I was in eleventh, and we fell in love."

"Great, it has been long!"

"Nine years!"

"So... when did you break it to your parents?"

"That is the most amazing part, *yaar*. Makes you believe that there is a God." I raised an eyebrow, just one. "You know what, she is a south Indian. And her dad is a professor at IIT Madras."

"Good... he must be impressed by you."

"No, no... nothing of that sort. He is conservative like hell, and wouldn't have allowed Nivedita to have a love marriage. IITian or with anybody else. He comes from a school that says –

Love is a pest,

And papa knows best."

"Then?" I asked, interested. He had all my attention. His case was not dissimilar to mine, and was having a happy ending. I wanted to know it all. "You won't believe it, just when she and I were wondering how to put it across to him, a marriage proposal came to my house."

"Then? You surely tore it off!"

"Exactly, that was my first impulse. I told mom I'll have nothing to do with proposals. I hate them."

"So do I."

"So I told her to tear the photo, but she somehow convinced me that the girl was beautiful, and deserved a look."

"You had it? No harm in looking at pretty faces..."

"Exactly, I thought, might as well look at a pretty girl..."

"Yes, then?"

"The roof fell over my head, and the ground escaped from beneath. It was her."

"Who?"

"Nivedita!"

"What?"

"Yes," he said, and I sank back into the seat like a boneless mammal. I understood, now, why he had said one in a million. Make it one in a billion. Add it to the wonders of the world list. Christen him the luckiest man on this planet. I shuddered to compare my life with his. Son of fortune, he sure was. A thought that often comes to my mind, when witnessing love stories other than mine, flitted in again – if only my life was so uncomplicated.

"What happened to you, Tejas? All well?" he asked, seeing me droop like that.

"Her parents never came to know about it, for nine whole years?" I asked incredulously.

"No, we played really safe, and we don't intend to tell him even now. Wonder how he'll react! Why take a chance?"

The man had proven his theories of life in an exemplary fashion. It was as solid a proof as the one given by Mr. Newton about something called gravity, when he let an apple fall. Why-take-a-chance motto was a hit surely, and I wouldn't wonder, if in a short time, hordes of children come out on the streets, singing the slogan. It would certainly become a rage. I felt bad, thinking how I had made fun of this genius of a man, and his ingenious motto. Chicken-hearted he might be, but it had served him well. I looked at him with a new found respect. He had evaded the attention of his future father-in- law for nine years, and I had barely managed two. I was just a minion compared to him.

"Will you mind telling me what happened?" he asked again, "You seem to be suffering from jaundice, all of a sudden." He had put it well, for my face had been robbed of its colour. I mustered all my courage to speak.

"Do you know why I am going to Chennai?"

"I am not much of a face reader!"

"Then let me tell you, you'd be glad to know that my story is very similar to yours, except that there is one major difference – Her dad knows, and I blame it all on you. If only you had met me before, oh the wise one! If only..."

And I told him all, as I have told it all to so many others. I also told him how much I appreciated his why-take-a-chance motto, but how I was incapable of following it. I was too impulsive to not take a chance. He empathised with me. Said he understood my pain and position, but told me again that I was taking another chance in going to meet my beloved. He added that it was worth it, now that her father knew, as he won't let her meet me otherwise.

He told me to be careful. I assured him I wouldn't take a chance once there, and he was happy. "That's the way to go," he said. He also said like so many others had, "You really love her, man!" and coming from a veteran like him, one whose relationship had lasted a solid nine years, and would go on forever, no doubt, it was an honour and I smiled meekly.

"You must come to the wedding, Tejas, obviously, if you can spare time from your dates," he said.

"Oh, I definitely will, I'll meet her only during the day. You must know how it is with girls, when it comes to coming out of home at night."

"Yes, especially with Nivedita; her father is a freak. You know how professors are! He has such crazy ideas, always. Now sample this. The dates of all the functions had been decided long back, but just about a week before the marriage, this man gets such insane ideas."

"Like?"

"The marriage is next Sunday and only yesterday he tells everyone that a *pooja* must be organized!"

"I don't prefer them much either. God's everywhere, but, surely, not much of a pain. Just a small *pooja, yaar*!"

"Small? Your head will burst when I tell you this. The *pooja* is to take place somewhere in Mahabalipuram, not for one-two hours, but spread over three days!"

"Three days?"

"Three days! And when I try to drive into his head that God will see not whether you have prayed for one or three days, but only how pure your heart is, he just doesn't get it. Says it is imperative for our future!"

"These superstitions sometimes kill you!"

"I know, and to receive such a shock out of the blue, just when I was thinking of enjoying a break after a long time, drives me to depression. You see, I am a man who likes to enjoy his time. I decided to travel in train especially, as I love it. I enjoy life's small-small joys, and this man kills them. When I was all geared up to have fun with my family and all, this man comes with this preposterous plan and stabs me!"

"Say stab in the middle of a sound sleep."

"Perfectly put!"

I sympathized with him. Being a victim of the whims and fantasies of a girl's father myself I could understand what he felt like. If there is ever a man, whom you would give anything to avoid for the rest of your life, it would be a girl's father. Your girl's, of course. I gave him a friendly pat.

190

"Don't worry, my friend, it'll all be alright. It's just a matter of three days!"

"Oh, I don't know what I'll do," he almost cried, "The only solace is that I'll have my sister there. May be, we have some fun. Oh, that reminds me... the last time I talked to her, Shreya didn't sound alright. She said there was something important..."

"Who didn't sound alright?" I asked. I was half dead.

"My sister."

"I mean, what is her name?"

"Shreya, why?"

That completed the murder. Rajit Ahuja *urf* Shreya's Raju *bhaiya*, the one who used to carry her piggyback all day long, the very brother who was getting married. I wondered, what prevented her from calling him Rajit *bhaiya*; wasn't too long; and I cursed the Indian tradition of keeping pet names.

I closed my eyes and fell into my seat. It didn't seem like a seat at all, instead a million mile deep pit. I fell fast and hit the bottom hard. I didn't feel anything after that for quite a long time. Numbed, that is what they call it, I was.

The train had assumed what must be its fastest pace after the shock of the discovery of bandits on its chassis. Most of the people had succeeded in their persevered attempts of beating the demons out of their heads, and had gone off to sleep. Thus, darkness reigned in the Chennai Express, and the night was once again still, if the expression can be used in the case of a moving train. However, amongst all this darkness a singular light shone on and illuminated the bogey S – 4. A traveller who might have been irritated by this disturbing light, as passengers in trains so often are, and decided to teach the illuminator a good lesson with his what-the-hell-are-you-doing-at-five-in-the-night speech, would have seen two pale faces— paler in the yellow light of the train— looking at each other dumbly like ducks. What he would've done afterwards doesn't bother us for, in reality, no body came and disturbed the ducks. They were alone in their compartment, which usually fills itself along the journey and, from the look on their faces, it seemed they were in the middle of, what is called, an awkward moment. I, as one of the ducks, can tell you for sure that I didn't have a clue about what to speak, and my brother-in-law was not doing much better either.

Presently my friend closed his eyes, trying to gulp in the shocker, and he did have difficulty in doing so, as was evident from the lump of the size of a basket ball, which had formed in the middle of his throat. I didn't blame him for his reaction. It was natural. I empathized with the poor soul, as I saw him writhe in his seat like a trodden snail. Of all the bally shockers, if there is one that sends the chilliest of chills down your spine, it is the one that deals with the discovery of your darling sister's love. "When did she grow so old?" is a question that each brother asks himself, wondering at the ways of nature – so fast, so furious. Till yesterday, the cute little girl who was so high, he says to himself pointing to his knees, has become big enough to start falling in love! Unbelievable, it seems. Years flash past so fast; he reflects and curses them. He takes his own sweet time, thus, to try and swallow the fact as it stares in his face— the realization that 'yes, it is for true, and, no, nobody is joking here, and that there is no use of running away from it.'

I appreciated his dilemma, probably, better that anyone else could. I have sisters myself, and though the news of their falling in love hasn't yet been conveyed to me, I can imagine what convulsions it would produce in me whenever it does happen. A brother wouldn't like to hear an explanation from his sister that "My dear brother, you, yourself are in love!" The brother doesn't see any sense in this parallel. He says to his sister, "Don't give my example. I am wise. But you are an innocent girl, and any bad guy can fool you. After all, the world nowadays is brimming with them!" Brothers, I tell you, are extremely protective, and don't like such news at all. But eventually, one does see the sense in it all, and the shock does get swallowed. One says, giving up and accepting life, "It had to happen someday. After all she won't remain so high forever. And may be the boy is good", but the time that it takes for this realization to surface is a wee bit long.

Meanwhile, as I mused on my friend's mixed feelings, I began to muse on my mixed feelings as well, and, juggling so many feelings, was as silent as a clock that has lost its batteries. I didn't know whether to feel unlucky or lucky. A part of me called Mr. Fate names, as it has done so often in this journey. "Nothing can stop me now," I had said to myself at the Pune station. Merely a train journey away from my love, tell me, wasn't I right in assuming that? But first the bandits, and now this! I could hear Mr. Fate laugh sinisterly, flashing his pointed incisors, and shout derisively, "You foolhardy soul, seems you'll not give up; take this."

In desperation, Mr. Fate had finally switched strategies, and now concentrated on Shreya's end. Cheap tactics, I tell you, to harry a delicate girl Unchivalrous, to put the poor girl at her wit's end, by conjuring up, out of the blue, this whole *pooja* business. My darling must've been busy with her dress rehearsal, already in a muddle whether to choose the blue *salwar-kameez* or the pink skirt to wear on the first day, when the news must have arrived. Her sweetheart was coming to meet her, traversing the length of the country, encountering the roughest of storms, and here she was helpless, about to be exported to some foreign land. My heart went out to her. She, probably, would have fainted on hearing this. Even the phone lines were all messed up the previous day, rendering a conversation impossible. Oh, how she would have coped with it! "Take me on, Fate, man to man, but stop harassing my little girl!" was what I wanted to shout out.

But my second voice told the first to calm down. After all, wasn't it Fate that had placed me and the hero of the very show, which might have prevented me from meeting my darling, in the same compartment? The use of 'might' here may seem a solecism to you but I assure you it is not. I use 'might', for the *pooja might* have foiled my plans, but now that I knew about it, it'd be a different script. I *was* going to meet Shreya if not in Chennai, then in Mahabalipuram or, for that matter, in Timbuktu, which not many people know, is a place in northern Mali, Africa. Therefore, this wise voice told me not to curse Fate, but instead to look at the brighter sides of life – a thing, if there is one, I'd want you to remember from my story.

If this man hadn't been planted below my berth by Fate, I would have waited for Shreya outside IIT Madras, where we were supposed to meet, peeping desperately into passing autos, only to find nothing like her in them, for God knows how long. Thus, Mr. Fate, though, had ruined quite a lot, was also doing his best to resurrect it all. Once again, I went into the pensive mode, thinking about the past and deriving hope from it. Numerous times along the journey everything had been shattered and, each time one saw the hand of Fate. But at all those times, hadn't he, not without my efforts, changed sides, proven himself an ally and put all the pieces together?

One needs perseverance and effort, thus, at all times in life. "Buck up", one needs to say to oneself, "and think." In the present dilemma, however, not much of thinking was required. There was only one man who could help me meet Shreya. And that man sat right before me. I looked at him once again. He still looked pale; his eyes were closed, but his breathing was getting back to normal. I decided to break the silence. I put a comforting hand on his shoulder and he opened his eyes. What he saw, must've been eyes full of pity and prayers. Pleading, begging, imploring for help.

"I know how it feels like, brother. I have a sister too," I fumbled with my opening lines. He kept looking at me unbelievingly. He didn't speak.

"I really love your sister; that is the only assurance I can offer you, right now," I added. He was still silent.

"I hope you understand, Rajit." He kept on looking, mutely. I didn't know what to do. He *had* to understand, he himself was a criminal, if love was a crime.

"You are the only one who can help us!"

At that he straightened himself and moved his eyeballs in surveying me from top to bottom.

"Not bad!" he declared at the end of it, reminding me of his sweet sister, and smiled. "You know what, you look like a school kid," he said, a little disapprovingly, I thought. I sympathized with the poor blighters, who have to go through that extremely unpleasant round of being examined by the girl's parents. My heart went out for them. "But," my friend added, "That is good, as Shreya looks just like a tenth grade girl. You'll look good together." He smiled again, and I managed a small one too, relieved at the positive assessment.

"I am happy for her. You really love her, *yaar*! Stay that way, always, I tell you, or else I'll break your legs," he said, forcing menace into his voice.

"Break them; do whatever you want to, but, right now, help me. I have told you, already, how difficult it has been to come this far, and now your *sasurji* has messed it all, both for you and me. I *have* to meet Shreya! At any cost!" I prayed.

"I wish I could cancel the *pooja*!"

"Can't you?"

"Not until the old pig-head is there."

"Can't we do something about him?" I asked in a sinister tone, implying an execution.

"I'd love to do many things to him, *if only* Nivedita didn't love the buffoon so much..." he said frustratingly, like a police officer, who has been ordered to bring the gangster back alive, and only alive. Oh, how much he'd want to cut him up, but the bloody authorities hold him back. "If only..." he repeated, and I related to his thinking. Many boys have felt that way about their girls' dads down the history line. 'If only' is the thing that comes to the seething lips at such times, and I felt for my friend.

"But something needs to be done..." I said.

"Now I see why Shreya was so worried yesterday, when I talked to her. She said there was something important she wanted to tell me and right then the phone lines went off..."

"Exactly what I wanted to ask you, how did you talk to her? I tried calling her up so many times yesterday, but the call wouldn't connect. Not even to her friend's number. Neither did I get a call from her. There was some problem with the lines..."

"Yes, I only spoke to her at seven in the morning. *Sasurji* has this habit of giving his *brilliant* news right in the morning... to set the tone for a brilliant day; so when I hung up on him, I called my *mausi* (Shreya's mom), to discuss with her and my mom, my dilemma! After that I also couldn't connect, and then I was busy at office."

"My God, I tell you, we should call her right away from the next station and see if it connects. She'll be worried like anything."

"At five in the morning?"

"She'd be awake, I am sure," I said.

"I am sure too," Rajit smiled, "Reminds me of old times... waiting whole night by the phone... just for one call. Amazing... love is!"

"I know!" I said, dreaming about Shreya.

"But right now, what we should worry about is how to get you to Shreya!"

"Point!"

"How, how, how..." he said meditating.

"Why did God have to give me this school kid face, I can't even play your friend."

"That just proves everything has its pros and cons."

Just then the train whistled and began to slow down. I looked at my new friend and he looked at me, and we both shot towards the door and looked outside. It was a station. It looked like a deserted island, save for a single bulb that lent its light to a tea stall. The whole station was just about the length of our train. There were hardly three-four persons on the platform. Our train stopped and we both jumped out, and dashed for the tea stall. A man sat there smoking *beedi*, wrapped in a shawl, but there was no sign of a phone there. My heart sank. Rajit asked the stall owner, "Any telephone booth here?" The owner looked at us suspiciously, and then like a magician produced from behind him a bruised and battered phone. "No meter sahib, will charge ten rupees per minute as per my watch, and you better call quick; the train will start soon, it is three hours late," he said in a coughing tone, and lifted his wrist to look at his watch. I dialled the number quickly and waited. Nothing happened. I dialled again. This time a message, "All routes are busy, kindly call later." The phone lines had to choose this time to fail us! I shook my head in disappointment, and Rajit took the receiver from my hand. He dialled the number. I waited, keenly studying his face to spot any sign of success. It showed none. But suddenly he said triumphantly, "It is ringing," and I heaved a sigh of relief. He thrust the receiver against my ear. She picked up the phone.

"Hullo," she said.

"Hullo…"

"Oh thank God, you called, Tejas, I have been calling you since yesterday, but the calls wouldn't connect…" and she broke down. She started crying like a baby.

"Don't cry, Shreya, don't cry!"

"You don't know what has happened!"

"I know. I know it all; you stop crying. I know you have to go to Mahabalipuram."

"How do you know?" she asked surprised, still crying.

"Always told you that I have a sixth sense!"

"Oh shut up, tell me!"

"Don't have time, Shreya, the train will start any time. You just don't cry and be strong. Don't worry, I'll meet you; it'll all be fine. I told you earlier that this all messing up is important for our book. How else will it be interesting? Life's nothing but a story, darling. So just enjoy the story that we'll tell our grandchildren. And sleep now, I know you haven't slept at all, and eat well for I know you have been skipping meals..."

"But will you tell me... how'll you come?" she asked, and at that I gave the receiver to her brother.

"Hullo," he said, "Yes, it's me, sis, can you believe it? With Tejas... God is great, sis, now don't worry, we'll chalk out some plan... but wait till I get there... I'll see you... you didn't tell your dearest brother *anything* about your extremely entertaining love story... after all his tales that he used to tell you... disappointing..."

The train began to move. I fished in my pocket for money. A hundred rupee note came into my hand. I signalled Rajit to hang up. He gave the receiver to me. "Okay, bye, Shreya; don't cry and don't worry. Didn't I tell you that I am on my way? And so I am more than ever; just wait for me and I'll be there soon, clutching you in my arms and... and right now I hate to hang up but the train is picking pace. Oh, how much I love running after trains. Done that for ages... Love you, bye..."

"Love you too, and get in safely," she said.

"Anything for you, ma'am," I said, and hung up. I pushed the hundred rupee note in the stall owner's hand, and ran with Rajit, shouting, "Keep the change..."

The call was priceless.

⌒

We were both really tired when we reached our compartment, and decided to sleep. There was the whole of next day to chalk out some plan. Presently, what the body needed was a nice sleep to get the mind in shape, to work out yet another plan that'd bail me out of yet another crisis. I felt happy after talking to Shreya. At least she wouldn't worry now.

As I closed my eyes, words of the song that I had written came back to me:

"There's one thing you've got to learn,
Life's full of twists 'n turns,
You've got to break the rocks in the hot sun,
For the tide to turn.
If there is night, there has to be dawn.
Life goes on."

Life was indeed brimming over with twists and turns, and that is how one has to live it. One can't run away from it. I waited for my dawn.

And then another song, brilliantly written by Sir Paul McCartney, made itself heard:

"When it will be right, I don't know.
What it will be like, I don't know
We live in hope of deliverance
From the darkness that surrounds us."

As I told you, there is a song for every occasion. I waited for the messiah of God that would bring me deliverance.

Still December 13, this year. Morning.

There was a bang. Yet again! And yet again while I was sleeping. I was sleeping like a corpse and the sound rushed me back to life. I jumped, fearing that the stubborn bandits were back again. But to my relief, and to my friend's entertainment, I was wrong. I saw Rajit near my ear, laughing.

"What on earth was that?" I demanded. You all know by now, how much I hate being woken up, and being woken up like that, well...

"That," he said, bringing his hands together, "Was this," and then did it again... the loudest clap I had ever heard. Even when awake it sent a shiver down the body. The train which was shaking as it normally does threatened to derail. The world, I tell you, is no more a safe place to live in, when people are equipped with tools like those. I marvelled at my friend's talent. One doesn't need guns or bombs, when one has hands that clap like thunderbolts. I wondered why my friend feared those gunshots. To him those should have been no more than drops falling soothingly into a bucket. Life is strange, it proves again, full of ironies.

"Man, you have got hand-grenades instead of hands!" I said, impressed.

"You got scared, didn't you?" he asked childishly. What a waste of a question!

"Of course I got scared, I don't live in a minefield, used to be woken up by bombs instead of alarms or cocks."

"Good, I got you then!"

"Got me?" I said unbelievingly.

"You were acting such a hero when the bandits came in, you coward!"

"Excuse me," I cleared my throat to clear the misunderstanding, "Courage is not defined by how you wake up to stupid sounds. Even *Angulimal* would've been shaken by your brute of a clap. Courage is about character..." My lecture on what courage was all about was nipped in the bud.

"Alright, *Teesmaarkhan*, I got it. I just wanted to get even."

"Even?"

"Remember how you scared me when you hung your head down like a ghost. *This* was for *that*."

"Alright, so we are quits. But please don't do this to me again, one more dose, and I may have a heart attack."

"Fine! You are spared. Now get up, don't you want to plan?"

"Yes," I said yawning, "What's the time?"

"It is nearing eleven and I heard that we are approaching another station. Train will stop at some place called Wadi. We are about four hours late."

I hopped down with my tooth-brush and soap, and made my way to the wash-basin. I washed my face and brushed my teeth, and made my way back to the berth. Meanwhile, the train that had started losing pace finally stopped. I got out lazily to enjoy the hustle and bustle at the station. The air was cool, the atmosphere electric, and I made my way to a cold drink shop.

The station in these parts, I have already told you, is like a splash of colours, and presently on this canvas, a particular *sardarji* stood out. His colours, by which I allude to the colour of his clothes, struck my eyes like a ball of fire. He was busy haggling with the owner of a bookshop

201

some fifteen meters away, with his back to me. He wore a red turban of the richest red, under it a green shirt of the richest green, and still below brown trousers, needless to say, of the richest brown. In short he looked like an apple tree, and a drunkard could not be blamed for attempting to pluck, what he thought, must be an apple. That no drunkard was in his vicinity was a thing that our *sardarji* must be thankful for.

With my eyes fixed on the human kaleidoscope, I asked the Pepsi Man for a bottle of the beverage, and while he produced one, I saw *sardarji* try to slip his purse into his trouser's back pocket. Well, at least our *sardarji* intended to, only that he didn't quite succeed. *Sardarji*, one saw, was extremely busy reading the book he had purchased, which he held in his left hand. What Sherlock Holmes must have deduced, had he been there, was that our man, no doubt a keen reader, was also a fastidious fellow, who wouldn't like to waste time, precious as it always is, that it took for one to go from the book-stall to the train, in mere walking. He'd have also labelled our *sardarji* absent-minded and careless, for his purse instead of going smoothly into the pocket, went smoothly out, and hit the ground with a mild thud, which was lost in the din of the station. I apprised you a para or two back of the cool breeze at the station. Presently this naughty breeze, precisely a nanosecond after the purse had landed, encouraged a stray newspaper page to fly and land on top of the purse thus concealing it from the eyes of eager thieves that prowl about at the station.

I marvelled at the scene, constructed so beautifully by the forces of nature. But having been exhorted always by my mum and *dadi* to help fellow brothers, I didn't stand sightseeing for long, and called out for the human palette, who had turned left towards the train with the book still in his left hand, a fat black trunk in his right, and his eyes still transfixed on the God-knows-what-lay-in-them lines.

"*Sardarji*," I shouted, and at that the *sardarji* turned around.

There comes a stage in one's life, sooner or later, depending upon the kind of life one has led, when the goriest of horrors ceases to make an impact. The ground remains firmly beneath, the world does not go dark, and the tummy bears it all without inviting butterflies. Any lesser man, had he been in my place, would have fainted on seeing what I saw. But what this journey of mine had done, if I could put my finger on a single thing, it'd trained me to absorb the worst of the life like the good, without even the slightest bat of an eyelid. My nerves had been fully converted to steel and muscles to iron. I had shown surprise or dismay, when dealing with the previous shockers, but to this one I turned a blind eye. I drank it like a bitter medicine that had to be taken. I had to move on. Let it be the most appalling jolt of my life. It had to be dealt with.

It's time, I guess, to give away what or rather whom I saw. I bet the first thing that'll bump into your head, when I tell the whole thing is, "What the devil is he doing here?" and I don't blame you at all. It was the very thing that came to my mind. It was Professor P.P. Sidhu. Don't ask me – "How could he have arrived at such an obscure station?" I haven't a clue. He was headed, we all remember, towards Chennai alright, but boarding the train from here? Wadi? The only thing clear, however, and which must solely concern the brave soldier, was that his adversary was right there and there was no escaping that. Pinching or slapping would have proven that I was not dreaming, but I didn't have the time. The first thing to do on seeing him, as he looked hither and thither for the caller, was to do an about turn, the ones they taught us so well at school at the morning drills. I hated them back then, but presently a wave of appreciation swept me. How well the school trained one to face any situation! I shifted the weight on my left foot and did a neat one-eighty degrees that would have made the fussiest of brigadiers proud. I knew for sure, Pappi hadn't spotted me in the large crowd at the station. I just walked straight nonchalantly, and hid at a vantage point behind the Pepsi shop from where I could scrutinize his movements.

Lying in ambush, I saw Pappi, after his initial puzzlement at the call, proceeding towards the train. He was lost in his book once more, and moved slowly, always in danger of bumping into the hurrying and scurrying passengers. The train rested at the station for a good fifteen minutes and Pappi had all the time in the world to reach his seat. When he was out of the danger area, I quickly moved to the book shop, and there, after letting a coin drop inconspicuously, bent and picked up the purse along with the coin. I swiftly moved back to my base, the place behind the Pepsi shop.

I flipped open the purse and from its right compartment stared at me Pappi, smiling from his IIT I-card. He had an absent-minded face, but a genial one. I remember telling you, he is a jovial sort of fellow, and that's exactly how the photo depicted him. One assumes, no doubt, that the picture was from an age, when he hadn't rubbed his shoulders with me, and his face was kind – bereft of the ruthlessness only I had seen. I felt a strange empathy for him, watching his innocent photo. I knew I didn't hate him. All his actions could be justified. He was after all soaked in what he thought was alcohol. For the first time I felt I was not on a vengeance spree with him. Hitherto, I had always seen him as an enemy but presently I didn't. I don't know the reason for such an attitude change. May be outside the walls of IIT it is a different life. Outside his station a policeman meets his prisoner without the same harshness.

It was no time to philosophise but to do something. I searched the purse. There were a few hundred rupee notes, some visiting cards and there was the ticket. We were travelling in the same train. I looked down and could hardly believe my eyes. I didn't shout, didn't flinch; just pursed my lips and knitted my brows. Bogey S- 4, seat number 43 said his ticket. Bogey S- 4, seat number 44 said mine.

I moved carefully to the window of my compartment. I passed it once quickly and a fleeting glance showed me that Pappi was busy with his trunk. It was open on the berth opposite to which Rajit was sitting. I turned and trotted to the window again, and from the left corner, the one closer to Rajit, I waved my right hand while my left was engaged in putting a finger on my lips – a warning for Rajit: "Don't react!" He was reading some book and noticed me after about five seconds. He was taken aback to see me in that avatar of an asylum runaway – with my eyes wide open like a lunatic and my hand signalling frantically, like a lunatic, too – trying to tell him to come out. He, no doubt, thought that a bout of epilepsy had come over me and was about to say something like, "Have you gone mad?" when, sensing that, I withdrew my waving right hand and employed it too in unison with the left. Probably two fingers were better than one on the lip, I thought, and it did the trick. He didn't speak but kept staring at me mutely, probably wondering what his sister saw in this boy, who went mad on serene mornings, and who knows, on every morning! I signalled him again to come out of the train and having no other option, he did so.

"Have you gone nuts?" he asked surprised.

"No," I said.

"Then why in God's name were you behaving in that crazy manner?"

"I wanted to tell you to come out but I couldn't speak!"

"You are speaking well enough now..."

"I mean I couldn't speak there."

"Why?"

"All hell has broken loose..."

"What?"

"That man in there, in our compartment, on the seat below my berth and above yours is that professor from IIT Delhi..."

"A professor!" he said in excitement, happy as if a reunion of IITians was in progress.

"The professor..."

"What difference does that make? Strange that three IITians should be in one compartment, all by chance..." he would have no doubt added like Dr. Prabhakar – the ways of providence, 'strange and wonderful' – but I cut him short.

"If only you'd let me complete."

"Go on."

"He is the very professor," I started explaining to him as my story had evidently slipped from his mind, "Professor Pappi, I told you about, who was soaked in soda by my friend and who tried everything to stop me from meeting your sister."

And then it dawned on him. His eyes bore no more excitement but incredulity and horror. And then he spoke, spotting an anomaly, "But you said that he had been removed."

"I wish I had removed him, from the world," I said it just like that, "I forgot to mention that he too was going to Chennai to attend some marriage..."

"Yes, it's this season, you know..."

"I don't know all that, all I know is that he is right here, and of all the places, right under my berth, like a carefully planted time bomb!"

"So what to do?" he asked.

I had a plan. I was certainly learning to plot quickly. The journey had taught me to think on my feet; sharpen my acumen and all that. Thank you, I acknowledged inwardly and then shifted my attention to Rajit.

"I have a plan."

"Say."

"I have his purse," I said with pride.

"Who's purse?"

"The professor's purse, of course! What a stupid question! How can other purses help us?" I said irritated.

"You have his purse," my friend said calmly. But presently his ever changing eyes sported a look of disapproval. They had me confused.

"Yes, here it is." I showed him.

"Bad!" he said shaking his head.

"I know, battered old purse, torn at places, leather is cracking and fading. Calls for a change. An ideal birthday gift..."

"I didn't mean that the purse was bad."

"Then?" I asked perplexed.

"I said that for you and your ways. Now you'll steal purses too," and at that he shook his head again, intensifying the disapproving look and wondering again, whether his sister ought to be allowed to continue her romance with a guy that has a habit of picking pockets at stations, and who knows, maybe everywhere!

I wondered at the insanity of the notion. I was getting worked up. "Do I look like a pickpocket?" I demanded indignantly, though fearing that he might say yes.

"No, but then where did you get it from?"

I described to him that scene of beauty.

"Ah," he said satisfied, relieved that I was not a thief.

"Your 'ah' go to hell, just listen to what needs to be done."

"Tell me."

"You go into the compartment and somehow take the Prof. away from our berths. Best thing would be to take him to as far as the door on the right side. Meanwhile, I will sneak in from the door on the left and climb onto my berth, turn my head towards the other side, crouch and lie there. Then you can bring him back and he will not be able to see me."

He listened intently but after I said this, saw something amiss.

"How will that help you?"

"I cannot be seen, so he won't know that I am there."

"You will stay on the top like a dead body throughout the journey?

Won't you come down to eat, or go to the toilet and how on earth will we plan?"

"I haven't finished my friend; you are forgetting the purse," I said waving it.

"Yes, what about it?"

"You know what is in it?"

"Probably his money."

"And?"

"May be the photo of his wife and kids..."

"And?"

"Stop fooling around, I know what a purse contains."

"But you are missing the nub of the story. What must the purse of a train passenger contain?"

His eyes were now the eyes of an able conspirator. He saw it. He saw it all now.

"His ticket," he said moving his head slowly up and down like a fellow conspirator who has got the whole picture, finally.

"So that means his ticket is not with him, but with me."

"Super!"

"And what does that make him, comrade?" I asked. I felt like one of those rebels, hatching a plan to bomb the president's car. Only black overcoats, black gloves, black glasses were missing.

"A ticket-less traveller!"

"You are right, comrade, but I meant, what does that make him in the eyes of law?"

"A criminal," he said, and I couldn't have used a better word.

"A criminal, a law-breaker, a person, comrade, who the law clearly states, can be sentenced to some good time in jail or imposed some good fine, amount of which I do not recall."

"Neither do I."

"Immaterial, the nub again is that our criminal neither has the ticket nor the money to save his good self." My partner in crime looked at me with eyes of appreciation. Fit, he probably felt, is this boy for my sister. Has all the brains.

"So when the ticket-collector is about to arrest him for his offence, and send him off to an obscure prison in Honolulu to keep murderers and pick-pockets company, I'll save him the humiliation by descending down from my berth like God's Messiah incarnate, telling the TC that the man he looks upon as a swine from behind his spectacles, is actually my respected Guru from IIT Delhi accompanying me on a technical project. I'll then pay off his fine, thus becoming a..."

"Hero in his eyes..."

"Exactly, a hero, a God's messenger, an angel of humanity, a whatnot! And then he'll have no option but to be grateful to me and bury the past. Of course I'll tell him that I was not involved the least in that shower incident and that I don't even drink, and he will no doubt understand!"

"Genius!"

"I know! That I am," I said accepting the compliment.

"Hey, but will he not ask you, what are you doing on this train?"

"He will."

"What'll you tell him?"

I opened the purse and showed him Pappi's photo. "Don't you think he is a nice man? Just look at his eyes!"

"Yes, he seems to be. I talked to him a little; seemed a pleasant fellow."

"And a pleasant fellow he is! He was angry with me only because he *thought* I insulted him. But after I clear his doubts, he will be a darling again. Don't you think such a man, touched by my act of deliverance, will understand my story?"

"May be."

"I think he will. After all, a professor ceases to be a professor outside the four walls of his college. Just like a policeman ceases to be a policeman after his beat is over. Society teaches us well to play these dual roles, my friend. A professor he might be, but when not delivering a lecture, when not marking papers, he becomes just another human being – a father, a husband, and a friend. He is a normal human being now— a normal man who listens to music, reads novels, likes to joke; a man vulnerable to emotions, love, sympathy. Of course some men are brutes, but look at him. Does he look like one of those? I am sure he doesn't. You get what I mean?"

"Best of luck!"

"So perhaps, I'll tell him all, or may be not, but right now let us rush in; the train has started to move. I'll be standing at this door; you bait him to the other one."

"Right away," he said and we climbed the train. It had started moving again. Oh, how much I love running and climbing into moving trains!

⌒

It had been a good two hours. Two hours and no TC! My back was aching from the crouching position I had got into in order to avoid detection by Pappi who, occasionally, stood up and walked past me. Initially, when I was fresh, I felt like a tiger hiding masterfully, ready to pounce on its prey. But now as time was tiredly trudging past, I was reminded of a frustrating 'hide and seek' game I had once been involved in. I was hiding in a similar awkward position in a cupboard of a reeky attic, but the one giving the 'den', as we used to call it, never turned up. He told us the next day that while counting till hundred under the old Peepul tree, he had scarcely gone till thirteen, when he had seen a ghost and run away. I remembered how I couldn't straighten myself for weeks after that experience. It was as though the cupboard had permanently been attached to my back. Now I felt the same in the berth.

I wanted to sleep but couldn't afford to. The arrival of the TC couldn't be missed. There had not been much talk between Rajit and Pappi. They were both busy reading.

As I was yawning, a voice made itself clear. "Ticket please," it said, and it sent a wave of fresh energy into my body. The TC seemed two-three compartments away, and I waited for him to land in our midst, once again with the air of a tiger. And he arrived shortly.

"Ticket please," he said.

I produced my ticket from above, without getting noticed by Pappi, who was busy searching for his. Rajit also showed his ticket. The TC indeed turned out to be a man with glasses and had a menacing look. He had a red *tikka* smeared on his forehead. His glasses balanced themselves on the very tip of his nose, from above which his eyes looked piercingly at our professor, waiting for him to produce his ticket.

I couldn't help looking at the professor sitting on the opposite side, restlessly checking all his pockets for his purse. Finding that it was not in its place, the professor asked Rajit nervously, "Have you seen my purse?"

"No," he replied, concerned.

"Just wait a second, sir, it might have fallen off," he said to the TC as he bent down and looked underneath. He rose. It was not there.

"I don't know where it has gone!" he said to the TC.

"I know," said the TC with a suspicious look.

"What?" asked Pappi.

"I know where your purse is mister and I know you well. Wait and watch!"

"You are getting me wrong, sir, I am a law abiding citizen..." and then suddenly Professor's eyes lit up. Hope was back. "Sir," he said to the TC, "I might have kept it in my trunk, let me check," and then he moved towards his trunk.

Horror filled the TC's eyes and he shouted, "Wait!" A man from the pantry, on his rounds, had stopped to watch the entertaining scene and seeing him the TC ordered,

"Hold him! Hold him tight, don't let him move, I'll be back," and at that he lifted Pappi's trunk and rushed off. I wondered where the TC had gone, probably to get a chalan slip. But why with the trunk? The pantry man hung on to Pappi like a lover in a fit of passion and it was funny. Pappi offered no resistance, yet the man held on to him as if he was a mass of sand. I braced myself for descending, in my role of the deliverer. I saw the TC come and told myself, "Here you go!"

I was in the process of getting up but I had to stop. Behind the TC were two policemen and a *hawaldar*. The petty offence surely didn't require three of the police force! A policeman came forward and told the pantry man to release Pappi. He did so and stepped aside. The policeman looked at Pappi in a ruthless manner and Pappi squirmed under his glare. The Professor opened his mouth to speak but before he could do so the policeman spoke, "Welcome, Mansukh Lal, after all these years, what a brilliant disguise but what a foolish mistake..."

The frightened look on Pappi's face turned to a confused one. And I was shocked too. What on earth was the policeman talking about? Who the dickens was Mansukh Lal? And what the devil was a brilliant disguise?

"Sir, you are mistaken, I am not Mansukh Lal, I am Professor Prabjot Pal Sidhu, a professor at IIT Delhi and I have lost my purse. I want to look in to my trunk for it, but the TC..."

The policeman laughed loudly, "Ha-ha, ha-ha, ha-ha..." He looked at his subordinates and they joined in too, "Ha-ha, ha-ha, ha-ha," roared the voices in our bogey. I wanted to laugh too at that comic scene, only that it was too big a mystery to me. It was apparent that police was confusing Pappi with some Mr. Mansukh Lal, but the million dollar question was – Who was Mansukh Lal?

The policeman banged his truncheon against some metal and it was all dead serious again.

"Look into your trunk indeed! No use, Mansukh, in dodging me! Ten years! After ten years we have closed in on you and your gang. And you want me to allow you to open your trunk, take out your pistol and run away again, you scoundrel! I had alerted all the officials to report to me in case of any suspicion. I knew I'd catch you the moment we shot two of your gang on the train, and wasn't I right? You are under arrest!"

The confused looking Pappi was a horror-struck Pappi now. Gone was the look of apology in his eyes for not producing his ticket. 'Ticket-less,' they might insult him with, but certainly not a 'scoundrel'. He was a man of dignity.

There was a change, meanwhile, in my plan. I couldn't descend and tell the officer that he was my professor. The police would want a proof and the purse would have to be produced. I had to wait for the moment when I could plant it somewhere. I couldn't just come down with it and announce, "Here it is!"

"Excuse me, officer," said Pappi, "You are mistaken. I told you I am not Mansukh, and I will have no more insults. I am a professor and demand due respect. What proof do you have that I am Mansukh?"

"Proof, forsooth!" shouted the officer, "You think you can dress like a *sardarji* and get away. The disguise of a Sikh, you must have thought, was the ideal one for the head of the *'Takla* Gang' (the gang of the bald). No body will ever suspect you with a turban and a beard! But you are wrong! I appreciate your genius, but by losing your ticket, you have committed a folly. Hawaldar," he addressed his subordinate, "Tear off his beard!"

⌒

"Shoot, before they tear off his beard!" Rajit said seconds after Pappi was taken away.

"Oh God!" I said and ran after them. Flashing the purse in my hand, I shouted, "Wait!"

They all stopped. The professor's beard was in place and I thanked God. Pappi looked at me unbelievingly. The officer shouted back, "What?"

I moved towards them and then asked Pappi, "Is this your purse?" His eyes lit up as he cried, "Yes!" He showed them the ticket and his I-card. The policemen turned pale. They pleaded with Pappi not to report this incident but Pappi swore he would. The Police had no doubt been rash and rude, which they nearly always are these days, but I didn't know how much to curse them. After all, they had helped my cause. I'd now be an even bigger hero in Pappi's eyes. Life is full of ironies, I reflected again. And strange indeed are the ways of Mr. Fate. How beautifully he had become my ally again, I marvelled.

The professor turned to me after finishing his discourse and said, "Thanks a lot! You saved my life! Where was the purse?"

"It was stuck between the berth and the wall; I saw it just in time."

"Thanks a million, Tejas, I don't know how to repay you. It was so humiliating. I'll teach those dogs a lesson!"

"It was my duty, sir, I wanted to tell them in the beginning only that you are my professor, but they wouldn't have believed me. I thought if I could find your purse, it'll help you more, and if I couldn't then of course, I would have told them!"

"But where were you? I never saw you!"

"Sir, I was on the berth above yours, sleeping when the policemen came!"

It was all well again. Pappi was impressed by my deed but suddenly an oddity struck him, "What are you doing here? What about the Industrial Tour?"

"Sir, I'll tell you all that in a while, let us return to our seats!"

"Alright," he said and we moved.

"Hmmm," he said drawing a deep breath. I had told him the real sequence of events of the soda-shower night. He looked almost satisfied but still not completely.

"Sir, honestly, I had nothing to do with that incident. It was a mere coincidence that I was present in that room..."

"Sir," said Rajit, "He is a fine boy, I know him well. He isn't lying. Let us try to see things from his point of view. How can he be blamed for someone else going mad! I have also studied at IIT and so have you. Do we not know that these things go on in hostels, and one has to live with them? You live like a family in hostel and even if you don't drink, you have to mix with people who do. And sometimes, some youngsters do go overboard. Part of our age, sir! I am sure you must have come across similar scenes in your days!"

"Never ones in which professors are splashed with..." he said and one had to agree. Such scenes are rare, probably one in an aeon.

"Sir, it was a coincidence that you were there at the door," I pleaded again, "And indeed, that I was there in that room. But didn't you mention some time back, 'It is a beautiful coincidence that three generations of IITians should get together in one compartment'? Sir, please see the parallel!"

"Hmmm, but one feels that your generation is losing it all..."

"Sir," began Rajit, "I know this generation is a little rash, and seems to be undisciplined and heading the wrong way! But isn't that the case with every generation, when looked from the point of view of the earlier one. Sir, in all generations some people are good and some bad. We cannot generalize and apply the epithet to a whole generation. I too did some crazy things in my days but you appreciate how well I am doing in life. Sir, we all find our way sooner or later! Please don't blame all of us and especially Tejas. I know him really well..."

"Alright, alright," Pappi interrupted, "I get it. Probably you are right! One needs to be a little more accommodating..."

"Exactly, sir," we both concurred.

"We all have our problems in college days," Pappi said, and I was particularly interested in listening to his mishaps. He was back to being the jovial Pappi again. "But you see, a professor has to be a little strict so that the students don't take too much liberty. Now, Tejas, am I not one of the 'coolest' professors, as the students call us? But that incident shook the whole faculty and I admit it forced me to be a little vindictive, for the first time..."

"Sir, I am sorry again!" I said.

"Oh, I have forgiven you, son, you saved my life today!"

"Thank you, sir; now please change the topic and tell us something interesting about college life..."

"Oh, leave that..."

"Sir, please..."

"Nothing, *yaar*..."

"Sir, I won't tell anyone," I said.

He laughed. "It is not that, son. I would love to tell you my tales. We all have been students. You people think we were born professors! Of course you only see me as an absent-minded professor. And didn't I prove it by losing my purse?" he laughed again, "You see me working, all absorbed on my projects, my bus, and you assume that is what my life is all about. Not true! I work on my projects so intensely because I love my work. It is my dream to have a viable alternate fuel, but then don't you have a dream? Yet, you treat professors as beings from some other planet. I also thought the same before I became one," he smiled dreamily, "But, son, besides being a professor, I am a husband, a father, a human being. But unfortunately we are all trapped in our images. Sad, but that's how it is. In my time there was so much interaction with our professors that they were like our friends, but these days there is none. It is depressing." I agreed with him. We always saw professors as ones who trouble us.

It was nice to listen to him. The professor might be absent-minded, might have the lousiest dressing sense, but he was a good man. I was back to liking him again, he was again the Pappi of old. "And," he went on, "A major reason is the lack of respect towards Gurus these days. Due to so little interaction, the students and professors are always on different planes, never understanding each other. So professors these days have become a little *khadoos*," he grinned, "But students who have interacted with me will tell you I am not. Besides, I was also a naughty student. I have gone through it all too – bunks, crazy things, love..." and at that my heart leapt. He had mentioned love. My eyes brightened, he must surely understand my position, just like Dr. Prabhakar had.

"Sir, love?" I asked teasing.

"Yes, son, love but we won't go into the details."

"Sir, just tell me, is your marriage love or arranged?" It was a question on which hinged my future.

He smiled, just like Rajit had earlier, and that told the tale. Amazing was life. Here in bogey S-4, sat three IITians, all of whom had at some point of time been smitten by love. Amazing, indeed!

"Love," he said smiling and in a childlike manner, "No more talks on this topic." And I wanted no more. That was enough. Well, we certainly underestimated teachers, I thought. He was right; we thought they were from a different planet, but I cannot tell you how good I felt at that moment. It is always a pleasure to find people who have loved, and to find uncles, professors – these respected elders – who have loved, is a feeling which I call 'most satisfactory'.

"You know what, sir, why Rajit is going to Chennai," I asked excitedly and then answered. "Sir, it's his marriage; and a love marriage! Been in love for nine years!" I added, and both of them smiled.

"Congratulations, son! What a coincidence, again," Pappi said incredulously, "I am also going to a wedding." We knew that.

"Life is all about coincidences, sir," I said wisely. I had seen them all.

"By the way, Tejas, you still haven't told me, how you are here and not on the tour?"

"Sir, I'll tell you the truth but don't punish me!"

"Hmmm," he said, "I won't, but you should tell me the truth. You told me your brother was getting married..."

"No, sir, I lied to you..."

"Then tell me the truth."

"Sir, I don't know how to say..."

"You love someone?" he asked so coolly that it startled me. I don't know how it happens, but there is something about love that makes people who themselves have been victims, just look into the eyes of others and learn the whole story. You can't hide it. The gleam in the eye, the smile, the blush – it is all too obvious. I merely nodded my head.

"Be brave, son, you don't have to be afraid. I am not a professor here; treat me as your friend. Now tell me, why are you going to Chennai?"

I told him in brief. It was so queer talking to a professor about love. But I was beginning to see the human side of my professor now, and was treating him as a friend.

"God bless you," he said at the end of it and smiled genially. I smiled back and acknowledged. "But sir, how come you boarded the train from Wadi?"

"Oh, I have a sister there. I was at IIT Bombay for some presentation; so I thought I must visit her. Wadi falls in the route and it'd been long since I visited her!"

"And, sir, what about the Biobull?"

"Oh, the project is almost complete. One purpose of going to Chennai is to test it!" I remembered what Vineet had told me about his partner. "You see, two of us are working on the project. My partner is a professor in IIT Madras. We've been working as a team – he working on some areas, I on some. But we decided to make two buses, one in Chennai and one in Delhi. My bus still has some issues, but this man has completed his."

"So, you are going for the bus as well as the wedding?"

He laughed. "Oh, you can say that they are one and the same. You see this Mr. Iyer is a crazy man, but we have become friends while working on the bus..."

He had to stop. And the reason was that our friend Rajit had uttered a squeal, almost like that of a pig. His eyes were threatening to pop out of his sockets and he was coughing with such force that his lungs were in danger of coming out through his mouth. I patted him on his back. The professor had a bottle of water. He drank from it and only then did he find that his larynx was alright. He spoke in a hoarse voice, "What was the name you said, Professor Sidhu?"

"Mr. Iyer, Anant Iyer. Why what happened?"

"Yes, what happened?" I asked too.

"I tell you, I can hardly believe this; all three of us are going to the same destination. Mr. Iyer is my father-in-law!"

"What!" said the professor.

"What!" said I, and sank back again like a boneless mammal into my seat. All limits had indeed been crossed. First I land in the same compartment as Shreya's brother. Then Professor Pappi also lands there. And then as if this was not enough, we come to know that we are going to the same party. Ways of providence, I had to admit, were strange and wonderful! You can never guess what surprises life has in store for you the very next second. Pappi had a partner in IIT Madras. The partner was Rajit's father-in-law and Rajit was Shreya's brother. Shreya, who of course is my love. It completed the circle. It was all as if a jigsaw puzzle had been carefully constructed by God, and only now were the pieces falling in place. An invisible thread had linked us right from the beginning of the journey, only now it made itself visible. It is true not only for this journey, but for every journey, for life itself. We go on about our lives, each doing his share of work and never know who we will meet or what we will get, until Mr. Fate chooses to break the news, and how!

The other two had also sunk back and were perhaps thinking along the same lines. It suddenly came to me that during my journey, everything strange and peculiar had happened for a reason. And so this thing must have a reason, too; it should help me meet Shreya. Yes, I was sure, that was its purpose, and then I saw light. I was on my feet in a flash with tremendous excitement.

"Sir, you said that the bus and the wedding are one and the same. Why?" I asked.

"Oh, you see, Mr. Iyer wants to inaugurate the bus on the occasion of his daughter's marriage. Says it is auspicious. So he has this insane idea that the bus, in its first drive, should carry the whole marriage party, and go to Mahabalipuram for a *pooja* he is conducting. You must be aware of it. The *pooja* will serve two purposes, he says, it will bless the wedding and the bus. He is a little crazy... told me about the plan only three days back, and hasn't told anyone in his family, says, it is a surprise, a wedding gift for his daughter. So, Rajit, don't tell her about this. Okay?"

"Yes!" shouted a voice. It was not Rajit's approval but a yelp from me. I had found a way. To meet Shreya, and an ingenious one.

"What happened?" asked my fellow IITians.

"Sir, I didn't tell you everything about the trip. This extremely long and taxing trip was on the verge of being decimated. And I'll tell you why! This Mr. Iyer of yours is indeed a crazy man, slightly foolish if I may say in front of you!"

"Alright with me, but is it with him?" he said pointing to Rajit.

"Oh sir, he cannot agree more, in fact he can supply much stronger expletives. Isn't it?"

"Bang on," said Rajit.

"So I was saying that this sudden plan of his, his obnoxious habit of springing surprises..."

"On early mornings..." added Rajit.

"On early mornings," I repeated, "this must be taken into account..."

"And in tight times..." added Pappi.

"And in tight times," I added, "No doubt put you both off, wrecked your mental peace, and for that he must not be spared; but for me, sir, for me he spun the most distressing predicament."

"What?" asked Pappi.

"Don't you get it, sir, in arranging this sudden *pooja*, he transported Shreya, like a black magician, from Chennai to Mahabalipuram!"

"Who is Shreya?" he asked absent-mindedly.

"Sir my..." I said blushing.

"Oh, I get it, but why is she going to Mahabalipuram?"

"For the *pooja*, sir!"

"Why will she go for the *pooja*?" he asked incredulously. At first I thought it was his absent-mindedness in full form. But then I realised I hadn't told him this. I had told him Rajit was a good friend in the beginning. Nothing more.

"She is my sister!" it was not me, of course, but Rajit who said that, and the professor had his circle of coincidences complete. He uttered a squeal similar to that of Rajit and dropped back, unable to digest any more. The same elixir, the bottle of water, which was used to revive Rajit, was tried on our sir and it succeeded yet again. His eyes were back to their places and his back-bone was straighter.

"Sir," I began, "You must muster all your energy and excitement as you are the only one who can help me! I know the mystifying chains of providence have taken a toll on you, as on all of us, but you must help me!"

"How?" he asked feebly.

"You say that everyone will go to Mahabalipuram in the same bus!

"Yes."

"So you must take me along too as some sort of an assistant student who has worked closely with you on this project, and who you thought must be there for the first drive."

"Is there no other way?" he asked.

"No sir, I cannot pose as Rajit's friend as I look too young, and there is no better way, sir, I am sure you can do it!" I waited for his 'yes'. I knew it would come. He was a nice man.

"Fine," he said, "Don't worry!" and at that I gave another yelp and hugged my favourite professor. He was a gem indeed. And then Rajit hugged me. It was a time to celebrate. What a journey it had been! How Professor P. P. Sidhu had started as my enemy and how he had ended as my saviour! How much I used to curse Biobull in the project days, but how it had saved me, time and again! Only Mr. Fate could do it all and presently, I hailed him and prayed that he should remain my ally for some more days.

"Which of you plays the guitar?" asked Pappi, seeing it from the corner of eyes, lying on the top berth.

"I do, sir," I admitted and he was impressed.

"Do you know how to play '*Main Hoon Jhum Jhum Jhum Jhum Jhumroo*'?"

"Yes, sir, one of my favourites, Kishore *da* is loveable!"

"Then bring down your guitar, a nice song for the occasion, and the music will help restore my nervous system."

"Mine too," added Rajit and I brought my guitar down. I strummed the chords when Pappi interrupted me.

"Wait!" he said, "Wait a while, son!" and he lifted his trunk, opened it and started rummaging inside. A book caught my eye, 'The Golden Bat' by P.G. Wodehouse.

"Sir," I interrupted, "Is that book yours?" I said pointing to it.

"Yes! Just bought it from the station. It is an early Wodehouse work, rare. So strange that you find such books at the oddest of places. Never found it in Delhi." Now I knew what the urgency was in reading the book at the station itself. It was Wodehouse after all. I would have done the same.

"Sir, will you lend it to me after reading it? I myself have been searching for his school stories."

"Oh, sure! Nice to know that you like Wodehouse too," and saying that, he produced a mouth organ. He put it to his mouth and started playing. I was stunned. 'We certainly underestimate professors', was the thing that resonated in my ears again.

"Sir, will you play too!" I said unbelievingly.

"Why? Can't I?"

"No, sir, by all means."

"Then start playing."

Thus the song started – Professor on harmonica, me on guitar, and Rajit singing well enough and adding the beat of his *tabla* that he played against the train wall:

"Main Hoon Jhum Jhum Jhum Jhum Jhumroo
Phakkad Ghoomoo Banke Ghumroo,
Main Yeh Pyaar Ka Geet Sunaata Chala,
Manzil Pe Meri Nazar, Main Duniya Se Bekhabar
Beeti Baaton Pe Dhool Udata Chala.
Yoodleyiii…"

Thus the train rattled and swayed on, brimming with joy and excitement. And the compartment with the three IITians made the maximum noise. I looked out of the window. Both my friends had slept, but I was too excited to do so. The compartment now had other passengers too. I watched as the meadows and farms rushed past. To understand what India is, I reflected, one must travel in a train. The window in a train is not an ordinary window; it is a window to the richness and diversity of India. How vegetation, terrain, people change effortlessly as one passes through the country in a train is an amazing spectacle. Nothing provides a more complete panorama of India as the window of a train does. And of course looking out of the widow has other advantages. It tells you that you are getting closer and closer to your love.

Chennai. December 14, this year.

The driver inserted the key while Professor Sidhu, Professor Iyer and Professor, oops, Tejas, just Tejas looked over his shoulder. The coconut had been smashed, a brief *pooja* performed with some professors and students, and the splendidly shining green Biobull smeared with a vermillion *tilak*.

"Turn the key slowly, Pandey," said Prof. Iyer to the driver, closing his eyes and muttering a prayer.

Pandey turned the key. The engine roared and roared and then went "Phussss..."

My heart sank, "Not another problem now!" The Biobull, besides being important to me, was also important for the nation. Finally, the dreams about alternate fuel were being realized. I prayed to God and so did the other two professors.

"I told you to go slow, Pandey," rebuked Mr. Iyer.

He then took charge himself. He turned the key as gently as he could and the engine roared again, and this time went on and on. Pandey pushed the accelerator, the engine roared more, and then putting the bus into gear, he pressed it again. The bus started moving! It was a success. A landmark! Both of them hugged each other and then hugged me in that moment of glory. We were on our way.

Thus we emerged out of IIT Madras, which is a beautiful green place with a bio-reserve too, to pick up the other family members. We were to meet them at a shrine on a beach adjacent to ECR, the East Coast Road. Mr. Iyer had convinced everyone to assemble there and after the surprise, the party was to move in the Biobull to Mahabalipuram. There were limited guests, which included of course, my friend Rajit and his pretty sister Shreya. The wedding was to be a simple one and only very close relatives had been invited. I had been successfully introduced as Professor P.P. Sidhu's favourite student and added to the party.

The Biobull, in spite of all its advantages, had a major drawback. At least presently it had. The professors had ordered Pandey not to go above the speed of twenty kph. And when one is on his way to meet one's love, and after such a long time, and after so many impediments, the speed of twenty is a torture. One cannot be satisfied with a speed of hundred at such a restless moment, and seeing rickshaws and cycles overtake the bus, one feels like jumping out and running to his destination. But I controlled my emotions. "Be patient," I told myself, "You have waited for six months, sixty minutes more will not kill you."

After we moved out of the terrible traffic onto the East Coast Road, the journey became delightful. Shreya had told me about the beauty of the road, and I couldn't agree more. It was a pleasure to drive on that road even at a speed of twenty. The road was wide and straight, and after some time, I saw the sea appearing on my left, just as promised by Shreya. It was an exhilarating view, watching the sea glitter in the sun. The bus, it seemed, sailed on the sea. I was beholding a sea after around ten years, and I longed to be on the coast. With Shreya. I had always dreamt of it.

The bus turned left and after a short distance halted near a shrine. It was a wide open area of brown sand. I could see about twenty people from the bus. They were about a hundred meters away. Among them would be Shreya. I started feeling a bit nervous. I adjusted my shirt a little and then looked in the rear-view mirror to see if my hair were alright. Dishevelled alright, I mean. I then felt the paper-packet in my jeans pocket. It was there. In it were ear-rings for her. How I would give them in front of so many people, I didn't know, but I knew I would. Her dad would also be there, I thought, but I was cool. After all, he had never seen me. We moved towards them, with the professors leading the way. I tried to be normal while walking. I was conscious of my movements. She would be staring at me from somewhere. I looked at the group, now that I could see them all clearly. I began scanning them from the left; she was not there, then I came to the middle; she was not there; surely she must be on the right. I looked to the right and she was not there either. How could that be possible? I looked about again but she was no where. I could see them all. I recognized Shreya's mother and father but there was no sign of her. And then I realized that nor was the prospective groom present. If it was a prank, I'd teach them a lesson. We finally reached and I was introduced by Professor Iyer, as Rohit, name changed due to obvious reasons, a brilliant student.

"Where is Rajit?" asked Mr. Iyer.

"Oh, he has gone for a while to the market with his sister... will be back soon!" said someone.

So that is where they were. That increased my agony and anger. "Oh, I had a surprise for my son-in-law," said Mr. Iyer, "But since he is not here at the moment, I will show something to you all, we don't have much time! The auspicious moment shouldn't pass," He broke his surprise of the bus. There was commotion and cries of congratulations everywhere.

Everybody moved towards the Biobull, and my frustration increased. Just then my cell rang. The number was an unknown one.

"Hullo, Tejas?" said the voice.

"Yes, who's that?"

"It is me, Rajit."

"Thanks for calling, Rajit," I said annoyed.

"Have you reached the shrine?"

"No, I am shopping in a market! Of course, I have reached. Your *sasurji* is exhibiting his bus to everyone! And how is *your* shopping getting along? Buy something for Shreya too, she loves gifts. What an occasion to shop!" I said out of irritation.

"We are not shopping, you idiot!"

"Then?" I said coldly.

"We are at the beach!"

"Oh, at the beach! Some carnival going on?"

"Will you stop making your foolish comments?"

"Yes, I will, but tell your sister that I don't want to meet her. I reach here... facing so many problems, and you two decide to fool around..."

"No one is fooling around... Listen; your bus must have taken a left turn from ECR to reach that shrine. Come on to the ECR and then walk straight; there will be another road turning left after some distance. You'll see a board saying 'Private Road'. Don't worry about that and walk right in. The road leads to the beach. Now come quick!"

"Why all this fuss?"

"Fuss! This world is not meant for good people who try to help others! Instead of thanking me you say, 'why all this fuss'. You wanted to meet Shreya for the first time in front of a thousand people? Here I arrange a sweet little rendezvous for you, and you go on and on with your nonsense."

"Sorry," I said cooling down and realizing his exemplary motives. White, one could say, shining white.

"Mr. Tejas, don't imagine that you are the only one intelligent in this world. Others also know a couple of things. I think I have some experience of love, humble though it may be before yours, to know how and where two enamoured souls should meet."

228

"Now don't say all that," I said embarrassed.

"Alright, then rush, your darling is very restless!" I could hear Shreya fighting with him for that teasing remark. My heart skipped a beat. I was so close to her.

"Will be there in a flash! Bye."

I whispered to Prof. Pappi about the new development and darted off. Once on the ECR, I didn't know whether to run or to walk. I decided on walking fast, real fast. As nervousness was increasing again, I saw the turn with the 'Private Road' board. I turned and saw Rajit standing far off, leaning against a wall; the road was really long. I could see the sand on the beach, but not the sea. I could only hear the waves. I walked quickly to Rajit and greeted him, embarrassed.

"Hi Tejas, you look smart!" he said smiling.

"I am sorry; my mood was a bit off on not finding you both there..."

"It is okay, now go straight, brother, on to the beach and you'll find her on the right... run to her..."

"Where are you going?"

"Do you want me to stand there watching you both? I don't mind!" he said bantering.

I smiled. "No, you look better here!"

"I know, now vanish and take her in your arms and well... do whatever... you have around ten minutes, you'll find me at that 'Private Road' board. I'll keep an eye, if by chance someone comes!"

"See you," I said and started walking towards the beach. It was a beautiful road with palatial houses on both the sides. There were some lovely farms too. The road opened on to the beach and I could still see only the golden sand. A strong but beautiful, that is the only way to describe it, wind was blowing. As I walked the sound of the waves became louder. There was no one else on the road. The moment was closer than ever. Soon I'd see her. I wondered what she would be wearing. She looked beautiful in everything. The sea was now visible to me. I could see the waves rush to the shore and my heart was filled with bliss. The road had now come to an end. I was out in the open. I saw her walking by the sea, her hair blowing in the wind. She saw me and stopped. I started walking towards her. She remained where she was. She was wearing a white *salwar-kameez*, embroidered beautifully with blue thread, and looked very graceful. A blue *dupatta*, like the blue of the sea, went around her neck and flew in the air with her hair. Her hair had grown a little longer and was as beautiful as ever. And well, she was as beautiful as ever too.

I had reached her. I looked into her beautiful brown eyes, outlined by *kajal*. They were happy eyes, sentimental eyes. I took both her hands in mine and brought her closer, and she submitted herself to my arms. No one spoke, only the waves lent their music. I looked at the sky above; there was not a cloud! I thanked God. I looked at the majestic sea; the waves were almost kissing our feet. I looked at the beach and there was no one there till eternity. Everything was perfect, pure bliss. I could feel her breathing against my chest. Finally, our dream had come true. If only we could stay there forever without speaking a word, our souls completely lost in each other. I felt something wet on my neck. I released her a little and saw her eyes. A lone tear had trickled down her cheek. I brought my lips close to her cheek and kissed away the tear. The wind had gained momentum and the waves were threatening to submerge our feet. I looked into her eyes; eyes that said so much. She closed them as I brought my lips close to hers and touched them. The wind, the waves; the sky, the day, had all ceased to exist.